I Know I've Been Changed

ReShonda Tate Billingsley

POCKET STAR BOOKS
New York London Toronto Sydney

A Pocket Star Book published by
POCKET BOOKS, a division of Simon & Schuster, Inc.
1230 Avenue of the Americas, New York, NY 10020

Originally published in trade paperback in 2006 by Pocket Books

ISBN-13: 978-1-4165-1198-4
ISBN-10: 1-4165-1198-9

This Pocket Star Books paperback edition February 2007

10 9 8 7 6 5 4 3 2 1

Cover design by Kristine V. Mills
Cover church photo by Fraser Hall/Getty Images

Manufactured in the United States of America

For information regarding special discounts for bulk purchases, please contact Simon & Schuster Special Sales at 1-800-456-6798 or business@simonandschuster.com.

For my girls,
Mya and Morgan

acknowledgments

I have been so blessed in my literary endeavors and there are so many people who have made my journey what it is. But first and foremost, thanks to God for opening doors and giving me the faith, strength and talent to walk through them.

It takes a strong man to deal with a woman like me, an I-want-it-all-and-know-I-can-have-it type of woman. Thanks to my strong man, Dr. Miron Billingsley, for weathering the storms and sticking by my side as I carve my niche in the publishing industry.

To my wonderful children, Mya and Morgan. I know I have to bribe you all to get you to deal with Mommy's constant trips on the road, but know that I do it all for you. And I promise, it'll all get better.

To the two most special women in my life, my mother, Nancy Blacknell, and my sister, Tanisha Tate. For so long it was just us three against the world. Both of you have been in my corner, listening to my stories, reading my work since I was ten years old. Thank you for everything.

Mama, maybe I'll sell enough books to finally buy you some new carpet (smile).

In this business you always hear people complaining about their agents and editors. I have no complaints because I have one of the best agents and editors in the industry. Sara Camilli, thank you for believing in my work and looking out for me along the way. Selena James, thanks for shaping my stories into bestsellers. I also have to say thanks to Brigitte Smith and everyone else at Simon & Schuster/Pocket Books. Thank you so much for believing in me. I hope I make our company proud.

To the best dang publicist this side of the Mississippi (okay, make that the world). Angie Pickett-Henderson, what can I say? You be puttin' it down. (I wonder if my editor will let my Ebonics slip through?) Seriously, thanks for pushing my career to new heights, and pushing me (even when I didn't feel like being pushed). What would I do without you?

To my girl, my dear friend and literary colleague, Pat Tucker Wilson, your time is coming. Keep your head up. You are a talented writer and it's just a matter of time before the world knows it too. To Jihad, thanks for the feedback and motivation in everything from writing to running. Thanks to all the other authors trying to do this literary thang with me and providing inspiration, support and advice along the way: Nina Foxx, Toschia, Victoria Christopher Murray, Zane, Eric Jerome Dickey, Monica Carter, Norma Jarrett, T. J. Butler, Cydney Rax, Yolanda Joe, Carl Weber, Karen Quinones Miller, Eric Pete, Curtis Bunn, my Strebor family and all the members of the Divine Literary Tour.

As always, much love goes to my chapter sorors: Jaimi

Canady, Raquelle Wooten, Kim Patterson Wright, Clemelia Humphrey Richardson, Beverly Davis, Leslie Mouton, Kristie King, Trina McReynolds, Finisha Waits, and all of the other illustrious women of Alpha Kappa Alpha Sorority (especially Mu Kappa Omega), who have shown a sista nothing but love since my self-published days. To all of the other Divine Nine, especially the men of Omega Psi Phi Fraternity, thanks for supporting my work.

To my Arkansas family in Smackover, Norphlet, and Mt. Pine, this is a work of fiction. Any resemblance to actual family members is purely coincidental. I don't want no drama at the family reunion. Special thanks to Aunt Birdell and Aunt Mel for all your love and support throughout the years.

To my sisters-in-law: Jacqueline McFadden, Della Jones, and Shawn Billingsley, thank you for supporting me and constantly promoting my books. To Xavier Billingsley, Sui, Roscoe, and Queena Jones, thanks for all your help while I was doing my book thing.

To all the book clubs and bookstores . . . man, I wish I could list you all, but there have been so many that showed me so much love, that it would take another book to list them all. So to those book clubs that had heated discussions over my books, I say thanks. I especially want to say thanks to those who invited me out: Brentwood Baptist Church, Brookhollow Baptist Church, Covenant Glenn, Mt. Horeb, St. Lukes, Afterthoughts, North Harris Community College, Cy-Fair Community College (especially Ivra Black), Cush City, Onyx, Cover to Cover, Seasonal Readers, Ladies of Expression, CPT, Go On Girl, Black Orchids, Ivy Readers, Sistahs in Harmony, Coffee, Tea and Read, Divas Who Read, and Kismet book clubs.

It was wonderful to hear you talking about my characters like they were real! And to the bookstores, thanks for helping catapult me to the bestseller lists. I hope we can do the same for *I Know I've Been Changed!*

Of course, I cannot forget all my colleagues at Fox 26 News in Houston, especially D'art Bebel, Kathy Williams, Erin Anthony, Linda Drummond, Ray Williams, Ulonda Kirk, Dana Davis, Patti Shieh, Aprille Meek, Bernadette Brown, LaShauna Sewell, Damali Keith, Melinda Spaulding, Isiah "Get Man" Carey, Joe Lanford, John Donnelly, Greg Groogan, Xavier Kirts, Torrey Walker, Todd Smith, Ray Cortez, Carolyn Mungo, Jesse Casteneda, Charles Hobson, Harry Husley, Ruben Dominguez, Joe McGinty, Jose Grinan, Joel Mathaisan, Christina Garza and Lisa Whitlock. A big, big thanks to Rodney "Big Rod" Pearson, for reluctantly giving me story ideas even though he thought we were just talking. (Don't worry, no one will know which stories are yours unless you tell them).

Also thanks to the Houston Association of Black Journalists and everyone at the *Houston Defender*.

Saving the best for last . . . the biggest thanks of all goes to you. The readers who bought my books, passed the word, and continued to show me support. I am what I am because of you. Thank you.

You know, the acknowledgments are more difficult to write than the book itself. That's because I know I'm forgetting someone and I know I'm going to hear about it. But that's the beauty of having such wonderful friends, family, and colleagues . . . If I left out your name, you know to charge it to my head and not my heart.

Until the next book . . . enjoy and thanks for the love.

I Know I've Been Changed

prologue

1995

I'm outta here and I don't care what anyone has to say.

Shondella, Reno, Auntie Mel. Even Mama Tee. I don't need none of them. Tell me I ain't gonna make it. I'll show 'em all. They can have this funky town.

Here I was, standing in front of Eddie's Filling Tank, the lone gas station bus stop in town, with all my belongings stuffed into four tattered suitcases. There was no turning back, not that I'd even want to. I was tired of Sweet Poke and all that it *didn't* have to offer. The one-stoplight town didn't even have a movie theater or a mall. The only three stores in the town were the five-and-dime store, McConn's, an overpriced old-people clothing store, and Piggly Wiggly. We didn't even have a freakin' Wal-Mart. If you wanted a decent pair of underwear, you had to drive twenty minutes to the next town to get it. And the nearest major city, Little Rock, was an hour and a half away. Sweet Poke was simply not a place where you could thrive. And it definitely wasn't a place for someone like me.

Shondella, my jealous older sister, had laughed when I'd first announced my intention to leave and go work in Tyler, Texas. She said I would probably end up hooking on the street. Then there was my great-aunt Mel, who had helped my grandmother raise me since my no-account mama had decided she didn't want to be a mama anymore and left me, Shondella, and my twin sister and brother, Jasmine and Justin, at this very bus stop. Auntie Mel had prayed over me like I needed to be exorcised or something. Mama Tee wouldn't even say good-bye. She just acted like I was goin' to the corner store or something.

I glanced at my watch. The bus was over an hour late and the wind was kicking my tail, messing up the $40, spiral-curl hairstyle that I'd had to sleep sitting up to maintain. People were always telling me I looked like former Miss America Vanessa Williams, so I'd tried to copy the hairstyle she always wore.

Some of the dust being kicked around by the wind got lodged in my throat and gave me a coughing fit.

"Just another reason to get out of this place," I muttered. Sweet Poke, Arkansas, was known for its twisterlike dirt clouds. And that about summed up all this town had to offer. On the list of progressive places in the country, Sweet Poke would rank at the very bottom. That's why I had to leave. Ever since junior high school, I've known I was bigger than this place. My family, friends, Reno, none of them could ever understand that. Some of my relatives called me uppity, but they just didn't understand. It wasn't only the slow pace that was driving me insane. I simply couldn't live in poverty. Since the average salary in this town of three thousand people was just over $14,000 a year, poverty was very real. Growing up, we were dirt-poor, although you'd never know it because Mama Tee was always hollering 'bout we was rich in spirit. Yeah, right. Tell that to the light company. They ain't trying to hear nothin' 'bout no spirits.

No, my future would be nothing like my past. I refused to be like Mama Tee, struggling to make ends meet, yet still singing every church song in the book. Forget that. Don't get me wrong, I haven't completely stopped believing in God, I just don't think He makes frequent stops in Sweet Poke. If He did, everyone here wouldn't live such miserable lives.

I used to pray that God would make things better for us, that he would bring my mama back. That was a pipe dream. All the nights I cried, all the nights I prayed for hours, begging God to bring my mother back didn't make a bit of difference. I wanted, no I *needed* my mother in my life so much I tried to bargain with God, saying stuff like I'd get straight A's and never trouble Mama Tee again if He would just bring her back. Yet, it never happened. So despite what Mama Tee is always saying, to me it don't look like God answers prayers. Least he ain't never answered none I sent up.

That's why I stopped waiting on God to change my situation and set out to change it myself. I was headed for bigger and better things. I was going to show the world that I wasn't some discarded little girl.

I pulled my scarf over my hair. I definitely didn't want any dirt getting in my hair. After I was sure I had it adjusted to where it was covering my entire head, I stepped out into the parking lot and peered down the road. "Finally," I mumbled as I noticed the big gray bus making its way through the clouds of dust.

For the first time that day, a smile crossed my face. I watched the Greyhound bus pull into the service station, wishing it would just slow down long enough for me to jump on board, then keep going.

"Evening, ma'am," the portly bus driver said as he stepped off the bus. "Will you be joining us?"

"Naw, I'm just standing out here in a dust storm for my health," I snapped.

The driver narrowed his eyes. "No need to get smart, little lady."

"No need to ask dumb questions." I was not in the mood for cordial exchanges. I was anxious to get out of Sweet Poke, the place I'd called home most of my life. "Yes, William," I said, reading his nametag. "I'm waiting on you. I've been waiting for the last hour and a half." I thrust my ticket toward him.

William forced a smile and shook his head. "They don't pay me enough for this," he mumbled as he took the ticket.

"What?" I asked, my hands firmly planted on my hips.

"Nothing," William responded. "We'll be taking a five-minute break, then we'll be heading out."

"Fine." As irritated as I was, I had waited all my life for this. What was another five minutes?

The driver rolled his eyes, then made his way over to where my luggage sat and began loading it on the bus. My entire life, stuffed in four pieces of unmatching, frazzled luggage. One was a Samsonite I had borrowed from Auntie Mel, and the other three cheap pieces were Mama Tee's. She'd probably gotten them on sale at a thrift store.

I huffed and was just about to board the bus when I heard someone say, "So you really gon' do this? Raedella Rollins is really gonna just up and leave?"

I stopped and turned toward Reno, my boyfriend of six years. Make that ex-boyfriend. We'd broken up two months ago after I'd caught him coming out of the only motel in Sweet Poke with Ann Paxton, the town tramp. I was hurt by his actions, mostly because he knew in a town as small as Sweet Poke, he wouldn't be able to cheat and get away with it. Still, he did it anyway. In fact, it was my sister who had come running home, out of breath, to tell me Reno was at the motel. The motel clerk had called somebody, who called somebody, who called my sister. Since we mix like oil and water, Shondella took great pleasure in bringing me the news.

"I guess you thought I was joking," I responded as I made my way to the side of the bus where he was standing. "I told you, Reno, I'm outta here. I'm destined for bigger and better things."

"This is about Ann, isn't it? I told you she don't mean nothing. *She* kissed *me*." Reno smiled that crooked smile that had captured my heart when I was just a freshman in high school. His eyes twinkled as he stood there in his Dickies overalls, holding a can of Coca-Cola. I'd known Reno since I was a little girl. But he'd moved away when he was nine years old, after his parents divorced. When he returned to live with his mother, he came back a handsome young man who had every girl within a hundred miles of Sweet Poke feenin' for him. Even now, he was as handsome as he was the day he'd first stepped foot in my freshman English class. His honey-brown complexion, short-cropped hair, enchanting eyes, and deep dimples almost made me think twice about my decision to leave. Almost.

"Whatever, Reno," I said, snapping out of the trance his eyes were luring me into. "That was your tongue down her throat, not the other way around. Anyway, I'm not going down that road with you again."

Reno displayed a big, cheesy grin. I used to believe Reno was one of the good guys. He went to church all the time. He was loving, attentive, and honest, or so I thought. That's why his cheating hurt me so much. I never saw it coming. He tried to give me some line about Ann claiming she had dropped something down the sink in that motel room and needed his help to get it out. I told him he must think I was Boo-Boo the fool if he expected me to believe that.

Reno reached out and tried to take my hand. "But we're a team. Always have been, always will be. Even when you tried to play hard and break up with me, I knew where your heart was. We belong together."

"Save that crap for your next victim," I said, jerking my hand away. "We broke up months ago. And this is about me wanting more than this two-bit town can offer. So Ann can have you because I don't want you."

"Tell that to someone who doesn't know you." Reno laughed, infuriating me.

"Let me explain something to you," I said, wiggling my neck. "You are a country bumpkin, a low-down, stank dirty dog. That's why I wouldn't get back together with your broke behind. And you have no aspirations to leave this place. You're happy working your minimum-wage job at the railroad. But me . . . CNN is calling, baby." I stood with my head held high.

Reno narrowed his eyes, looking at me like I was crazy. "Shondella told me you're going to Tyler, Texas. That's a long way from CNN."

"But it's on the way!" I was sick of people degrading my decision to take a job as a reporter in Tyler. Auntie Mel said I was just jumping out of the frying pan and into the fire by leaving one small town to go to another. Both she and Mama Tee had blasted me for going away to a town where I didn't know a single soul. But I'd let my family talk me out of going away to college, even though I'd desperately wanted to leave this place. Between being broke and madly in love with Reno, I'd been suckered into commuting to college at the University of Central Arkansas at Conway, which was about thirty minutes from Sweet Poke. Still, I stayed focused, earning my degree in broadcast journalism and sending out audition tape after audition tape until I finally got a job offer in Tyler. "I have to pay some dues. Anyway, I'll only be there a few months before some big-time television station snatches me up."

Reno doubled over with laughter.

"Forget you, Reno. You ain't gotta believe in me. That's why I'm leaving your country tail. And you will be sick when you see me on CNN, or *Entertainment Tonight* or *60 Minutes*!" His disbelief made me even more determined to fulfill my dream of becoming a nationally known news anchor.

"Yeah, right," Reno said between laughs. "You call me country? Your behind still talking 'bout 'Can I *axe* you a question?' How you gon' be Barbara Walters and you can't even talk right?"

Reno eased his laughing and leaned in, running his

hand across my face, which was on fire with fury. "Baby, face it. Sweet Poke is where you belong. You just a little ol' country girl. Your people are here," he stressed as he leaned in closer. "It's where you were born, where you gon' die. You can't run from it. It's in your blood."

His words made me shiver. This couldn't be my destiny. I'd get away from Sweet Poke or die trying.

"Lady, if you're catching this bus, you best get moving."

I hadn't even noticed the driver get back on the bus. I shook myself out of the trance Reno's words had put me in. "We'll see who has the last laugh," I said.

With that, I turned and boarded the bus, leaving Reno standing in the midst of the dust storm.

Within minutes, I was settling into a seat near the front of the bus. As the bus took off I leaned my head back and closed my eyes tightly. I refused to look out the window at Reno or Sweet Poke. All of that was my past. I was headed to my future.

chapter 1

"You have five minutes!"

I cut my eyes at Simone, the production assistant who was bellowing at me from the doorway of the dressing room. Another wannabe. She was young and attractive. Her sandpaper complexion, sandy brown hair, and model features made her prime television news-anchor material. I'd even heard Richard, my news director, talking about giving her a shot at reporting through some new reporter-training program.

That was a bunch of bull. She needed to go to a small town and pay some dues like the rest of us. I had seen her audition tape, and granted, she did have a natural talent, but that didn't mean she deserved to start out in a top market. Cities were ranked by what we in the news business called market size, with small towns ranked lower and big cities ranked higher. Houston was a major television market and you had to have your stuff together to work here. It had taken me seven years to get here. Seven years of toiling in small, pissant towns for little or no pay. I worked in Tyler two years, almost going crazy in that hick place. Then I went to be a reporter and anchor in Rochester, New York, then Phoenix, Arizona, before coming to Houston four years ago to work at KPCR, the NBC station. I'd been around the country. And here comes little Miss Thang who thinks her looks will get her a free ride straight to the big time.

I made a mental note to tell Stan she had to go. Stan was the general manager and Richard's boss. We had a special relationship. He called me his Chocolate Star. Some people would call that racist, but I know Stan. He doesn't have a racist bone in his body. Only one color matters to him and that's green. And my new talk show had been bringing in the money. *The Rae Rollins Show* aired every day at ten in morning and was rated number one in the market. There were even talks to take the show into syndication. Watch out, Oprah! In addition to my talk show, I did special reports for *Dateline* and the *Today* show, and I anchored the six-o'clock news. It was a demanding schedule. My days could get pretty hectic, with me running from sunup to sundown, but I was one of the most popular local on-air personalities in the country. I had received job offers from ABC and CNN. But when I threatened to leave, NBC offered me the talk show. And since I just knew that would take off, I stayed in Houston. The move had paid off, so what I want definitely matters to Stan.

And I definitely wanted Simone gone.

Screw that mentality about reaching back and helping out. This was a cutthroat business and there was only room enough for one chocolate star at this station. And I was that woman. Had been for the last three years. I'd come a long way from my days in Sweet Poke. I'd achieved everything I'd set out to do when I left that backward town. I was living my dream and I wasn't about to be replaced by some starry-eyed, do-anything-for-my-job college graduate who would work for a tenth of what I made.

"Rae, did you hear me? Five minutes to air," Simone repeated.

"I know what time it is," I snapped.

"Sorry," Simone muttered. "I was just doing my job."

"Well, go do it somewhere else." I flicked her off and looked at the girl applying my makeup. "You think you can finish this today?"

"I'm done. I was just—"

I stood up, cutting her off, then peered into the mirror examining my makeup. "How many times do I have to tell you I don't like my lip liner that thick?"

The makeup girl, a permanent fill-in for whenever Sasha, the station's make-up artist, was on vacation, cowered and started stammering. "I'm s . . . s . . . sorry. I can redo it."

"Just forget it," I said, frustrated. I fluffed up my copper-colored hair and made sure my eye shadow was accenting my light brown eyes. I noticed Simone's reflection in the mirror. She hadn't budged from the doorway. It was eerie, she looked like a much younger version of me. "I said I was coming! I know what time my show starts!"

Simone slithered away and the makeup girl looked at me like she wanted to cry. I know I can be brutal sometimes. But after all I've been through in my life, I think I'm entitled.

I will admit, though, that phone call today from Mama Tee had shaken me up. It had been three months since I'd talked to her, and she'd called me back then to tell me Auntie Mel had died. Mama Tee couldn't understand why I didn't come back for Auntie Mel's funeral, but I'd told everyone when I left Sweet Poke, I wasn't going back. There's only been one exception, and that was four years ago when my baby brother, Justin, almost died from leukemia. I'd taken my then boyfriend with me and it had been a disaster. I left there more depressed than I'd ever been.

When Mama Tee had called earlier today to tell me Justin had taken a turn for the worse, I couldn't imagine going back again. Justin had been battling leukemia his entire life. But since his near-death episode, he had been getting better, or so I thought. The news that he was relapsing had really shaken me up, especially because I knew I hadn't been there for him like I should. Out of everyone in Sweet Poke, Justin was the only one I truly missed. While several of my relatives called me at the station whenever they wanted something, Justin and Mama Tee were the only ones I really talked to and even that was sporadic.

I raced toward the studio, trying to shake off my sad thoughts about Justin. I'd just have to send him some money to see a specialist or something, but I wasn't going back. I couldn't go back.

I grabbed my earpiece, stuck it in, and plopped down into my seat just as the director gave me the one-minute cue. He shot me an ugly look. I shot one back, letting him know I wasn't the least bit fazed about him being upset.

I shook my head and quickly got into my TV mode. If there was one thing I was good at, it was that—shaking off everything and putting on my TV face. It's what made me so good at this business. Today, I had to be better than normal because I was doing the show solo. My coanchor was out sick. But I knew running the show alone wouldn't be a problem once I put thoughts of my family out of my mind.

An hour later, I was finished. I pushed back from the set and headed back to my office. The show had gone smoothly, despite all my worries about Justin.

I checked my messages. My sister Shondella had called two more times. She had coerced my private work number from Justin several years ago and didn't hesitate to use it whenever she needed something. I deleted both messages without completely listening to them. There were several messages from fans and one from Myles. We were set for dinner tonight. He stood me up last night because he had to work late, so I'm sure he had something special planned to make up for it. Myles was a city councilman and the love of my life. Just thinking about what lay in store tonight brought a smile to my face. That smile quickly faded when I listened to the last message.

"Uppity tramp. You ain't all that!" The phone slammed down. I felt shivers run up my spine. That was the third call like that this week. The voice sounded familiar, but I couldn't make it out.

"It's just an obsessed fan," I muttered. One of the drawbacks to the job. Crazy people were always accosting me. Still, something about those calls had me uneasy. I jumped when the phone on my desk rang. I snatched it up.

"Channel Two. This is Rae Rollins."

"So, you too good to call somebody back?"

I silently cursed before taking a deep breath and answering. "Yes, Shondella. May I help you?"

"May I help you?" she repeated mockingly. "You ain't gotta put on no airs with me. I know your tail is country. And all anybody got to do is listen close enough and they can hear that Sweet Poke twang in your high-falutin voice. No matter how much you try and pretend, you still ain't high society." She laughed.

"Shondella, I'm busy. What do you want?" I was so not in the mood to deal with my older sister. We had never gotten along. I've always felt she was jealous of me. And that's not just my confidence talking. We had different daddies. Hers was one of the darkest men in Sweet Poke and she had inherited his skin color. Personally, I thought her deep black-brown skin was beautiful, but she had always had issues with it. Between that and being about forty pounds overweight, she had some severe self-confidence problems. I was a smooth caramel color, a sexy size eight, and Shondella was forever making comments about my looks. Aside from the physical traits, we just didn't like each other. Following in our mother's footsteps, Shondella had four kids by three different men.

"Are you coming to see Justin?"

"I talked to Mama Tee. There's nothing I can really do, and it's not like my being there will help. Besides, I'm swamped here at work." I eyed my desk, which bore no pictures of my life in Sweet Poke.

"Oh yeah. You and that high-falutin job of yours. All that money to sit in front of a camera and read," Shondella taunted.

Okay, time to cut her off. Shondella never hesitated to belittle my job. Like ringing up packages of Marlboro 100s at Jr. Food Mart was top-of-the-line work.

"You know what," I told her, "I'm hanging up."

"Wait, wait!" Shondella yelled before I could hang up the phone. Something, I don't know what, made me pause.

"Look here," Shondella whined, "I ain't mean to start no fight with you. I'm just upset because of Justin and all, and you act like you don't even care."

I let out an exasperated sigh. My family just didn't understand me. Why couldn't they let me live my life and I'd let them live theirs? Honestly, when I was in high school and Auntie Mel would embarrass me by coming up to the high school and picking up cans, I'd imagine that I had been switched at birth. My real mother would discover the mistake, come find me, and rescue me from my pitiful existence. Of course, it never happened. And when I shared my dream with Reno, he'd told me to stop watching so much Lifetime television.

"I do care," I said, snapping back to my conversation. "I just don't know what I can do for him, that's all." I should probably have made arrangements to go back for Justin, but I hated that part of my life and just wanted it to be over.

"Okay, I see your point."

I leaned back in my chair and crossed my legs. Shondella never saw my point about anything. "Shondella, what do you want?"

"Why I gotta want something?" she replied in the sincerest voice she could muster.

"Don't act like we have a sweet sister relationship and you were just calling to chat."

"You know what? I get so sick of your self-righteous behind!" she snapped. "I just wanted to see if you were coming home to see Justin."

I inhaled deeply. I knew she really loved Justin. Everyone did. "All right. I'm sorry. It's been a long day."

"Cool. Apology accepted."

A silent pause hung between us. "Well, I really have to go," I finally said. "Thank you for calling."

"Hey . . . ummm . . . before you go, I was wondering . . . my lights are about to be cut off and, ummm . . . Lexus wants to go to this band camp . . . so I was wondering if you could spot me a little sumptin' sumptin'."

I felt my blood boiling. I should have known. The only time she called me was when she wanted something. I have loaned—no, let me correct that—I have given (because none of them have paid me back one damn dime) my relatives so much money, it is ridiculous.

"Shondella, I knew you wanted something."

"Come on, Sis. It ain't like I done asked you for nothing recently," she pleaded.

"That's a lie. I just sent you five hundred dollars."

"That was four months ago. I ain't asked you for nothing in the last month."

"You didn't pay me back that five hundred. Or the three hundred before. Or the thousand before that."

"Dang, it ain't like you need it! I'm gon' give you all your funky money back when I settle this lawsuit."

I shook my head. Shondella had been counting on

money from a lawsuit since a Frito-Lay truck had hit her more than a year ago. She wasn't even hurt, but she'd taken three months off from work, gone to therapy every day, and was sure she'd be able to get a hefty payoff.

"Whatever. I'm sick of this. I wish . . . I wish—"

"You wish what? That we'd just go away? I'm sorry, little sis, but we're family. For life. You can run all you like, but there's no escaping that." Shondella laughed.

"Shondella, I just don't have it."

"Stop lying! You know you make all that money."

I knew that bidding war the stations had gotten in to get me would come back to haunt me. It was all in the papers how NBC had shelled out nearly half a million dollars to have me join their team. Couple in signing bonuses and extra pay, I made close to $600,000 a year.

"You just gon' let your nieces sit in the dark 'cause you got a beef with me?" Shondella asked after I didn't say anything.

There she went again, playing on the only other thing besides Justin she knew I cared about in Sweet Poke. My nieces. I didn't talk to them often, but I did love them. I felt sorry for them, not only because they had car names—for the life of me I couldn't understand why Shondella would name her children Lexus, Mercedes, Camry, and Porsche—but because I believed they were doomed to repeat the cycle in Sweet Poke.

I finally concluded that the sooner I agreed to send her the money, the sooner I could get her off the phone.

"How much?"

"So you'll loan me the money?" she asked excitedly.

"How much?"

"I need about eight hundred."

"Fine." I leaned forward and pulled my checkbook out of my purse. I wanted to write this check and get it in the mail today. Shondella would be calling me every day until it arrived.

"I meant nine hundred," she said quickly.

"I will send eight hundred tomorrow."

"Can you send it Western Union?"

"Shondella, you better be grateful I'm sending it at all, especially since you didn't pay me back the last three times."

"Okay, okay. Thank you. I'll pay you back this time. I promise."

"Yeah, yeah, yeah. Bye."

I didn't even give her time to respond. I placed the phone back on the cradle, wondering what I had done in a former life to be sentenced to a family like mine.

chapter 2

Every woman ought to have a man as fine as mine.

My eyes ran up and down Myles's body—a body that seemed to be made of steel, chiseled at the hands of Michelangelo himself. There was not an ounce of fat on his muscular physique. His hazel, seductive eyes, defined chin, and plump lips were just the icing on the cake.

Can I say it again? My man is fine.

Not just that, though. He's a rising star. The youngest man ever elected to Houston's city council, Myles Jacobs knew how to play the political game. He was charismatic, intelligent, and knew how to work a room. People were already pushing him to consider running for mayor. Some even said he had what it took to be the first black president, although I didn't foresee that happening in this lifetime.

Even so, I'd look good as a first lady.

"Girl, you know you're gon' make me late, lying there

looking all good and stuff." Myles popped me on my behind. I was sprawled out across my king-size bed, the morning paper spread out in front of me.

"Boy, you're silly," I said as he leaned in to kiss me. I turned my head before our lips met. "And definitely in need of some Scope. Oh my goodness." I fanned my face.

Myles playfully pounced on me, blowing his breath in my face. "There, take that."

"Ughh," I screamed, trying to wiggle from his grasp. "Quit playing."

Myles laughed, pulled himself up and headed into the bathroom.

"Let me get in the shower before I really am late," he said. "And I'll make sure I take care of this halitosis you claim I have."

"Yeah, baby, that was brutal. You might want to use Scope *and* Listerine," I called out after him.

I heard the water running as I got up out of the bed. I picked up my sundress, which I had left in the middle of the floor last night. I smiled as I reflected on our unforgettable night.

As expected, my baby had had a wonderful evening planned. First, we ate dinner at Bellagio's on Westheimer. Then he took me on a carriage ride through a recently renovated downtown Houston. After that, we went back to my place for a romantic completion to the night. We don't get to spend much time together, but when we do, Myles makes sure it's first-class. He didn't make much money as a councilman, but his thriving real estate law firm afforded him the ability to treat me as the queen that I am.

I slipped my robe on and poked my head in the bathroom. "You better get going. How would it look if Mr. Councilman is late for his constituents' breakfast in his honor?"

"Yeah, yeah, yeah," Myles said. Within five minutes he was walking back into the bedroom. "I still wish you were coming with me."

"I do, too, baby. Really I do. But you know I have to tape today and Malcolm's people said this morning was the only time he could do the show."

"So you're kicking me to the curb for ol' black Malcolm Long, just because he's a big superstar?"

I laughed as I laid back down across the bed. "Now, baby, just because Malcolm is deep mocha fine doesn't mean I'd choose him over the sexy future mayor Myles Jacobs. I would much rather be with my baby. Besides, I don't cut for Malcolm like that anyway because he doesn't like black women. He says we're too bossy."

Myles slipped into his crisp, white Armani shirt and began buttoning it up. "You are. Do this, Myles. Do that, Myles. I'm going to get me a nice, obedient Asian woman, too."

"Don't get cut," I said, half-joking. I could have a jealous streak when it came to Myles, but it was only because I couldn't have anyone jeopardizing my master plan.

"I'm just kidding. I wouldn't trade my Nubian sisters for anything." He leaned down and kissed me on the lips. "Now, I need to finish getting dressed before you get me all worked up again."

I watched his backside as he disappeared into the bathroom. I flipped over on my back and smiled. I had a dream job. A dream man. A dream life. A life so far removed from Sweet Pok

"You only have about fifteen minutes," I called out to him.

"I'm hurrying!"

I closed my eyes. It was hard to believe we'd only been together a year. I'd seen Myles around town when I was out covering stories. But we didn't officially meet until the NAACP Freedom Awards banquet a year ago. I was the emcee and he was receiving an award for his achievements in the political arena. We immediately clicked. He asked me out to lunch the next day and we've been going strong ever since.

Myles was everything I had ever hoped for: intelligent, sexy, and successful. We complemented one another. The power couple. That's how the various newspaper and magazine articles that featured us described our relationship. We were even slated to appear in an upcoming *Ebony* magazine article. I loved that man to death. And I had no doubt that his love for me ran just as deep.

Myles's family loved me, too. His father, who was deceased, had started their law firm, Jacobs & Jacobs, Inc., knowing his son would follow in his footsteps. Myles's mom, a successful Realtor, bragged about me like I was her own daughter. And his younger brother, although not as successful as Myles, was still trying to make his mark in the film industry. It felt so good to be a part of such a together family. Such a normal family.

On the other hand, Myles hadn't met my family. It was definitely not from his lack of trying. In fact, I hadn't even been completely honest about my background. He took it personal that I didn't want him to meet my people. But the last thing I wanted was my family worming their way back into my life and ruining my relationship with Myles like they did with Alex.

The last time I went home, four years ago, I took my boyfriend, Alex, a wealthy surgeon from a blue-blood background. We never went farther than the hospital, yet my cousin Tank stole Alex's wallet. Shondella beat her oldest daughter right in the hospital lobby, and Aunt Ola and Uncle Otis got into a fight in the parking lot. Alex was so mortified by the way my people acted that he broke it off with me when we returned home. Initially, he just became distant. Finally he admitted that our families would never be able to mix, that his family would be disgraced if we ever got married, and he was worried about "his lineage" if he ever had a child with me.

After that fiasco I vowed to never let another man meet my family. So taking Myles to Sweet Poke was not an option. Shondella would be jealous and find a way to sabotage everything. Mama Tee would probably say he was uppity. My cousin Nikki would try to get him into bed, and heaven only knows what other secrets would be uncovered should we set foot in Sweet Poke. While Myles wasn't as anal as Alex, I simply didn't want to take that chance. Nope. Myles was best off believing I was estranged from my family. In fact, I hadn't even told him where I was really from, instead lying and telling him I was from Little Rock. I didn't want him getting any bright ideas. I felt bad about lying to Myles, but ultimately, I didn't see any other way to handle it.

The ringing telephone snapped me out of my thoughts. I rolled over and answered it just as Myles blew me a kiss and headed out the door.

"What's up, girl?" It was Shereen, the only real friend I had at the station. No, make that the only real friend I had in Houston.

Shereen was director of community service at Channel 2 and didn't let my ways get to her. She didn't let much of anything get to her. She was a cross between hippie and ghetto, a wild-child sister-girl. But she had proven to be a really good friend since I'd met her.

"Hey," I responded.

"Girl, turn on the TV and look at Lorna's hair."

Lorna was the black anchor at the ABC station. She was my only real competition.

I grabbed the remote and flipped the TV set on.

"Oh . . . my . . . God."

Shereen laughed so hard I could barely hear. "I know. Can you believe she dyed her hair blond?"

I joined in her laughter. Lorna looked like an idiot. "Girl, I hope she keeps it. It'll make the few viewers she has turn away and over to us. Not that I need her five measly viewers." I laughed.

"Rae, you are too much."

I liked that Shereen understood my confidence and wasn't turned off by it. That's just another reason why we got along so well. Shereen was about five-three, 220 pounds, and wore minidreadlocks. She had no desire to be on air, so I didn't have to worry about her stabbing me in the back.

"So, are you ready for Malcolm?"

"Yeah, I'm about to get dressed now," I said as I pulled myself off of the bed.

"Me, too."

"I thought you were off today."

"I am, but I have some work to do. Yeah, that's it," she stammered.

"Yeah, right."

"Okay, so you got me. But how will I ever get Malcolm to father my children if I can't get him to meet me?"

I snickered. "Yeah, okay." Like Shereen had a snowball's chance of Malcolm even looking her way. But Shereen was my girl, so far be it from me to tell her that.

"Why don't you hook a sister up? Tell him I got the cure for his jungle fever. Once he tastes me, no other he'll want to see."

"A poet you're not. Good-bye, Shereen."

"Tell him that once he samples this black, he'll never go back."

"I'm hanging up now."

"Help him get it through his head that big girls are better in bed."

I laughed again and hung up the phone. I was grateful for Shereen's friendship. Ever since I'd left Sweet Poke, I'd been a loner, too scared to let anyone get close to me because I didn't want anyone to find out about my past. Of course, Shereen had asked about my past, but I'd told her the same thing I'd told Myles, that my father was dead and I was estranged from the rest of my family. I think she knew I was lying, because she gave me this crazy look, but she never called me on it, only telling me that whenever I wanted to talk to her about anything, she was there.

I scanned the racks of clothes on the far side of my closet. I had suits for days. Dana Buchman, Donna Karan, Albert Nipon, Tahari, you name it, it was hanging in my closet. I had come a long way from when Mama

Tee would sew our clothes and hand them down from Shondella to Nikki to me. By the time I got them, they were usually hanging together by a string.

"Those days are long gone," I mumbled as I picked out a deep green BCG jacket and skirt. The suit alone cost $700. That's more than Mama Tee probably spent on all my clothes my entire life. I put Mama Tee, Sweet Poke, and my previous life out of my mind as I held the suit up to my body and surveyed myself in the full-length mirror. I looked good. I felt good. And as I twirled around in the middle of my closet, I couldn't help but feel like I was on top of the world.

chapter 3

I was still floating as I gathered my things to leave the studio. The interview with Malcolm had gone well. Extremely well in fact. He had even asked me to have dinner with him before he headed back to New York. Shereen, who had showed up at the station anyway, came over and introduced herself to him, but as I'd expected, he didn't pay her any attention.

She had mouthed, "Oh, well, his loss," before sashaying her big ol' behind off. I laughed and was grateful that she didn't see him as he turned his full attention to me. Although guys always flock to me whenever Shereen and I go out, she's never fazed.

Anyway, I told Malcolm no can do. I could tell he's used to getting whatever woman he wants because he acted surprised that I wouldn't take him up on his offer. But I calmly explained to him that I was madly in love and my boyfriend wouldn't approve of me dining with another man, even if that man was Malcolm Long.

Even though I am completely faithful to Myles, it feels good when other men show interest. It lets me know I still got it. And judging from the number of letters, e-mails, and calls I get from men asking to take me out, I've definitely still got it.

And tonight, I wanted to use it all on Myles. I had secured tickets to the Broadway play *Aida* at the Wortham Theatre. I planned to surprise Myles and take him there, then back to my place, where I was going to practice these new tricks I'd read in Zane's latest book.

I decided to call Myles to make sure he came straight home. I planned to swing by my place, grab some clothes to wear tonight, then just meet him at his place since I had a key. It had dang near taken an act of Congress to get it, but after weeks of me pouting and protesting he'd given in.

As soon as I got in my car, I pulled out my cell phone and dialed Myles's office. After I'd played nice with his secretary, she patched me through to him.

"Hey, baby," I said, after he picked up the phone.

"Hey yourself."

"Working hard or hardly working?"

"You know I'm working like a Hebrew slave."

As much as I loved his work ethic, sometimes I wished he would just slow down. "Well, stop what you're doing and meet me at your place. I have tickets to *Aida* tonight."

"What's that?"

"The Broadway play. You know, the one I was telling you about that's playing downtown."

"Oh, yeah, I remember. Well, you're going to have to call Shereen or something. I can't get away tonight."

I closed my eyes in frustration. It quickly dawned on me that I was in the middle of traffic, so I whipped my eyes back open just in time to slam on my brakes to keep from running into the Honda Accord in front of me. "What do you mean, you can't get away?"

"I'm in the middle of a project and I probably won't get out of here until late tonight."

"But, Myles . . ."

"Babe, I can't just drop everything."

"Do I ever come first to you?" I whined.

Myles sighed. "Please, not that tired old argument again."

"It's not tired."

"It really is. You knew what I did for a living when you met me. Now, you're constantly complaining because I'm always working." Myles huffed.

"You should be able to find a happy medium."

"Good-bye, Rae. Have fun at the play. I'll hook up with you tomorrow."

Then he hung up the phone on me. I was furious. *How dare he hang up on me?* I viciously punched his numbers into my cell phone.

The secretary answered again. "Jacobs and Jacobs."

I knew Myles had a direct line, even though he denied it. I couldn't stand always having to go through his damn secretary. "Put Myles on the phone."

"Excuse me? May I ask who's calling?"

This heifer knew who was calling but I was not in the mood to argue with her. "It's Rae."

"Oh, Miss Rollins." She quickly changed her tone.

"I'm sorry, I didn't catch your voice. Mr. Jacobs is in a meeting right now. May I take a message?"

"He is not in a meeting! I just talked to him!"

"I'm sorry. May I take a message?" she softly repeated.

I contemplated cursing her out, but I didn't want to give her anything else to gossip about. Besides, she was probably only doing what Myles had told her to do.

"You know what?" I said. "Don't worry about it, okay? Just don't worry about it."

I flung the phone on the floor on the passenger side of my car and gripped the steering wheel tightly. Myles had pissed me off again. Now some perfectly good tickets would go to waste because I was in no mood to go see a play.

chapter 4

We had been back and forth over this issue so many times my head hurt. But I refused to budge.

"This is ridiculous, Rae," Ian, my producer, said. He turned to my news director, Richard, who was sitting in the conference room with us while we went over ideas for upcoming shows. "Richard, tell her it's just a show."

Richard, who hadn't even been paying attention, looked up from the notepad he was doodling on. "Huh?"

"Tell her this is a great idea and she's just being difficult," Ian said.

"Uh, Rae, listen to him. It's a great idea and you're being difficult."

I shook my head, disgusted not only by Richard's lack of management skills lately, but by his overall appearance. "Richard, do you even know what he's talking about?"

"Yeah, of course. Um, he wants us to um, do a show,

um, and uh, I'm just here to listen and supervise," he snapped.

We both looked at him strangely. His eyes were deep pink, his hair disheveled and he looked like he was totally spaced out. Richard had shocked us when he even showed up to our editorial meeting because normally he left the story planning up to us. But he had been acting stranger by the day.

I blew Richard off. It was obvious his body was in the meeting room with us, but his mind was totally somewhere else. "Find another topic," I told Ian. I rubbed my temples. I was still upset about wasting those play tickets last night.

"But it will be Mother's Day and what better topic to do than mother/daughter relationships. I think it would be great for you to bring your mother on. We'd even fly her in from . . . where does she live again?"

I tensed up. I couldn't even remember what lie I had told him. That's the trouble with lies, you have to remember them. "Ian, just drop it. I'm not doing a show with my mother."

"Fine, I can understand you don't want to have your own mother on, but what's the big deal about having other mothers on?"

"The big deal is I don't want to do it and I'm not going to do it," I snapped. The real reason was I couldn't stand to look at some happy-go-lucky mother and daughter talking about how great their relationship was. I didn't need any reminder of how screwed up my own relationship with Rose was.

"Will you at least consider the idea?" Ian pleaded.

"No! Let's move on already! There are a lot more pressing issues going on. You need to find them." My head was throbbing and Ian was getting on my last nerve. "I have to go."

I stood up, nearly knocking over my chair, and paced along the conference room table. I didn't need to deal with memories of my mother on top of all this drama with Myles. I called him until four in the morning, but he didn't answer my calls. I only knew he was home because I drove by his house at two. I should've gotten out but I didn't want him to think I was checking up on him, so I went home to wait for his call. It never came. That truly pissed me off and made my tolerance level really low.

"I think you're being unreasonable, Rae," Ian said.

"You want unreasonable, I'll show you unreasonable." With that, I turned and stormed out, leaving Ian sitting in the conference room. I ducked into my office, grabbed my purse, and headed out the back door to my car. I needed to get away. Go somewhere and calm down. Just escape. It was only ten o'clock and we weren't taping my show today, so I had plenty of time before having to do the newscast at six. An afternoon of pampering at the Escape Day Spa was just what I needed.

Despite my best efforts, as I sped down Interstate 45 toward the spa, I couldn't get my mother out of my mind. Images of D-day, as Shondella had referred to it, ran rampant in my head. Drop-off day.

I was eight, Shondella was thirteen, and Jasmine and Justin weren't even a year old. Mama, or Rose as she made us call her, had left our hometown of Lake Charles, Louisiana, and driven for what seemed like an eternity. Finally, we arrived in Sweet Poke. I only knew that because I saw the huge WELCOME TO SWEET POKE sign lit up as we were pulling into town. Rose had pulled into the gas station and parked, and we sat there in that parking lot for over two hours. Rose had been acting strange all day, and snapping at each of us if anyone uttered a word. Justin and Jasmine napped in their car seats. Shondella and I were sitting in the backseat, quiet and scared. We knew something was up; we just didn't know what. Rose was chain-smoking cigarettes, the car was clouded with smoke. We were too scared to even cough. Rose would puff a cigarette, run her fingers through her hair, bite her nails, huff, and sigh. It was so strange. I tried to ask her what we were doing, and she told me to shut up and just sit there until she figured out what she was going to do. After a little while, she got out and used the pay phone. We couldn't hear what she said, but when she got back in the car, she was crying.

"Mama, what's wrong?" I asked softly, forgetting her request to call her by her first name.

"Just be quiet! Okay? Why the hell can't you just do what I tell you to do?" she snapped viciously. I sank into the seat, fighting back tears and vowing not to say another word.

We all sat in silence for what seemed like eternity. Rose finally spoke. "Get out."

Not understanding what she meant, none of us moved.

"I said, get out. Sugar Smack, get the twins." Sugar Smack was my nickname. Given to me, Rose said, because all I ever wanted to eat was Sugar Smacks cereal. "Shondella, get your suitcase." Rose stared straight ahead as she spoke. Shondella opened the door, got out, walked around to the back, and pulled out one huge suitcase from the trunk. We had watched Rose throw all of our meager belongings into that one oversize, raggedy suitcase. We didn't question her then. Just like we didn't question her now. Shondella slammed the trunk closed. I still hadn't moved.

"Sugar Smack, I'm not gon' tell you again. Get the babies and get out." Rose still didn't turn around and look at me.

I jumped and quickly started removing Justin from his car seat. He had woken up and was giggling and laughing, oblivious to what was going on. To be quite honest, I didn't have a clue either. I handed him to Shondella, then unstrapped Jasmine and pulled her out of the car seat. I looked to Shondella for answers, but she wasn't much help. She was standing there with a scowl across her face.

"What's going on?" I whispered as I took my place next to her.

"Stop asking so many questions," she snapped.

I was getting frustrated. Here we were in some strange place called Sweet Poke, at a dirt-filled gas station in the middle of the night, being ordered out of the car by our mother.

Rose rolled her window down. "Come here," she called out.

I adjusted Jasmine on my hip and followed Shondella to the car window.

"Look, I thought long and hard about this. And I ain't got no choice." She swallowed, then took a deep breath. "I love y'all. Don't let no one ever tell y'all otherwise. Someone will be here shortly. They family. They gon' come through." She sounded more like she was talking to herself than to us. "I'm not a bad person, I just made some bad decisions. Having you kids was a bad decision."

"This is because of Sam, ain't it?" Shondella shouted. She was on the verge of tears. That just added to my fear because my sister was hard, even as a little girl, and she seldom cried about anything. "I heard him! I heard him tell you he couldn't be with you 'cause he didn't want no damn kids."

Rose thrust her finger toward us. "I know you better watch your mouth, little girl. I'm still your mama."

"Mothers don't leave their kids at gas stations in strange places in the middle of the night!" Shondella stormed off and went and leaned against a gas pump.

I thought Rose would go after her and beat her real good. I just knew our mother wouldn't tolerate Shondella talking to her like that.

I loosened Jasmine's grip on my hair. "Mama, you not gon' leave us here, huh?"

Rose lit another cigarette. "Sugar Smack, you just too young to understand." She inhaled deeply on the cigarette, then exhaled, blowing the smoke in little rings into the air. I used to think it was cool to see my mama do that. But at that moment, I wasn't impressed. "Shondella just mad right now," Rose continued. "One day you will understand why I'm doing this."

I started to cry, which caused Jasmine to cry as well. "No, Mama. Please don't leave us!"

Rose took another long drag on her cigarette. "I called your grandma. She said she wouldn't come, but she will. I know she will." Rose started the car up and my tears started coming faster. I threw myself on her car door, almost dropping Jasmine. "Mama, please, don't leave us here!"

Shondella had appeared beside me. She shifted Justin in her arms and rubbed Jasmine's hair with her free hand. "Stop all that damn crying. And stop begging her. Let her go."

"You're just being mean again!" I screamed at Shondella, then turned back to Rose. "Mama, we'll be good. We promise. Shondella, tell her. Tell her you'll stop being bad!"

"Stupid, she would rather be with that old, baldheaded, fat-ass boyfriend of hers than take care of her own kids, so forget her," Shondella said.

I was speechless. Shondella was about to get it for sure now. No way could Mama let her get away with saying something like that, let alone curse.

I felt the car move and looked as Rose put the car in drive. A tear was trickling down her cheek. "Nooo! Mama, she didn't mean it. Shondella, tell her you didn't mean it!"

"I meant every word." Shondella's nostrils were flared. A defiant look was across her face and she was desperately trying to fight back tears. Justin and Jasmine had both started crying as well. The silence of the night had been pierced by the sounds of my sister cursing, my baby brother and sister wailing, and my sobbing. Then, finally, there was the sound of tires as they screeched out into the street.

That was the last time I'd see my mother for seven years. She and Sam moved from Lake Charles, and nobody, including Mama Tee, had any idea where they went. The sad part was Sam had not only been my daddy's best friend, he was the man who had taken his life. He had shot my daddy to death in a game of craps and got off because he convinced a judge it was self-defense.

Even still, I tried reaching out to Rose when I was twelve, after we found her secretly living in Camden, Arkansas, another small town just two hours away. Somebody was visiting relatives up there, spotted Rose, and told Mama Tee. I only found out about it because I overheard Mama Tee talking to Auntie Mel about it.

I was excited when I found out where Rose was. I really put forth an effort to establish a relationship with her, writing her letters after I discovered her address written down in Mama Tee's phone book. None of my letters was ever answered. I even hitchhiked one time to her home, only to find out she'd moved again. Then on top of that, Mama Tee beat me silly for leaving Sweet Poke.

The night Rose dropped us off, my grandmother did show up. She came shortly after Rose drove off. She must have called Rose everything but a child of God. We had sat in silence as we made our way back to Mama Tee's house. We had only visited Mama Tee once, when I was about four. She and Rose didn't get along, and Rose hated Sweet Poke. So we didn't even know what to expect.

Mama Tee took us in and eventually we healed from Rose's desertion. Or healed as best we could. For years, Rose never called us. Then one day, when I was fifteen, she just showed up out of the blue. We found out Sam had run off with another woman. So I guess she wanted us back. Shondella wouldn't even stay in the same room with her. Justin had no clue who she was, and me, I tried to listen to what she had to say, even though it was going in one ear and out the other. When she asked where Jasmine was, I lost it, and Mama Tee finally made her leave. She didn't even know her own child had died. How pathetic was that? Then, before she left, she had the nerve to ask us to call her Mama.

I shook off thoughts of my family as I pulled into the Day Spa. I said a silent prayer that they would be able to squeeze me in. I should've called on my way over, but I was lost in thought and it hadn't even crossed my mind. But for all the money I spent there, they'd better fit me in.

"Good afternoon, Miss Rollins," the receptionist said as soon as I walked in. She looked down at her appointment book. "I didn't know you had an appointment today."

"I don't. But I need a session with Raul."

"Oh, he's pretty booked today."

"I have to have a session with Raul," I pleaded.

She looked at me and I guess the stress showed across my face because her expression softened. "You know what? Since you're such a valued client, I'm sure Raul would be willing to forgo his lunch break to squeeze you in. Let me check."

I smiled gratefully. I was willing to beg Raul, pay double, anything to lie in the relaxing seascape room while Raul worked his magical hands up and down my body.

A few minutes later, the tall, handsome Italian masseur emerged from the back. "Madame Rollins." He took my hand and gently kissed it. "So wonderful to see you. I was just about to meet a friend for an early lunch, but since you're so much cuter than him, I will reschedule." He flashed an enchanting smile.

"Raul, I am forever indebted to you."

"Come, come. Let me ease that tension from your body."

"That obvious, huh?"

"It is. But I have just the thing for that." He wiggled his fingers in the air as I smiled and followed him into the back.

chapter 5

"You still mad at me?" Myles was leaning up against the frame of my front door.

"May I help you?" I tried to be cold, but the truth is, seeing Myles standing there in his three-piece, tailored suit warmed me from the inside out.

"Oh, so it's like that, now?" A sly grin spread across Myles's face.

"It's how you make it." I leaned against the door, still not moving.

Myles sighed and motioned toward my living room. "May I come in?"

"You sure you have time?" I didn't mean to be difficult, but I was getting sick of Myles only fitting me into his schedule when he found time.

"Okay, since you want to be like that, I guess I'll just have to take this and go give it to the homeless woman I passed on the street on my way over here." Myles reached into his jacket pocket and pulled out a long, rectangular Tiffany box with a huge white bow on it.

I pursed my lips and, just as he was about to turn away, called out, "I guess you can come in."

He smiled again. "That's what I thought." I opened the door all the way and let him pass. He strutted in, took off his jacket, and threw it across the chair. He reeked with confidence. It would have pissed me off if he weren't so dang cute. "Now, why should I give you this?" he asked as he waved the box around.

It was my turn to smile. I felt like a giddy kid at Christmas. "Because it's your way of apologizing for being an insensitive jerk." I reached for the box. He pulled it back just out of my reach.

"I don't believe I was insensitive, but I do apologize that you had to go to the play by yourself."

"I didn't go at all. My tickets went to waste. You owe me two hundred dollars. Now give me my present."

Myles handed the box to me, letting his hand linger on mine. "I hope you'll accept my apology."

I took the box, tore the ribbon off, and opened it. It was a pink ruby tennis bracelet. It was beautiful.

"Ooooohhhh," I squealed as I gently pulled the bracelet out of the box. "You should have." I slid the bracelet around my wrist.

"You know I give my baby the best of everything." Myles pulled me to him and kissed me passionately. I could never stay mad at Myles long. He would shower me with gifts and whisper sweet nothings until I forgot what it was I was mad about in the first place.

I reached down and started unbuckling his trousers. "Let me show you how much I appreciate you giving me the best of everything," I said with a wicked grin.

Myles reached down, took my hands, and stopped me. I looked confused for a minute until he pulled my hands up to his lips and gently kissed them. "No, I'm the one who was in the doghouse. So let me show you."

"You should make me mad more often," I giggled as I nuzzled Myles's neck. We were lying on the zebra-skin rug in my living room.

"Naw, baby," he said as he gently stroked my hair. "I just want to make you happy."

We lay there in blissful silence for a few minutes before his cell phone went off. I silently blasted whoever had invented the cell phone before rolling over out of the way so he could answer it.

"Aren't you going to get that?" I asked when he didn't move.

"No, the rest of the night is yours. And yours only."

I shrieked with delight. Yes, Myles could be a jerk sometimes, but when it all boiled down to it, I couldn't help but feel my relationship had been made in heaven.

chapter 6

I could really get used to this. I stood proudly next to Myles while he cut the ribbon for a new homeless center in a part of town called Fifth Ward. It was a historically black area that had become dilapidated over the years. It was part of Myles's district, and he had been the spearhead behind getting the new homeless center built.

Now, as we stood outside among a sea of smiling faces—Myles, the noble, debonair councilman, and me, the doting, beautiful girlfriend—I couldn't help but feel that this was how life should be.

Myles extended his hand toward me and I smiled as I stepped forward. I politely waved at the crowd. I could hear the generous applause. A scraggly figure in the back of the crowd caught my eye, mainly because she was wearing a long overcoat, a scarf and shades in the middle of May. My mind immediately went to all the nut cases my station had covered. Don't ask me why, but she looked out of place. Myles always says I'm morbid and paranoid, but when you've covered as much death and destruction as I have, you can't help but be that way.

I eased back behind the podium. If she started firing, I didn't want to be first in the line of fire. But just as quickly as I noticed the woman, she was gone. I shook off my paranoia and turned my attention back to the press conference. Myles was talking about how much the district meant to him. Unfortunately, it was all an act. Myles had grown up a sheltered, spoiled rich kid, getting the best of everything. But my man had game. He knew what he wanted and knew how to get it, and it didn't hurt that he was helping people in the process.

After the ribbon-cutting ceremony, I watched Myles continue to work the crowd. I didn't stray too far from him, wanting to make sure everyone knew we were together.

"Miss Rollins, I love your work on Channel 2." I hadn't even noticed the petite woman standing before me. She had a huge grin on her face and was clutching a pen and paper in her hands. "May I have your autograph for my son, please?"

"It would be my pleasure." I took the pen and paper from her. I scribbled my name and station call letters on the paper before handing it back to her.

"I like you so much better than that Lorna lady at Channel 13," the woman murmured.

"That is so sweet of you. You must give me a call at the station so you can come by for a visit."

The woman smiled excitedly before scurrying off. I

would try to return her call if she followed up on my invitation, but with the amount of calls I got each day I didn't know how realistic that actually was.

Myles had maneuvered his way several feet from me, and I couldn't help but notice the way his secretary, Karen, was fawning all over him. I felt my blood rising as she brushed some lint off his jacket shoulder. Her hand lingered a little too long.

I eased over to where Myles was, making sure to drape my arm through his, and push Karen out of the way. I ignored the sneer on her face and put on my television personality as I continued to greet people.

We had just finished saying our last good-byes and were about to get into the car when a man stopped Myles and started talking to him. I made my way on toward the car, anxious to get home. The driver had just opened the door when I noticed the woman in the overcoat again, walking toward me. She still had on the shades and scarf, so I had no idea who she was. I was just about to jump into the car when she called my name. Normally, even that wouldn't have stopped me, but she called me by my whole first name.

"Hey, Raedella." She removed her sunglasses and was now standing directly in front of me. I motioned for the driver to go on and get in the car, which he did. "It's me, Laila," she said after I didn't respond. Honestly, I couldn't respond, because this could not possibly be my cousin standing in front of me. The Laila Evans I knew was a robust young woman with a beautiful smile and warm personality. She was my auntie Mel's oldest granddaughter. But this woman standing before me now was anything but beautiful.

I knew I was standing there with my jaw hanging open as I looked her up and down but I couldn't help it.

She chuckled. "I know I look different now, girl. Big-city living will do that to you."

She was saying that as if it were a good thing.

"Well, ain't you gon' say something? It's been what, ten, fifteen years?" She hit my shoulder, almost knocking me over.

"What happened to you?" was all I could manage to say.

"Dang, is that any way to greet your long-lost family?" She scowled.

I know it was rude, but I kept staring at her. She looked like she couldn't weigh any more than a hundred pounds, and that was soaking wet. Her skin looked like it was hanging off her face. There were dark circles underneath her eyes. Her teeth were yellow and she was missing a tooth in the front.

"I got a little hooked up on some drugs, but I'm clean now." She held out her arms and started pushing up her coat sleeves as if I were actually going to examine her arms. I was still stunned because the Laila I remembered had always been a straight-A, prissy young woman. "I came down here with my boyfriend—you remember Janky?" She paused, I guess waiting for me to confirm or deny I knew this Janky person.

"Anyway," she continued after I failed to respond, "that bastard got strung out then had me strung out too. He's up in county now, left me out here to fend for myself. I had to turn a few tricks and thangs, but I don't even do that anymore," she proudly exclaimed. "Now, I'm getting myself together. I live in that halfway house right over there." She pointed to a dilapidated building across the street.

"I don't have any money." I was wishing she would move on before Myles wrapped up his conversation.

She hit me on the shoulder. "Girl, I don't need your money. I just wanted to come say hi, that's all. I'm happy your boyfriend got this building for us. We need it." We stood in uncomfortable silence for a few seconds.

"Okay, then," I said, trying to ease closer to the car.

"You know, since Mama died, I hadn't been back home, so I was just wondering how everyone was doing." She lowered her head and her voice got soft. "I don't want to go back till I'm completely cleaned up."

I felt a twinge of sympathy for her, but I still knew I had to wrap up our conversation. "I don't know how anyone is doing. I don't talk to them anymore." I looked around nervously and noticed Myles heading to the car. "Oh, well, see you around." I reached for the door to try to hurry and ease into the car.

"Maybe we can get together some—"

I slammed the car door before she could finish her sentence.

Myles joined me in the car. "Man, I'm tired. I can't wait to get home. Who was that homeless person you were talking to?"

"Nobody. Just someone begging for money."

Myles leaned back in his seat and loosened his tie. "I can't for the life of me understand why those people don't just get a job."

I nodded my head in agreement.

chapter 7

There had to be something major going on. Everyone in the newsroom was gathered around the big monitor that hung at the front of the room. I had just gotten in, late as usual. No matter how hard I tried, I just couldn't get to work on time. Usually, I didn't care what anyone thought, but today, I was thankful for the diversion. I know people have been whispering about my hours and I just wasn't in the mood to add fuel to their fire. I glanced at Richard's office. The light was off and the door was locked, which meant he wasn't even in today. I relaxed a little.

"Oh, no! He's gonna crash," one of my colleagues shouted.

"He's going down the freeway the wrong way!" another one screamed.

It sounded like they were watching another high-speed chase. I glanced up and saw the chopper camera aimed at the U-Haul flying down Interstate 610. *Why do we insist on carrying those things live?* I wondered as I made my way into my office.

"Don't you want to watch this?" one of the photographers asked as he passed by my office.

"No. Unlike you people, I don't get off by watching high-speed chases," I snapped.

The photographer, Todd, laughed. "This is good. This dude just escaped from prison, held up the Bank of America downtown, shot a security guard and a six-year-old kid. Now, he's about to kill somebody else flying down the freeway like that."

I ignored Todd and grabbed my coffee cup before heading to the break room to fill up on my daily dose of java. I passed by the studio set where Keith, my male coanchor, was giving a play-by-play of what was going on.

After filling up my cup, I took a slow sip and savored the hot liquid as it slid down my throat. Myles was pleased with the ribbon-cutting ceremony so he'd wanted to go out to a jazz club. We were up late celebrating. I was absolutely worn out.

I glanced up at the TV in the break room and shook my head again at the way our helicopter camera followed every move of the U-Haul.

I was making my way back out to the newsroom when one of the reporters stopped me. "Rae, that guy has the same last name as you." He laughed, pointing to the mug shot that was flashing on the screen. "You sure that isn't your brother?"

I prepared to roll my eyes when I glanced up at the TV set. The next thing I knew, my cup of coffee had slipped from my hand and crashed to the floor. The noise made everyone jump and turn toward me, but the panicky voice of the helicopter pilot quickly diverted their attention.

I couldn't take my eyes off the TV. Kevin. Oh, my God. That was my cousin's mug shot plastered across that set. What the hell was going on? How could I be dealing with two of my relatives within the same week? I hadn't seen him in years, but there was no denying it. Those were his features, the narrow, cleft chin and eerie-looking eyes. Then they flashed his name on the screen—Kevin Rollins—and I swear, I thought I would pass out right there.

I managed to compose myself and ask Keria, one of the assistant producers, what was going on.

"Girl, this guy overpowered a guard in a prison work-release program in Huntsville and escaped. They say he's from Arkansas and a dangerous felon. He supposedly killed four people." Keria's wide eyes remained glued to the set.

I felt my throat dry up. I was so grateful no one knew I was from Arkansas.

"You know, I feel sorry for his family," Keria said, shaking her head. "I don't understand what kind of upbringing breeds a cold-blooded killer."

I could barely talk. Kevin's mother, my aunt Ola, my mother's oldest sister, was a churchgoing, God-fearing woman. She had done her best to raise her one girl and eight boys. But seven of the boys turned out terrible. And her only daughter, Nikki, was the biggest slut this side of the Mississippi. I wondered if Aunt Ola had any idea it was to this extreme with Kevin. This would kill her.

"Rae, are you all right?" Keria asked. "You look like you've seen a ghost."

"What? Oh, yeah. I'm fine. I-I just have to get back to work."

"I think the whole newsroom is on an official break while they watch *America's Most Wanted,*" Keria joked.

But I was in no laughing mood. That was my cousin, a wanted murderer/bank robber/escapee/God-only-knew-what-else, speeding down the highway.

I moaned as I walked back into my office. I couldn't bear to watch anymore. If I ever needed confirmation that getting away from my relatives was the best thing that had ever happened to me, this was it.

chapter 8

I was still stunned over seeing Kevin this morning and had been holed up in my office all day trying to get my bearings about me.

I wondered if Aunt Ola knew; a question that was answered as soon as I checked the voice mail messages in my office.

"Raedella, it's Mama Tee. Just letting you know your cousin Kevin done up and broke out of jail," Mama Tee said in the message. "He robbed a bank, hurt some folks and we heard he was down your way. Lord, Ola 'bout to lose her mind. If you see that boy, you ask him what in the world is he thinking and tell him to take his butt back to that prison. Oh yeah, Shondella got promoted to manager at Jr. Food Mart and Mrs. Miller gon' have to have her leg cut off. I told her that diabetes was gon' get her if she didn't take care of herself. You call me back and—" My machine cut her off. Her message actually made me smile. Not only because she just kept calling me with these crazy family updates, but I wondered if she actually thought I'd see Kevin—other than video of him running from police.

I shook my head as I deleted the message. I was contemplating whether I should call Mama Tee back when I glanced up to see Simone standing in my doorway. She had a hesitant look across her face.

"Yes, what is it, Simone?"

She looked like she wanted to say something but didn't know whether she should.

"Can't you see I'm busy?" Actually I wasn't. I was about to read the latest issue of *Essence*. But she didn't need to know that. "If you have something to say, spit it out."

"I . . . I was just wondering if you would take a look at my audition tape and give me some feedback," she stammered.

So I was right on target. She did want to be on air. Probably wanted my job. I frowned up at her.

She spoke again. "It's just, well, I respect your work and would love to, umm, get some constructive criticism on how I can improve."

I leaned back in my chair. The girl was brave. Part of my persona as this high-powered diva was being unapproachable, yet she still felt compelled to come ask for my opinion. If she wasn't trying to take my job, I might have some admiration for her. Might. "I don't know, Simone. I'm really busy."

Simone stepped into my office, a pleading look across her face. "I know that, so just whenever you get around to it, if you could maybe take a look at it . . ."

I sighed, making sure my irritation was evident. "Sorry, you'll just have to ask someone else."

Simone managed a smile. "I understand. I just thought I'd ask." She turned to leave.

I thought about it, then stopped her just as she reached the door. Maybe I needed to see what she had. "Simone, give me the tape. I can make time. I'll do all I can to help another sister out." I gave her a phony smile.

Simone quickly turned around, beaming with excitement. "Oh, thank you so much! I really appreciate this." She handed me the small Beta tape. "I won't harass you about it, just whenever you get a chance to look at it would be good."

"Umm-hmmm. I'll get around to it." I threw the tape down on my desk, then turned back to my computer, acting as if I were engrossed in my screen.

"Thank you, Rae. And I am thick-skinned. So I can take an honest assessment."

I waved her off. Believe me, I was going to be honest. The girl had to learn the hard way that this was a cutthroat business. If down the line she ever hoped to compete with someone of my caliber, she would have to be able to endure the hard times.

I glanced over my shoulder, making sure she was gone, then I got up, walked over, and closed my door. I grabbed the tape off my desk and popped it in the outdated Beta machine in the corner of my office. I pulled up a chair, sat down, and pressed play.

"Knock, knock."

Shereen's voice startled me. She walked in, shutting the door behind her. I glared at her. "Most people knock, then wait for an answer before they come in."

"I'm not most people. Whatcha doing?"

I grinned. "I'm about to watch Simone's audition tape. You in for a good laugh?"

Shereen pulled up a chair next to me. "I'm always down for a good laugh. I didn't know Simone wanted to be on air."

"Don't they all? The tape just started." We turned our attention back to the TV. I turned up the volume. Simone was already in the middle of her first story. It was about the police department being under fire for shoddy procedures at the DNA lab. She did a stand-up—the part of the story where you see her walking and talking to tell us something about the story—and in this case, showing how a leak in the roof had allowed rain to drop on critical DNA evidence. I remember seeing the story on air. She had actually told my boss about it, but because she was just a production assistant, they gave the story to another reporter to do. I guess she put a story together herself for her tape.

The next two stories were also rehashes of stories that had aired on our news. But they were actually written better than the ones that had aired.

I stopped the tape before her last story could finish.

"Damn," Shereen said, looking at me with her mouth open. "That heifer is good."

I got up and turned the TV off. "She's all right."

"All right? Man, she's better than half the reporters we have on air right now. I'm in awe." Shereen was shaking her head.

"She wasn't that good. Did you see the way her hair looked on that first report? She really needs to see a stylist to do something about those split ends."

Shereen laughed. "All you can find negative to talk about is how she looks? Come on, you know those stories were da bomb."

"Shereen, nobody says *da bomb* anymore."

"I do. Anyway, it's just a matter of time before someone snatches her up and puts her on air. I wouldn't be surprised if she got a job in a nice-sized city real soon."

"Please. She needs to take her little tail to Victoria, Texas, and pay some dues like the rest of us."

Shereen's smile faded. She got up, then walked over to my desk, plopping down in the chair in front of it. "Can I ask you something? Truthfully, why do you treat her so bad? She's a really nice girl."

I rolled my eyes. I didn't feel like getting into this with Shereen, but she was the type that wouldn't let up, so I decided to go ahead and be real. "Look, I know her type. Little yellow girl who thinks she can break into this business because of her looks. She's in for a rude awakening and I'm just trying to prepare her." I had been where Simone was, bright-eyed and ready to conquer the world. She had to be tough to make it, and believe it or not, I was really trying to toughen her up.

"But you have to admit, the girl is good," Shereen said.

"I don't have to admit anything. Even if she is that good, which she's not, she doesn't need to get a big head."

"Like you?" Shereen smiled slyly.

"I'm going to pretend I didn't hear that. Look, I used to be Simone. Cute, thought I was full of talent, and ready to take on the world. I got to Tyler and reality hit me smack dead in the face. I was the only black person working there, and those people treated me like dirt. I was nice and people ran over me left and right."

"You don't seem like you were ever nice."

"Shut up and let me finish."

Shereen shrugged.

"As I was saying, I cried myself to sleep so many nights. I turned to the only other black person in the business and she was mean to me, too. But you know what? It made me a stronger person. That's all I'm trying to do."

"You're doing it well."

"Whatever."

"It just seems to me that as people of color, we should be more supportive of one another, not fighting like crabs in a bucket," Shereen said matter-of-factly.

"I'm no crab," I protested.

"Hmph. If you say so."

"That little Miss Thang has nothing that I want. She's the one who wants my job."

"Don't be ridiculous. I'm sure that eventually she'd like to have your job. But I doubt very seriously she wants to take your job from you right now."

"Not that she even could."

"Exactly. So why do you feel threatened?"

"Shereen, no offense, but you work in promotions. The news business is a different creature. I don't feel threatened from that little wannabe. But all my life, no one has given me anything. I have had to work for everything, twice as hard. So, I'm just trying to prepare that girl for the hard days ahead."

"Oh, so this is all about you caring for her?"

"Something like that."

"Yeah, okay. Tell that to someone who doesn't know you like I do." Shereen got up and walked toward the door. "You don't care about nobody but yourself."

I resented that comment. And why was my so-called friend going off on me?

Shereen stopped in the doorway. "Oh, yeah, you care about me, too." She smiled. "I don't know why, and even though you try and act hard, I really think you care about our friendship, which is why I'm still hanging around. So, stop pouting at me for being real with you. And don't forget, you're going to church with me Sunday."

"I never said anything about going to church with you Sunday."

"Ummm, yes, you did. I told you last month I wanted you to come with me on the twenty-first because my niece was singing a solo. You promised."

I raised my eyebrows. I remembered making that promise, I just never thought Shereen would hold me to it. She knew I seldom went to church.

"If you don't go with me, you can forget about me being your friend," Shereen playfully threatened. "I'm always there when you call. Maya is your biggest fan and I told her you'd be there. So do this one thing for me. Okay? Thanks, you're a doll." Shereen blew me a kiss, then sashayed out.

I reluctantly smiled. Shereen was my girl. Even though I didn't agree with some of the stuff she'd said earlier, I knew she was frank. She loved me despite my faults and I couldn't help but love her as well. If she wanted me there for her niece, I'd be there.

chapter 9

I studied the numbers in my checkbook register once again. I couldn't for the life of me figure out why I kept coming up short $200. I eased out my calculator and tried to balance the numbers again.

Shereen leaned over toward me and hissed, "I can't believe you're sitting up in church balancing your checkbook."

"What? I need to do something. This man is about to put me to sleep," I whispered back. I knew I shouldn't have let Shereen talk me into coming to church with her today. Even though I'd grown up in the church, I just didn't get anything out of coming. I hadn't regularly attended since I'd left Sweet Poke and hadn't even set foot in a church since Easter Sunday last year. My disdain probably came from Mama Tee forcing us to go to church every time the dang doors opened.

Shereen poked me in my side and motioned for me to

put the checkbook away. I reluctantly slid it back into my purse. I should just leave. Shereen's niece Maya had already performed her solo, which was absolutely beautiful. So, I'd done what I'd promised I would do. But I knew Shereen would have a fit if I tried to leave. Besides that, we were seated right in the middle of the pew and I'd have to cross over several people to make an escape.

I sighed, leaned back, and tried to turn my attention back to the preacher. He looked to be in his mid-fifties, strikingly handsome with a salt-and-pepper beard. Shereen had told me he was a widower; his wife had recently died from a heart attack. And from the looks of the women in the pews salivating over his every word, it seemed like the Reverend Simon Jackson could have his pick of women willing to step into the first lady's shoes.

"The problem is, God speaks to us all the time, we just don't hear him," Pastor Jackson said.

I leaned toward Shereen. "What's he talking about?"

Shereen huffed. "Something you most definitely need to be hearing."

"Anyway," I said as I sat back and tried to focus on his sermon.

"See, if God ain't saying something we want to hear or something we think can directly benefit us, we don't listen to Him. Tell me, church, are you listening to God?" The reverend continued.

"Yes!" several people shouted.

"Are you really listening? With your heart? Can you hear what He's really trying to say to you?"

"Yes!" they shouted again as the organist began playing.

I sighed in exasperation. Here we go, the dance and minstrel show.

Growing up, everybody and their mama at Greater Gethsemane back in Sweet Poke used to get the Holy Ghost. I could never understand why people had to dance and shout to give honor to God.

I tuned out all the shouting and began mentally making my checklist of things I needed to do this week.

I felt a bit of relief when I heard Pastor Jackson begin to wrap things up. It took fifteen more minutes before he finally dismissed the congregation, but when he did, I grabbed my purse and made a beeline to the door.

"The devil was hard at work on you today," Shereen said as she caught up with me in the church lobby.

"Since when did you become a Holy Roller?" I asked.

She laughed. "Why I gotta be a Holy Roller? Because I believe in God?"

"I believe in God."

"I can't tell."

"Why? Because I don't jump up and down and shout like I'm crazy?"

"No, because you don't act like it. When's the last time you prayed?"

"I pray," I said defensively.

"I mean really prayed? For something other than for Myles to act right."

I cut my eyes at Shereen. "That was a low blow."

"You know I keep it real with you, Rae. And as a Christian, it's my duty to tell you when I don't think you're living right."

"What? So now you're a soldier for God's army? Miss Sleep-with-anything-that-shows-me-attention." I was pissed now. How dare she try to challenge me?

Shereen looked at me like she wanted to curse me out

right there in the lobby of Zion Hill Missionary Baptist Church. Then she slowly smiled. "Okay, you got me back 'cause that was a low blow, too." She reached over and grabbed my hand. "Girl, you know I don't judge you. I can't judge you because my house is falling apart itself. I just feel like you're not really happy, even though you try to pretend you are. And I thought that if you sought guidance from God, it would help guide you in the right direction."

I rolled my eyes to the top of my head. Try as I might, I couldn't stay mad at Shereen.

I was just about to say something when we were interrupted by a loud voice in the corner of the lobby.

"Why you gotta bring her here, Bobby, huh?"

I looked toward the young woman. She looked like she couldn't be more than twenty years old. Her auburn-tinted curls framed her delicate face. She was pretty, too pretty to be standing in the church lobby acting a fool over some man.

"Oh, Lord, here she goes again," Shereen said.

"Who is that?"

"Girl, that's Reverend Jackson's drama-filled daughter, Rachel. Her baby daddy married somebody else and she ain't taking the news too well."

"Rachel, that's my wife and this is the church she attends," the man responded as he picked up a little boy who was the spitting image of him.

Rachel started crying. "You're supposed to be the man. Find another church! Do you know how much this hurts me?"

People had started to stop and stare. A handsome man in a choir robe walked over and whispered something in Rachel's ear before taking her hand and leading her out of the lobby.

I shook my head in disgust. That would've been my life had I stayed in Sweet Poke. Somebody's baby mama with no class whatsoever.

"You ready to go, or are you still mad at me?" Shereen's voice broke my thoughts.

"I'm fine." I followed Shereen out to her car, where we got in and rode in silence for a good ten minutes.

Shereen reached over and turned down the volume on the gospel radio station we'd been listening to. "Rae, don't get mad because I'm asking this, but why do you seem so, I don't know, disconnected from God?"

"What are you talking about?"

"It's just that you are so hard on everybody, yet you let Myles run all over you. On the outside you look like a strong black woman, but it's like you're miserable on the inside." Shereen exited the freeway and pulled onto the feeder road.

"Where are you going?" I asked.

She ignored my question and pulled into the Lakes at 610, a serene park on the southwest side where couples often came to talk and families came to play. Shereen parked the car and turned to me. "Now, tell me what's really going on."

I folded my arms and contemplated going off on Shereen, but finally decided that if she wanted the truth, I'd give it to her. "You want to know why I'm so disconnected from God, as you say? Huh? Well, I'll tell you. It's because I can't for the life of me understand what kind of God allows a mother to just drop her kids off like they're some old clothes she's giving to Goodwill. I can't seem to find praise for a God that will let those same children live a life of indescribable poverty."

Shereen listened attentively. I felt empowered getting everything off my chest.

"In case you haven't guessed, I'm talking about myself. My mother dumped me at a gas station in the middle of the night and I didn't hear from her for years. Granted, my grandmother raised me, but it was a horrible, poverty-ridden life. She struggled constantly, cleaning houses and taking care of people's kids just to keep food on the table. My sister and I had to grow up too fast. My brother has leukemia and could die at any time. And my youngest sister, Jasmine . . ." I turned my head and took a deep breath before continuing. "My baby sister died a tragic death when she was just six years old. I ran as fast as I could from my life in Sweet Poke, Arkansas, and I haven't looked back. I have had more than my share of tragedy."

I waited for Shereen to ask me how Jasmine had died and was grateful when she didn't.

"So, you'll have to excuse me if I find it hard to be faithful," I continued. Shereen still didn't say anything. "What?" I said, turning to her.

She gave me a faint smile. "Nothing. I'll keep you in my prayers."

I let out an exasperated sigh. "You do that, Shereen."

We rode in silence the rest of the way home.

My conversation with Shereen was still fresh on my mind as I sat at Houston's restaurant waiting on Myles. I knew she had some valid points about my relationship with God, but she just didn't understand. I didn't think she ever could.

I shook off the melancholy thoughts that had been plaguing me since Shereen dropped me off thirty minutes ago. I was here to have a good time and celebrate my Emmy nomination, which I found out about four days ago. I was up for another Emmy for best talk show host. I'd wanted to go out when I first found out about it, but of course, Myles couldn't squeeze me into his schedule until today. Even though this celebration was late, I was determined to have a wonderful evening out with my man.

"Well, if it isn't the second-best news anchor in town."

I looked up at the leggy, blond-haired woman standing over me, Channel 13's news anchor, Lorna Holliday. "Hello Lorna," I replied, not bothering to fake a smile. "I see you've been going to Madonna's hairdresser."

Lorna patted her hair and I could tell I had hit a sore spot. "I'll have you know, blonde is the latest fashion trend."

"Not on black women, it's not. But hey, I'm only an Emmy-nominated talk show host. What do I know?"

Lorna glared at me. "I see you've resorted to dining alone," she smirked.

"Lorna, it looks like your daughters are waiting on you?" I pointed at the two thirty-something looking women standing off to the side waiting on her.

"Those are my sisters," Lorna snarled.

I shrugged and quickly turned my attention back to the menu. I didn't feel like sparring with her and she was ruining my mood. The sad part was I'd never done anything to that woman. Well, except come in and topple her from her number one spot, but that wasn't reason enough to hate me.

Lorna didn't bother to say goodbye as she huffed and stormed off to her table.

I glanced at my watch. Myles was now forty-five minutes late and I was officially upset. Just as I was about to call his cell phone, my phone rang.

"Baby . . ."

"Let me guess," I cut Myles off, "something came up."

"Sweetheart, please don't be mad. I was going to try and make it to dinner in between meetings, but it's just not working out that way."

"Myles, this was supposed to be a celebration!" I caught Lorna looking my way, no doubt trying to be nosy.

"I know, baby. But I promise I will make it up to you. I just—"

I didn't even give him time to finish his sentence. I snapped my cell phone closed, grabbed my purse, paid for my strawberry margarita and hightailed it out of the restaurant.

chapter 10

I was so not believing this. I had just begun reading my e-mail at work and the first message had me fuming. It was from Richard, who had been missing in action, but I guess had stopped in the office long enough to send this e-mail.

> It is my extreme honor to announce the promotion of Simone Sanders from production assistant to reporter trainee. Simone has proven she is an invaluable employee and a solid journalist. Therefore, we will give her a chance to showcase her talents on air. She will train for six months before coming on board as a full-time reporter.

I was floored. How was she able to work that? It was just a week ago that she had had me look at her tape. I hadn't even given it back to her yet. She needed to take her little yellow tail to a small town and work her way up like the rest of us had. What in the world was Richard thinking? I was beginning to think he wasn't thinking. He didn't half come to work these days and when he did, he was always acting strange. And this was definitely a strange move. I mean, the girl had no experience. And it's not like we needed any more black faces. They had me, our weekend male anchor, and two reporters. If that little tramp thought she was getting her slimy paws on my job, she'd better think again. I would chew her up and spit her out.

I reread the e-mail, getting angry all over again and decided to call Stan. After his secretary patched me through, I didn't waste any time.

"Hey Stan, just trying to figure out what's going on with this reporter training they have Simone doing."

"Hello to you too, Rae," Stan replied, in his usual chipper voice. "Richard told me about that. It's no big deal. He's just trying to give the girl an opportunity."

"Since when did we get in the training business?"

Stan laughed. "Do I sense a hint of jealousy?"

I didn't see anything funny. "Don't be ridiculous, Stan. I'm just trying to get clarification."

"Rae, sweetheart, you have no cause to be bothered, feel threatened, or anything," Stan said. "You know you are the person who keeps the viewers tuned in. The company just started a reporter trainee program and Richard thought Simone would fit well in it. But trust me, it will be a long, long time before she's ever able to become my chocolate star."

I smiled. That's why I loved Stan. He knew just how to make me feel better.

"So don't you worry your pretty little head about anything other than taking home yet another Emmy. By the way, congrats on that. You just keep doing what you do and making us all rich," Stan said. "Look, my other line is ringing and I need to take this call. Are we okay?"

"We are. Thanks Stan."

I sighed, put the phone back on the hook and was just about to delete the e-mail when my phone rang. "Rae Rollins," I answered.

"Miss Rollins, you have visitors up front." The receptionist was whispering into my phone. "They're demanding to see you."

"Kay, you know I don't see people without an appointment. Get their names and numbers and send them on their way."

"I'm afraid it's not that easy."

"I told you her bougie ass wasn't gon' come out!" I heard a male voice shout.

"Hell, naw . . . she coming to see us!" a different male voice roared.

"Oh my God, Kay. Who are those people? Call security."

"Well, I was going to," Kay whispered. "But they say they're related to you. They say they're from some place north of here called Sweet Poke. And they aren't leaving until they talk to you."

I closed my eyes and prayed this was a really bad dream. This could not be happening to me.

"They say their names are Scooter and June Bug."

"Why, why, why?" I stomped my foot under the desk so hard, I almost broke a heel. Scooter and June were some of my cousins from Sweet Poke. Kevin's brothers. I thought Scooter was in jail himself. I hadn't talked to either of them in years. They were pure country thugs. Why in the world were they bothering me?

"Do you want me to go ahead and call security?" Kay whispered.

I knew Scooter and June would act straight fools. The best thing would be for me to go ahead and see what they wanted.

"No, just tell them I'm on my way." I placed the phone back on the cradle, took a deep breath, then headed up to the front office.

I was totally embarrassed when I saw them standing in the lobby. I was grateful that it was Kay at the front desk and not her backup, gossipy receptionist LaMonica. Kay was the epitome of professionalism. She wouldn't go running to tell everyone about my people.

I surveyed Scooter and June. According to Mama Tee, the thirty-four-year-old twins were still living at home with Aunt Ola. With all the gold in their mouth, they probably could've bought their own place. Scooter sported a long, dripping Jheri curl. He had on baggy jeans and a FUB (not FUBU) shirt. The *U* looked like it had washed off. The Jheri-curl juice had his face looking like he had smeared Vaseline across it. June was the better looking of the two. He had thick cornrows and wore some Karl Kan (yep, no *i*) overalls. One strap was left undone and hung loosely across his chest. I wanted to tell him people stopped wearing their overalls like that twenty years ago, but then I figured, why bother?

"Scooter. June. Isn't this a surprise?" I put on my best fake smile.

"What's shaking, Cousin?" Scooter said.

"You high society now," June added, looking at my picture on the lobby wall.

I simply smiled. "What brings you all down to Houston?"

"We need to holla at you 'bout a li'l sumptin', Cuz," Scooter said.

I looked at Kay, who had busied herself typing on her computer. I contemplated taking them into our conference room, but quickly nixed that idea. No way did I want anyone to see them.

"Why don't we step outside? Did you park out front?"

"Word."

I sighed and followed them out front. "Now, what's going on?" I probably should've asked about Aunt Ola, but I was anxious to get this over with.

"Look here, we know you don't like dealin' with us too much since you left," June said. "But, since you all big-time and stuff now, we thought you could help us."

"With what?"

"We need you to get Kevin out of jail."

I looked at them as if they were on crack. "Kevin, as in your brother Kevin? As in the Kevin that killed four people, robbed a bank, led authorities on a high-speed chase, hit an old lady crossing the street and shot at police? That Kevin?"

"Yep." Scooter nodded as if he had just given me a simple request like, can I borrow $5?

"They treating him like dirt in there," June interjected.

Yeah, that's usually what they do to criminals, I wanted to say. "Guys, I don't know what kind of power you think I have, but I can't help Kevin."

"Can't you do an expo on the jail or something? I seen

them undercover investigations the TV people be doing," June pleaded.

"That's exposé."

"Whatever. All I know is corruption is goin' on up at that prison and it needs exposing," Scooter replied.

"Look," June continued when he saw the utter confusion across my face. "Kevin would die if he knew I was telling you this, but some of them men up there, they funny."

I still wasn't getting it. "Maybe they use humor to pass the time."

June let out an exasperated sigh. "Not that kind of funny." He looked around, then fluttered his hand back and forth. "Funny, funny."

I wanted to scream. "And your point?"

"Kevin is scared them funny dudes . . ." He paused and cringed. "He's scared they might try something with him!"

"We got to get my baby brother out," Scooter exclaimed. "*You've* got to get him out."

I was still looking at them as if they were crazy. I couldn't believe they were wasting my time with this foolishness. Even if I did have the power to get Kevin out of jail, I wouldn't. I mean, good grief, four people were killed! "I don't know what you want me to do. But number one, I don't have that kind of power. And number two, he committed a serious crime, make that *crimes* with an *s*."

"It ain't him. He got hooked on that crack and it's messed him up," Scooter said, a pleading look etched across his face.

"I'm sorry." I shrugged and headed back toward the front lobby. I didn't know why I thought they would just go away. They followed me, no doubt trying to think of something to say to convince me to intervene.

"But he's in pain," Scooter protested.

"So is the old lady he hit in that chase, and the families of the four people he killed," I bluntly responded without turning around.

"What happened to innocent until proven guilty?" June said.

I stopped just as I was opening the door and turned to face my cousins. "It died with the invention of the video camera. Kevin is *on tape* holding up the bank, shooting the four people, and taking off."

"So, it's like that. You not gon' even try?" Scooter threw up his hands in frustration.

"I told you this bougie skank wouldn't help," June scoffed.

"You come asking *me* for help for your trifling convict brother and call me a skank?" I couldn't believe I'd even wasted my time with these ingrates.

"We're your family!" Scooter jumped up in my face.

Inside the lobby, I saw Kay stand up, phone in hand, ready to call security. She looked at me as if waiting for the word. I raised a hand to let her know I had the situation under control—for now.

"Look, I haven't seen any of you in years and you waltz in here asking the impossible. I'm sorry. I can't help you. Now, I'm going to ask you to leave before Kay calls security."

Both of them glared daggers at me.

"Snobby ass—" Scooter snarled.

June grabbed his arm and pulled him back. "Let it go. She gon' need us one day. You can bet on that."

I looked at him and almost laughed. Need them? For what? There wasn't anything they could do for me—except get the hell out of my station and take their country behinds back to Sweet Poke.

I watched them ease out the door and hoped that that would be my last time seeing them.

chapter 11

I whirled my pasta around my fork. Another dinner spent alone. As usual, Myles had called, saying he was running late. I was upset at first because this had become a regular habit with us. Here I was at his condo, two twelve-ounce steaks, jumbo shrimp, and angel-hair pasta sitting on the table, getting cold.

Myles could be so inconsiderate. I swear, sometimes I wondered how I could possibly love someone so selfish. I heard someone turning the doorknob and thought, finally, he's home.

I got up to greet him at the door. But instead of the door opening, the knob just kept viciously jiggling. Then a woman's voice called out, "Myles, you can't run from me forever. Open this damn door!"

I didn't know whether to be frightened or pissed. I hesitated before opening the door. "May I help you?" I asked after I swung the door open. A short woman with a closely cropped, blond Afro stood there, attitude all over her face. She had strong features and might have been attractive if not for the scowl on her face. She had a small diamond earring in her nose and wore a spandex miniskirt with a V-cut T-shirt that prominently showcased her double Ds.

"Who the hell are you?" she asked.

"Excuse me?" I knew this four-foot-tall heifer was not banging on my man's door, asking me who *I* was.

"I didn't stutter." She pushed past me and made her way inside. "You know what? I don't really care who you are. Where is Myles?" She looked around the room, her hands on her hips like she belonged there. Oh, no, she wasn't about to punk me in my man's home.

"Look, I don't know who you think you are, but Myles isn't here and you need to leave."

She crossed her arms and looked at me cockeyed. "Awwww, snap. I know who you are. You that news lady. Myles told me he was dating a local celebrity, but he never said who."

"Well, I'm glad you know who I am. But what you probably don't know is this pretty face can get real ghetto." I left the door open and stepped in her face, daring her to make a move. I wasn't the bravest of people, but I wasn't about to be played for a fool either. "I will make sure I tell my boyfriend you stopped by."

She smirked. "Well, can you tell *your* boyfriend that his *other* girlfriend doesn't appreciate being played. Now, I can deal with you, but I ain't about to deal with no other hos."

I looked at this woman like she had lost her mind. All this drama was making my head hurt. "Who are you?"

She uncrossed her arms and waved a hand in my face as she announced, "My name is Delana. And I'm what's known as the other woman."

I didn't know how to react. But Delana looked like she couldn't care less about my feelings.

Delana adjusted her knockoff Louis Vuitton bag on her shoulder and started wiggling her neck. "Look here. I told that sorry bastard that if he messed over me again, there would be hell to pay. So here I am. I hate to be the one to break it to you, but *our* man ain't no good."

Our man? Okay, this fool was straight trippin' and I was not about to listen to her madness. "You know what, Delana, you need to leave." I was trying to maintain some dignity, but this no-class tramp was making it real difficult.

"Naw, I ain't leaving until I say what it is I came to say. Myles ain't here to hear it, so you will." I sized her up. Girlfriend looked like she had some street in her. I could probably get one good punch in if I jumped her. Oh, who was I kidding? I'm no fighter. I talk a lot of noise, but that's about as far as it goes. This woman looked like she had been around the block a few times. I saw there would be no getting her out the door until she had her rant.

"Say what you gotta say." I walked over and shut the door before turning back to her. "But make it quick."

"That's what I thought," she said as she smacked on a wad of gum. "Anyway, my cousin's baby daddy's sister saw Myles at this motel tonight with some other woman. At first I thought it was you, his celebrity woman, but then I figured if you was so high profile, you wouldn't be goin' to no seedy motel. How you get on TV, anyway? I think I'd make a cute reporter." She stopped talking and struck a pose, then quickly returned to her defiant stance. "Never mind. We can talk about that later. Anyway, so I jumps in my car and hightails it over to the Diamond Inn off Highway 288. I sat out there honking my horn and calling his name until he came out. Then that fool gon' have the nerve to try and play me. Tell me to beat it! Call me a crazy ho. Oh, I'm a show him crazy." She pulled a switchblade out of her purse and began slicing up his leather sofa.

This was absolutely unreal. This woman had to be lying because I knew there was no way in hell Myles would reduce himself to the level of messing with someone like this.

I contemplated grabbing her arm, but sister-girl looked like she would've just kept swinging that blade. I decided this situation was beyond my control.

"Stop it!" I shouted. She ignored me and moved on to the love seat. "I'm calling the cops!" I finally yelled. That seemed to set in with her because she paused, the knife poised in midair.

"Fine. I'll leave, but you tell that low-down dirty dog this ain't over." She closed the switchblade, dropped it in her purse, patted her Afro, pulled her spandex skirt down a little, and strutted out the front door. I stood there in utter disbelief. Where was Myles? He had to come straighten out this madness. I just knew he would not jeopardize everything we had to mess with a freak like her.

I numbly made my way into the kitchen, where I tried to clean up the now cold dinner. After I finished, I walked back into the living room. I stared at the sofa. It was damaged beyond repair. Delana had sliced it to shreds. I fell down on the love seat, which had escaped her wrath. I buried my face in my hands, hoping that Myles would hurry home so he could tell me this was all a big misunderstanding. I didn't know what I would do if it wasn't.

It was well after three in the morning when Myles came home. I was still sitting on the love seat. All of the lights were out in the living room when I heard him ease the front door closed.

He jumped when he saw me. "Rae, baby, what are you doing up?"

"Where have you been?" I didn't look up at him.

"I told you I had to work late to go over the Metro Rail proposal."

I turned to him, my gaze intense. "Was your meeting at the Diamond Inn?"

"What is going on with you? Where'd you get that? And why are you sitting here in the dark?" He walked over and flipped on the light. His mouth dropped open when he noticed his sofa. "What the . . ." He looked at me for an explanation. "Why did you cut my sofa up?"

"I didn't cut your sofa up." I kept my eyes focused on him and my voice calm. "Delana cut your sofa up."

"How did she get in the house?"

"Oh, so you *do* know who she is?" I sat up, the calmness leaving my body.

He sighed heavily, like he'd been busted. "Um, yeah. She's this friend of mine."

"She seems to think she's more than just a friend."

"Look, Rae, I'm tired. My sofa is ripped to shreds and I can't do this with you."

I felt tears forming, but I was determined not to cry. "Myles, you owe me an explanation. Who is Delana and where were you tonight?"

"What is this? Am I on trial?"

Now my patience was wearing thin. "Who the hell is Delana and where were you tonight?" I yelled as I pounded the coffee table.

Myles rubbed his head. He hesitated before speaking. "Delana is no one. And I had a meeting tonight."

"A meeting at a motel!" I screamed. So now he was going to try to play me for stupid. I threw back the afghan that had been draped across my lap and stormed into his bedroom. I grabbed my duffel bag and started stuffing my things in it. I had never changed out of my clothes so I was still fully dressed. "I'm sick of this," I screamed as I stuffed my belongings in the bag. "You never have time for me! You're always disappearing for hours on end. And you and your flirtatious behavior 'bout to get on my damn nerves! Now some ghettofied tramp comes sashaying in here, mad because you're cheating on us!" I could no longer contain the tears. They started pouring down my face. Myles had followed me and was now standing in the doorway.

"What are you doing?"

"You're the genius, what does it look like I'm doing? I'm leaving." I walked to his closet and started grabbing my shoes, which were neatly lined up on my side of the large walk-in closet.

"So, just like that, you're going to take the word of someone you've never met over someone you know and love."

I stopped with an armful of shoes in front of me and

spun toward him. "So are you telling me she's lying?"

Myles smoothly moved toward me and gently removed my shoes from my grip. He threw them back in the closet. "Yes, she's lying. Come on, I'm a political star on the rise. Why would I jeopardize my career"—he caressed my cheek—"my life with you, for someone with as much class as my left foot?"

"Well, then, why is she your *friend*?" I was trying not to give in so easily, although I desperately wanted to believe him. She did seem so out of character for him.

"She's a woman I tried to help at the community center that developed an extreme crush on me. She got really ignorant when I told her there was no chance of us ever being together." He lifted my chin so that our eyes met. "A man like me needs and wants a woman like you. But more importantly, I love you and don't want anyone else. You do believe me, don't you?"

"I . . . I don't know. What about the motel? She says you were at a motel with someone else."

"Let me repeat, she is a liar."

"So where were you then?"

He removed his hand, then turned and walked toward the bedroom window. He gazed out into the darkness. "I did have a meeting, but if you must know," he said without turning around, "after that, I drove around thinking about us."

"Us?"

He turned toward me, a huge smile across his face. "Yes, us. I was thinking of how much I love you. And, well, I needed some time to make sure I was doing the right thing."

"Myles what are you talking about? Doing the right thing how?"

"Well, this isn't how I had planned on doing this, but since you think I was out cheating, I have to go ahead and tell you what I was doing." He walked toward me, then dropped down on one knee. My heart started racing.

"I don't have your ring yet because I wanted you to go with me to pick it out, but . . ." He took my hand and gazed into my eyes. "I have been missing a piece of me. For so long, I have felt incomplete. Will you join with me so that I can be complete?"

My hand was shaking fiercely. "What are you saying?"

"I'm saying, will you marry me, Rae Rollins?"

We had talked about marriage, but I had no idea he was anywhere near ready for it. In fact, whenever I brought it up, he changed the subject so quickly it wasn't funny.

"Are you serious? Don't play with me."

"I'm as serious as a triple bypass."

I studied his face, hoping that he wasn't just proposing to get out of trouble. I don't know if it was because I wanted it so badly, but I swear I saw the sincerity in his eyes. Deep down, I think I didn't buy what Myles was saying, but I started thinking about being Mrs. Myles Jacobs and decided it wasn't even worth arguing about. If he did mess with her, it was just something to do on the side. No way would he want anything real with her. Don't get me wrong, I'm not stupid. There probably was some grain of truth to what Delana said, but most men are going to cheat anyway. As long as I can have one that I know loves me and who can give me the life I need, then that's all that really matters.

"Yes! Yes!" I pulled him up toward me and hugged him tightly. "Yes, I will marry you!" I began kissing him fiercely as I envisioned our life together, a life so far removed from Sweet Poke.

chapter 12

The last three weeks were the best of my life. Myles had been everything I ever dreamed of, attentive, loving, affectionate, and optimistic about our future. We had even taken a spontaneous four-day vacation to the Poconos this past weekend.

I was back at work, trying to come down off my high. I had pretty much been closed up in my office all morning. I was sifting through folders full of e-mail when the assistant producer, Keria, waved at me through the window of my office door. I motioned for her to come in.

"Hey, welcome back. How was your vacation?" she asked.

"Great. Hated to come back."

"I didn't know if you read the e-mail about today's meeting?" Keria said.

I shook my head. "No, I was just making my way through all my e-mails. There's over a hundred here."

"Well, we're supposed to have a meeting this morning, and I hear it's supposed to be a big announcement."

"Oh, really?"

Keria looked nervously around before stepping farther into my office. "Yeah. You know how Richard is always blowing up at people and coming in late for work?"

"Yeah, he's been on a leave of absence. Personal problems I heard."

"Personal all right. Word is he got arrested for DUI."

I was amazed that Keria was spreading office gossip, but I found myself intrigued. Since Myles's proposal, I'd been so out of the loop at work.

"Wow. I knew things had been crazy around here, but I had no idea it was that."

"Yeah, and I overheard two photographers talking about how this meeting was about the station cleaning house. But I need to get back to my desk. I just wanted to give you a heads-up."

I thanked Keria and leaned back in my chair to process what she'd said. Truth be told, I didn't really care if the announcement was involving layoffs. I wasn't too worried about their getting rid of me. I was the star of the show and getting rid of me would have been ratings suicide.

"Will the staff please gather in the large auditorium?" the security guard's voice boomed over the intercom.

I made my way out of my office and walked with the rest of the staff to the auditorium. At the front of the room I saw three men in designer suits, corporate-looking types. Stan, the general manager, stood next to them. A slender black woman in a tailored navy suit sat next to them, writing on a notepad. She had to be their secretary.

This must be pretty big if they were having their secretary tag along.

The tallest of the three men stepped up to the microphone once all of the staff members had settled in. "I'm sure many of you have heard about the personal problems involving Richard. We are here to inform you that he has chosen to step down and focus on getting his life back in order. Normally, finding an adequate replacement would take months, but we had someone we had been grooming to take over as news director for the Philadelphia station. Instead, we have done some restructuring and decided she would best fit here. She is a solid news journalist, a shrewd businesswoman, and just what we need to hold on to our spot as Houston's leader in news and entertainment. Ladies and gentlemen, allow me to introduce you to your new vice president of news, Dina Burns-Stanton."

The secretary stood up and walked toward them. My mouth immediately dropped open. She smiled at Stan and the other corporate flunkies before approaching the microphone.

"Hello. Let me begin by saying how honored I am to be given the charge of leading such a dynamic team. I have studied the numbers, and while we're a solid number one, I have some great ideas to keep us in that number one position. I look forward to meeting each one of you, talking with you, and getting your input on how we can stay Houston's news and entertainment leader."

She seemed together, poised, and in command. She was a beautiful woman who could well have had a prosperous career in front of the camera. I had never worked for a black woman before so I thought this would be pretty interesting. I sat back and surveyed her as the corporate types made other announcements.

Once they had dismissed the meeting, I approached her, flashing a huge smile. This sister was going to be calling the shots. I needed to put on my best face. "Hi, Dina. I'm Rae Rollins, the main anchor and host of *The Rae Rollins Show*. Richard used to call me the face of Channel 2." I giggled.

"I'm not Richard," she icily responded.

I bit down on my lip. This was going to be a lot harder than I'd thought. I couldn't believe this. "Oh, I didn't mean to insinuate that you were. It's just—"

Then that wench straight cut me off. "Excuse me," she said, before walking off to talk with someone else.

I stood there, dumbfounded. A couple of photographers had witnessed the exchange and were standing off to the side, snickering.

I had to save face and at least act as if I weren't the least bit fazed. I plastered a smile on my face and sauntered over to the other three company officials. They smiled and greeted me warmly. At least they knew how to treat their moneymaker. That Dina, she was gonna have to learn.

I watched Dina out of the corner of my eye. She was talking to a group of production people. She was all smiles as she shook each of their hands. I was definitely upset now. They were just production people, and here I was, her top talent, and she treated me like crap.

I watched Simone move in with ease, and Dina talked to her as if they were old friends. I could no longer stomach the sight of that witch all chummy with everyone else, so I excused myself from the meaningless conversation the three corporate suits were having and headed back to my office.

I contemplated calling Stan, but I figured I would give Dina a chance to redeem herself. I needed to get busy cleaning out my voice-mail box. I entered the phone number to check my voice mail, then punched in my code.

"You have seventeen new messages."

Everybody felt they had a story to tell, and I had seventeen new messages to prove it. My show was a mixture of light news, celebrity interviews, and any other entertainment I deemed newsworthy. But I was amazed at the number of people that would call about the craziest things. One man even called me last month wanting to come on the show and talk about how wrong it was that he had to pay child support because he didn't even, and I quote, "want the damn kids."

I sighed heavily, then pressed the button to play my messages. There were the usual ten people who had the "best, most pressing story" that demanded my immediate attention. I promptly forwarded all of those to my producer, Ian, without even completely listening to them. On the last message, however, I heard a faint "Hi," then the caller didn't say anything. It was a woman's voice. After she paused, she hung up. I was so sick of people playing on my phone.

I picked up the phone to call Myles, and to my surprise he answered his cell phone. "Hey, I didn't expect to get you."

"I saw your number on the caller ID and wanted to make sure I answered. I wanted to tell you how much I love you," Myles said.

I sank back into my seat, a huge smile plastered across my face.

"I love you, too. I needed to hear that. It's been a crazy day. Richard is out."

"Richard? Is that your news director?"

"Yep. He was arrested for DUI. He quit and corporate brought in someone new. A sister."

"What? They gave the job to a black woman?"

"Yep. But she was real nasty to me. Somebody better tell her," I scoffed.

Myles laughed. "They sure better, because nobody treats my baby, my soon-to-be-wife, like that. Anyway, does she not recognize that you're the station's bread and butter?"

I nodded my head like Myles could really see me. That was my man. He knew just what to say to make me feel better.

"Forget her, baby. She'll figure it out soon enough. Somebody will put her in her place. Besides, you have more important things to think about, like becoming Mrs. Myles Jacobs."

I smiled dreamily as I thought about our life together. Me and Myles, little Myles Jr., and Angelique, living together in our million-dollar home. We would be the perfect little family.

"Stupid jerk!"

Myles's yelling broke my little fantasy. "What did you say?"

"I'm sorry, baby. This fool just cut me off." I heard Myles pressing down on his horn. "Some people don't need to be on the road!" he screamed.

"Sweetheart, would you calm down? It's not that serious." I swung my chair around, almost knocking over my favorite picture of me and Myles in Bermuda. I caught the picture, smiled at it, and set it back on my desk. "Ummmm, so what time will you be home tonight?"

"I don't know, why?"

"Well, it's been three weeks now, and I was kinda hoping we could go look at rings."

Myles let out deep sigh. "Just chill; there's no rush."

Now it was my turn to let out a huff. "Myles, when you proposed, I thought you wanted to get married right away. I didn't know this was something you wanted to draw out. I don't even feel like I'm engaged. I sure can't tell anyone because I don't even have a ring."

"Is that what you're worried about, telling someone? Having a ring so you can show off?" Myles snapped.

He was getting defensive and I was getting upset. "Look, did you even mean it when you proposed, or was that just your way of getting out of the Delana situation?"

"Awww, here we go with that mess."

"I'm just saying—"

Myles cut me off. "Be ready at seven."

"Excuse me?"

"I said, be ready at seven. I'll be by the station to pick you up so we can go get your big rock so you can show it off to your one friend."

I ignored his sarcasm and squealed with delight. "You mean it?"

Myles's voice softened. If there was one thing he loved, it was seeing me act like a giddy child under his control. "Yeah, baby. I mean it. I'll see you at seven."

"I'll be ready and waiting!" I exclaimed. I was so excited, I wondered how I was ever going to make it through taping the newscast.

chapter 13

I stared at the glistening platinum-set rock on my finger. Three carats of pure precious stone. I hadn't stopped smiling since Myles and I had returned from picking out the ring. I'd wanted something custom-made, but I was too impatient to wait. When I saw this one, I knew I wouldn't have to. Myles scoffed at the $7,000 price tag at first, but when he saw how much I really wanted it, he gave in.

I made love to him that night, all night, wearing nothing but that diamond. I tried to make the night one he'd never forget. And by the way he had fallen into a deep slumber, my mission had been accomplished.

Now, I was at work trying hard to focus on reading over my scripts for the nightly newscast. But every time I'd read a line, my eyes would make their way back down to the ring on my finger. I hated that I didn't have anyone to share in my joy. Shereen was still out sick and wasn't answering her phone. I thought about going by her house, but knowing Shereen, she probably wasn't even sick and was chilling in Jamaica or something.

"Knock, knock."

I looked up.

Keria stuck her head in my office door. "Hey, Rae. Just letting you know I made some changes on the lead story. Can you please take a look at it and give your final approval?"

I had never talked to Keria other than about work-related stuff and the occasional office gossip, but she was better than no one. "I'll take a look at it in a moment. But take a look at this." I thrust my hand out.

Keria's eyes widened as she stepped into my office and walked over to examine my hand. "Wow! Are you engaged?"

"Yes."

"To the city councilman?"

"Yes."

"Well, congratulations. I'm happy for you."

"Thank you." She threw a genuine smile at me before heading back to her desk.

I had just pulled up the lead story to review when my phone rang. I grabbed it up. "This is Rae Rollins."

"Well, don't we sound all chipper."

"Mama Tee?"

"Last time I checked that was still my name."

I couldn't help but smile at the sound of her voice. I pictured her robust frame standing in her hallway—the only place she had a phone in the whole house—rocking back and forth on her feet, her soft gray hair parted down the middle and plaited into two long braids that hung to her shoulders.

It didn't matter how much I tried to avoid Mama Tee, she still called me regularly with family updates, talking as if nothing were wrong. After all she'd done for me, I could never bring myself to be rude, so I always took her calls.

"Since you don't know how to call me, I thought I'd call you. Still don't understand why I don't have your home phone number and always gots to call you on your job. And I'm not even gon' mention the fact that you didn't return my last phone call." Mama Tee sighed.

"Well, umm . . ."

"Don't even fix your lips to lie to me, gal. You doing okay?"

"I'm doing well." It was strange that Mama Tee would call me at a time when I had happy news I wanted to share. But somehow I couldn't bring myself to tell her about the engagement. She would want to come to the wedding and would tell everyone in Sweet Poke, and they would all want to come, too. And Lord knows, I didn't want my wedding day ruined by my relatives.

"Okay, fine. I figure you'll tell me when you feel like it. Just calling to tell you Justin is doing much better. The doctors let him come home and they say as long as he takes it easy, he should be fine."

"That's wonderful news. Give him my love."

"I will," Mama Tee said. "By the way, yo' cousin Nikki almost got stabbed last night. Messing round with some other woman's husband. Ola 'bout had a heart attack when she saw Kevin on the news. It was all on CNN. She ain't stopped crying yet. I told her she was spoiling them badass boys and they wasn't gon' amount to a pillar of salt, but she ain't never want to listen to me.

Shondella still fooling round with that no-good Baxter boy. Long as she don't come up pregnant, I guess I can't complain."

Why Mama Tee felt compelled to call me and give the rundown on my family was beyond me. I never asked about anyone other than Justin and Shondella's children. I hadn't seen the rest of my family in four years and didn't care to know what they were doing. But that never seemed to bother Mama Tee.

"Is that so?" I nonchalantly responded. "Well, look, Mama Tee, I'm kinda busy. I guess you need some money or something."

Mama Tee took a deep breath, then let out into me. "Raedella Dionne Rollins. Have I ever asked you for one thin dime? I don't need your money, don't want your money, and if I wasn't saved, I'd tell your ass what to do with your money. I been making it just fine all these years and I'm gon' keep on making it."

I felt her fury through the phone. "I'm sorry, Mama Tee. I wasn't thinking. It's just that I recently sent Shondella some money."

"That's between you and your sister. I don't want your damn money."

"I'm sorry."

"Umm-hmmm. I just wanted you to know Justin is doing much better. And, oh, yeah, I wanted to tell you we're having the family reunion down there next month."

"Here? In Houston? Why would you all have it six hours away from Sweet Poke?" I nearly dropped the phone.

"Had you been coming around, you'd a known that we decided to move it to a different city each year. You know your uncle Clyde is down there. So we gon' have it there."

I dropped my head and closed my eyes as I inhaled deeply. I had forgotten that Uncle Clyde lived here. He had called me when I'd first moved here, but I'd never got around to calling him back.

"So, we gon' see you there, right?"

"I don't know—"

"Good. 'Cause I'm telling you now, you don't show up, each and every last one of us is gonna come up to that fancy station and show out till you come out. And you know we'll do it."

I was silent. They would do it. And take great pride in doing it.

"Okay, Mama Tee. I'll think about it."

"Ain't nothing to think about. We'll see you in three weeks. I'm a send you the flyer on where the family picnic is. Least I do have your address." She paused. "I'm sho' looking forward to seeing you. And bring that handsome young man you seeing."

I was glad she couldn't see the flustered look on my face. "How do you know about Myles?"

"Chile, I know a whole lot more than you think I know." Mama Tee laughed. "A whole lot more. We'll see you in three weeks." With that she hung up the phone.

chapter 14

I rolled my eyes at Simone's report on the noon news. She was at some petroleum fire doing a live report. She was the lead story. What happened to training? How did she go from being a reporter trainee to being the top story in the newscast? It probably had something to do with how chummy she was with Dina. Every time I turned around, they were giggling like schoolgirls.

I know people might think I'm jealous or something. Really, I'm not. Simone was no threat to me. I just couldn't appreciate her being given a handout when I had had to work so hard to get where I am.

I started going through my mail. I had the usual assortment of fan mail, press releases, and so forth. There was also an oversize envelope from Shondella. I recognized her crooked handwriting immediately. Could it possibly be her paying me back some of the money she owed me?

"I seriously doubt that," I muttered as I grabbed my

letter opener and pried the envelope open. I reached in and pulled out the contents. It was the front page of the *Sweet Poke Times.* Why would Shondella send me the newspaper? Then I thought about it. My sister has always had an obsession with newspapers. It's crazy. In addition to the *Sweet Poke Times,* she reads at least three other newspapers a day. She had been doing it since she was a teenager. Personally, I think that allowed her to escape her bland existence, but that was just my two cents.

As soon as I unfolded the paper, I saw why she'd sent it to me. Reno was on the front of the paper with the headline "Local Coach Saves Drowning Toddler." He was holding a beautiful little girl. A homely-looking woman stood next to him, cheesing like a Cheshire cat. I immediately read the cutline under the picture. "Sweet Poke High School football coach Reno McBride poses with his wife, Edith Louise McBride, and Imani, a three-year-old he rescued from the Arkansas River. McBride was fishing along the banks when the little girl, who was with her family nearby, fell into the river."

A nostalgic smile spread across my face. Reno, a hero? I couldn't believe how well his life had turned out. Well, I guess good by Sweet Poke standards. I'd always thought he would end up with a dead-end job, a bunch of babies, and a boring existence. I looked closely at the picture of his wife. She looked vaguely familiar, but I couldn't place her face. She had one of those faces that you definitely wouldn't remember. She was as bland as dry toast. And what in the world was that she had on? Why would she take a picture in that frumpy dress? It was a yellow paisley number with a huge, matronly lace collar. Her honey-colored hair was pinned up in a bun on top of her head.

Huge bifocal-looking glasses sat on the bridge of her nose. Unbelievable. "Good grief, Reno. You couldn't do any better than that?" I muttered.

I was surprised at the tinge of jealousy I felt. Maybe it was because both of them looked genuinely happy. Maybe it was because I'd half-expected Reno to wither up and die when I'd left.

It's been seven years, get over it. I shook off thoughts of Reno. I guessed he would never truly be out of my system. After all, he was my first real love. The first man I'd ever made love to. The man who'd gotten me pregnant. I closed my eyes as the memories came rushing back.

"You're what?"

"I didn't stutter. I said, I'm having a baby." I was standing outside Reno's house, tears rushing down my face. Not only was I devastated that I was pregnant, I was also furious that I had let myself become a Sweet Poke statistic.

Reno scratched his head in what I thought was stunned disbelief. Until he broke out in a big smile. "So you're really pregnant?"

I couldn't believe this fool was standing there smiling at me like I'd told him we had just won the lottery or something. "Yes, and what are you smiling about?"

"I'm going to be a daddy!" Reno slapped his knee and started dancing around. I looked at him like he had lost his mind.

"I said, I'm pregnant. I ain't said nothing about nobody being a daddy," I snapped as I wiped away my tears.

Reno stopped dancing and glared at me. "What are you talking about?"

"Boy, I ain't finna have no damn baby. Be stuck here forever. Living on welfare. Are you crazy?" My heart was racing. I started to envision diapers and food stamps and everything I ever dreamed of going up in smoke.

Reno's expression turned serious. "No, Raedella, I think you're the crazy one if you're saying what I think you're saying."

He wasn't fazing me. No, I didn't ever want to be in this position, but I was here now. I knew what I had to do. I was shaking as I raised my head high. I swallowed the lump in my throat and said, "I'm saying, I need three hundred dollars and for you to drive me to Little Rock to take care of this. We don't have a choice and it's not open for discussion." I crossed my arms and glared back at him to let him know I was serious.

He continued to stare at me, dumbfounded. "So you would just kill our child?"

I felt myself shudder. I couldn't believe he went there. This wasn't easy for me but I saw the big picture.

"God wouldn't approve of this."

"Oh, don't go getting all holy on me. You wasn't thinking about that when you was having sex with me!" I huffed and fought back tears again. "Besides, God will understand. God knows this"—I flung my arms out—"He knows this is not my destiny! I'm about to finish high school. I'm going to college so I can get a degree and get out of Sweet Poke."

Reno reached out and took my hand. "Why are you always talking about leaving Sweet Poke? This is your home."

I jerked my hand away. "News flash! I'm bigger than this. And a baby will mess up my plans."

"Don't say that. This is a blessing."

I rolled my eyes and threw up my hands. My head was pounding and Reno was about to get on my last nerve.

"Reno, you graduated last year," I calmly tried to explain. "You don't have a job. You live with your mama and your eleven brothers and sisters."

"And?"

Now it was my turn to look at him like he was crazy. "*And*, where would we live?" I couldn't believe he was seriously thinking we should have this baby. As much as I loved him, he knew a baby wasn't in my future. At least not anytime soon.

"We could get our own place. I can get a job at the railroad and we could be one big happy family." Reno nodded his head like he had it all figured out.

"Yeah, and we can get us a farm, some chickens, and, hey, let's spring for some cows. And maybe I can gets me a job cleaning white folks' houses."

"Stop being silly."

"You the one being silly if you think I'm about to have a baby. Then I'll be pregnant again next year, then the year after that. You won't stop until I have seven kids and I'm stuck here in Sweet Poke the rest of my life." I sighed deeply, regretting that I had even told him about the baby. I should have just borrowed the money and gone ahead and had an abortion on my own. I don't know what I was thinking.

Reno stepped toward me and rubbed his hands up and down my arms. "What if I tell you I don't want you to do this. That I want you to have my baby."

I exhaled as I continued to fight off the tears. "I would say, let me hit that crack pipe you smoking."

"I'm serious, Rae." He tried to pull me toward him. "You graduate in a few months. We could do this."

I pulled myself from his grasp and pulled my emotions in check. "Reno, this isn't open for discussion. Are you going to give me the money or not?"

"So you would really kill our baby?"

I bit down on my lip. He made me seem like a cold-blooded killer. "You know what, Reno, go to hell. I'll take care of this on my own!"

With that, I stormed off, leaving Reno leaning up against his 1979 pickup truck. I refused to have this baby, mess up my life, and end up like my sister. With or without Reno's help, I was going to do what I had to do.

I shivered as I thought of that day. I had borrowed the money from a guy named Felton, who had a huge crush on me throughout high school. I had gone crying on his shoulder and he liked me so much he gave me the money. He wanted to go with me, but I wouldn't let him. I had gone by myself to Little Rock to have an abortion. It was the loneliest, most horrible day of my life. I had come close so many times to backing out. Reno's words about me killing our baby rang in my head all the way there. The only thing that kept me strong was my desire to leave Sweet Poke.

I cried like a baby when I left that clinic. In fact, I sat in the ladies' room of the bus station and cried for a good two hours. But I'd finally pulled myself together and headed home.

I glanced back down at the picture of Reno. He had been so furious with me. It had taken him almost a month before he would even talk to me again. But we did get back together and eventually things returned to normal. Neither he nor I ever mentioned the baby again.

Felton, on the other hand, had flipped out when he found out I'd got back together with Reno. He accused me of using him and even stalked me for a little while. But he ended up getting arrested for something and I no longer had to deal with him.

After that, I stopped sleeping with Reno. I just couldn't chance something like that happening again. Maybe that was part of the reason he went to Ann Paxton. I don't know, but at that point in my life, only one thing mattered and that was doing whatever it took to get out of Sweet Poke.

chapter 15

I hated the call-in segments of my talk show. We tried to do a talk-back show at least once a month. The viewers loved this segment, which is why management wanted us to keep it. I love my show, but this was definitely an area I could do without. We always got people rambling on about one thing or another. Or, even worse, you never knew what someone would say, and I didn't like surprises. The producer tried to screen the calls, but every now and then some prankster or mental case managed to sneak through.

I plastered on my fake smile at the psychologist who sat beside me, talking about mending rifts in families. The scholarly-looking, elderly woman seemed to know what she was talking about. But I'd be willing to bet my left arm she wouldn't be able to mend things in my family.

"And so you see, parents don't realize the impact their dysfunction has on their children," Dr. Shumaker was saying. She had been talking to some woman who'd called in whining about how she never got love from her parents, and now she couldn't give love, yada yada yada. This was getting on my nerves. Then, to top things off, I had been feeling sick to my stomach all day. I glanced at the clock. Ten minutes to go. I made a mental note to tell Ian these types of shows were out. Let the radio stations deal with the whiny callers. I had better things to do with my time.

I gave the obligatory nod, acting as if I were really interested in Dr. Shumaker's analysis of this woman. That's part of why my ratings were so good. Once I put on my TV persona, I could be more sensitive than Oprah.

"Thank you, Doctor," the caller said. "Is there any way I can get your number and talk to you some more?"

Why people wasted money on a shrink was beyond me. But I was grateful this call had wrapped up. I jumped in.

"Absolutely. You can see her number up on the screen right now, and, of course, you can always log on to our Web site at TheRaeRollinsShow dot com. Thank you for sharing and we sincerely hope you mend your relationship with your parents. Stay with us, everybody, we'll be back right after this."

As we went to commercial break, I looked at the production assistant holding up two fingers. That meant we had two more callers to go. I wanted this show to be over already.

Ian talked into my earpiece. "Good job, Rae. This show is really interesting. The next caller is Rose and she wants to ask Dr. Shumaker how she can repair her relationship with a daughter she abandoned. Try and get some emotion out of her. I need some tears to end this show on."

I froze. The smile left my face and I stared straight ahead. I must have heard him wrong. Dr. Shumaker noticed the look on my face. "Are you all right?" she asked.

I couldn't move. Ian must have noticed it in his monitor in the control room because he started yelling in my earpiece. "Rae! What's going on? Are you okay?"

Then I heard the director's voice boom, "Thirty away!"

Dr. Shumaker leaned in and touched my leg. "What's wrong? You look like you're in shock."

I shook my head, trying to get back to reality. This had to be an eerie coincidence. Rose would not have the audacity to call me live on the air. Ian was still yelling in my ear.

"I'm fine. I'm fine," I said, shaking my head. I was about to tell Ian he would have to find out some more information on this Rose before we put her on the air but the director didn't give me time.

"Rae, I need you to focus. Stand by! And five, four, three, two, one!" he shouted as he pointed his finger to let me know we were on.

The theme music for my show started playing and the camera panned toward me. *Shake it off!* I snapped to myself. I plastered on my smile, and when the red light came back on, I smiled toward the camera.

"Welcome back to *The Rae Rollins Show*. I'm your host, Rae Rollins, along with Dr. Elaine Shumaker from the Baylor College of Mental Health. It's talk-back time and we're talking to you about mending relationships with your family." I took a deep breath. "On the line now is Rose. And, Rose, I understand you're trying to mend your relationship with a daughter you abandoned."

I kept my smile pasted on, praying that this was not my Rose. At first, Rose didn't say anything and I was hoping she had hung up. But then, when she spoke, there was no mistaking it. That was my mother.

"Um . . . yeah. I-I don't know where to start. I was just wondering if . . . um, if the doctor could tell me, how do I get my daughter to forgive me?" Her voice was raspy, like she'd been crying.

It took everything in my power not to let my emotions show. I didn't know how I felt. Astonished. Angry. Hurt. Terrified that she would reveal who she was.

Dr. Shumaker jumped in. "Well, Rose, let's start with you telling us why you abandoned your daughter."

Rose hesitated again. I took that as my opportunity to jump in. "It appears we've lost our caller. Let's just move on to our next one."

Ian began yelling something and I was trying to discreetly motion for the audio operator to go to the next call.

Rose spoke up before I could get rid of her. "I'm still here."

I tried to keep the smile. "Oh, sorry. I thought we lost you." I leaned back in my seat, trying not to let the defeat show.

"Yes, Rose," Dr. Shumaker continued, "I was asking you why you abandoned your daughter."

"I was young and, umm, I guess being a parent just got to be too overwhelming for me. I just gave my kids to my mother, who I thought could give them a better life."

Keeping my smile was getting harder and harder.

"I also got . . . got hooked on drugs and, well, my judgment wasn't its best. I made a huge mistake and I'm so sorry for it, but how can I get my daughter to understand that?"

Dr. Shumaker was shifting in her seat. I could tell she was about to really get into this. "Rose, that is not uncommon. Oftentimes—"

I couldn't hold it in any longer. If Rose wanted to call my show and try to worm her way back in, I had something for her.

"Doctor, I'm sorry to cut you off, but I don't understand the rationale behind just giving your kids away. You give away old clothes. You give away toys you no longer want. You don't give away kids," I snapped.

A surprised look crossed Dr. Shumaker's face, and for once she seemed at a loss for words.

"I was doing what I thought was best," Rose whispered.

"What's best? I'm sure what would have been best for your kids was to have their mother," I remarked as professionally as I could. I noticed all the strange looks from the studio crew and snapped back to reality. "Umm, at least that's what I would think, but I'm not the expert. Doctor?" I said, turning back toward Dr. Shumaker, who was still looking at me in amazement.

"Um . . . yes. Rae is right. It doesn't take a psychology degree to figure out it probably would've been best for your children to stay with you. But that's only if you were able to provide them with a loving and stable environment."

"I tried my best to give my kids everything, but it just seemed like things kept working against me. Don't get me wrong, I don't blame anyone but myself, but how do I make amends for my past mistakes?" Rose asked.

"Did you truly believe you could no longer properly provide for your children?" Dr. Shumaker asked.

"I thought they would have a better life with my mother," Rose softly responded.

"Well, then, you probably did the right thing, giving them to someone who could give them a better life," Dr. Shumaker replied.

"But, Doctor," I jumped back in, "there are some women who abandon their children for a man. Say that man doesn't want kids. Some women will say, 'Okay, I'll get rid of the kids so I can be with this man.' " At this point I knew I wasn't being professional. I was angry and not worried about whether Rose would say something too revealing or getting in trouble or anything. I just wanted to let her know what was on my mind.

Dr. Shumaker looked like she didn't know what to say. I seldom interjected my opinion in these call-in shows. I could tell by all the strange looks everyone was giving me that I might have pushed the envelope too far.

"Of course, I'm grateful I come from a loving two-parent household," I quickly added. Don't ask me why I felt the need to lie. Rose had gotten to me and now I needed to clean things up. "My mother is a wonderful woman who showered me with love growing up. She would never dream of abandoning me, so that's why I can't understand the rationale behind your actions." I got back into TV mode. "Please forgive me, Rose, if I seemed a little defensive. I'm sure you had a great reason for abandoning your children. It's like you said, you did what you had to do. But I know there are some viewers out there who perhaps are in similar situations and you can provide some insight on how mothers can just discard their children."

Dr. Shumaker looked like she still didn't know what to make of that. But she nodded anyway. "Unfortunately, most Americans don't come from picture-perfect homes like our host here. Rose, there are others out there like you. And I would have to tell you, it's never too late to mend your relationship with your daughter."

Wanna bet? I wanted to say. But I kept my mouth shut.

Dr. Shumaker continued, "You just have to try to explain to her why you made the choices you made and tell her you're ready to be a mother to her."

"But what if she won't take my calls? Or see me? I even moved to the same city to be near her, but I've been too scared to even approach her. I know she has so much hate for me," Rose softly said.

"Can you blame her?" I asked.

"Rae!" I heard Ian snap in my earpiece. "What the hell are you doing?"

I ignored him and started twiddling with my bracelet. I had had enough of Rose and her funky apology/let's-heal-our-relationship rhetoric. As far as I was concerned, Rose was as dead to me as Elvis.

Dr. Shumaker told Rose something else, but I had tuned them both out. If I kept listening, I was sure to go off, so I just had to focus on something else. I looked up at the digital clock. We had just under a minute. The director gave me the cue to wrap things up. Thank God.

"Well, I know we have one more caller, but it looks like we're out of time. Dr. Shumaker, as always, thank you for such insightful advice," I said.

The doctor smiled and nodded, although I could tell she was wondering what was going on with me. I thanked everyone for watching, waited for the music and credits to roll, then hopped up off the set as soon as the director said, "Clear!"

I heard Dr. Shumaker call my name as I raced off the set. I didn't even turn around as I yelled, "I'll see you next month, Doctor. I gotta go. Great job today!"

I wasn't in my office two minutes before my door swung open.

"What was that?"

I was not in the mood for Dina. I had sat down on my sofa and was leaning back with my head against the wall.

"What was what?"

"That . . . that attack on our caller."

"I don't know what you're talking about."

Dina slammed my door so hard I jumped. "You know what the hell I'm talking about!" She stormed over to me, pointing her long, bony finger in my face. "I don't know what kind of drugs you're taking, but we don't pay you to analyze our viewers. That's why we bring in the experts. Your job is to sit there, try and look pretty, and move things along. It is not your job to beat up on people who take time out of their day to call in to our show."

I stared at her finger, which was two inches from my nose. I wanted so bad to reach up and just grab those Wicked Witch of the West–looking fingers and break them in half.

"You do not have to get all up in my face," I said calmly.

"I will get wherever I want to get!" Dina hissed. "I don't know what kind of royal treatment you're used to around here, but my newsroom doesn't operate like that. If I ever see some mess like that on my show—because contrary to your convoluted belief, this is not *your* show—if I ever see something like that again, I will fire your ass so quick you won't know what hit you!" She turned around and stormed toward my door. She stopped right before opening it. "Oh, and you can best believe this incident is going in your file." With that, she swung my door open and walked out, leaving the door wide open. I'm sure all the newsroom gossips were taking it all in, but at that point, I didn't really care. I rubbed my temples. I couldn't believe the nerve of Rose. I hadn't talked to her in years. All those years that she had made no effort to see me or my siblings on our birthdays, on Christmas, on graduation, nothing. Twenty-two years. Twenty-two years and she thinks she could just waltz up in here and win her way back into my heart? Forget that. Louis Farrakhan had a greater chance of becoming president of the United States.

I picked up the phone to call Myles's cell phone. I had already been feeling sick all morning; now this had my head hurting. I needed to talk to my baby, so he could make everything all right.

Myles picked up just before my call transferred over to voice mail.

"Hey, baby."

"What's up?"

"What's up? Is that any way to greet your lovely soon-to-be-wife?"

"Rae, what's going on? I'm heading to a meeting."

"Well, excuse me," I said, my mood souring even more. "Did you catch the show?"

"Do I ever catch the show?"

Smart alek. "No, you never seem to be able to find the time."

"That's because I work. I can't sit around and watch TV all day."

I took a deep breath. I couldn't fight with him right now. "Myles, I just had a really bad day, that's all." I hadn't shared with Myles my whole situation with Rose. I hadn't shared it with anyone except Shereen. So it's not like I could tell him exactly what happened. "The show didn't go well, then Dina came in here trippin'."

"Rae, we're going to have to talk about this tonight," Myles interrupted.

"What are you doing?"

"I told you I was heading to a meeting."

I heard the light jazz from the radio. Myles kept his car stereo on 95.7, the jazz station. "But you're in your car. Can't you talk to me until you get to your meeting?" I heard someone mumble something. "Is someone with you?" I felt my headache flare up.

"Yes" was all Myles would say.

"Who is with you?"

"I will talk to you later."

"Myles, don't hang up this phone!"

Myles sighed heavily. "If you must know, Rae Rollins, I have Councilman Willis with me. We are on our way to a budget meeting. We have some items we need to discuss before we get to the meeting. I am not going to deal with your distrust. If I can't ride down the street without you thinking I'm cheating on you, we have a fundamental problem."

I was quiet. Not only was Myles going off in front of Councilman Willis, he had called my whole name so the councilman would know whom he was talking to.

"I'm sorry. I just had a bad day."

"Well, don't take it out on me."

"Okay. I'll let you go. You'll need to pick up dinner tonight. I managed to get a doctor's appointment right after work."

"Doctor's appointment—for what?"

"I told you I haven't been feeling well. I'm throwing up, and yesterday, I blacked out."

"A'ight. Whatever. I'll see you later tonight."

I paused. "Myles. I love you."

"Yeah, okay." He hung up the phone before I could say anything else.

chapter 16

"Pregnant?"

The word hung in the air as if it were some vile, infectious disease. All the joy I had been feeling was soaked up in Myles's contempt at the idea of having a child.

"Six weeks." I beamed, despite his obvious disdain. Myles sat in stunned silence. "You aren't excited?"

Myles stood up and began pacing the floor, running his hand across his closely shaved head. "Excited? How can I get excited? We aren't even married yet. How is that going to look to the constituents, me having a baby out of wedlock?"

I looked at him in disbelief as the smile faded from my face. "Your constituents! You think I care about your constituents?"

Myles closed his eyes, inhaled, then opened his eyes back up. "But you were on your period last week."

"I know, that's why being pregnant never crossed my

mind. But the doctor said that you can get your cycle and still be pregnant." I lowered my head, sadness setting in. "I thought you would be happy." I had been so excited when the doctor had told me I was pregnant. I'd spent the whole evening thinking this was my chance to redeem myself.

Myles exhaled in frustration. "Rae, it's not just me. You're putting your career at risk, too. You already say Dina is out to get you. She won't want her top talent being unmarried and pregnant. What kind of example would that set?"

I hesitated. He had a point, but it's not like Myles and I weren't planning to get married. "Myles, it's not like this baby is the product of a one-night stand."

Myles continued with an exasperated look across his face. "Look, Rae. The election is in ten months. We had agreed to wait until after then to get married."

Now I was getting pissed. "You should have thought about that before you sent your little swimmers in search of fertilization."

Myles sighed, seemingly grasping at straws. "I thought you were on birth control anyway."

"I told you I was switching over to the birth control patch because the pills were making me sick. You were the one who said, 'Oh, baby, we'll be fine.'" I knew exactly when I had gotten pregnant. It was yet another makeup session after Myles had pissed me off because we hadn't been spending any time together. I had just switched to the patch and the directions were clear: use a backup the first month. When I had told that to Myles, he'd groaned, complaining, "Condoms block the feeling."

"Rae, this just isn't a good time," Myles said, shaking his head.

"So what are you saying, Myles?" I looked at him for an answer. He didn't respond, but I could see it in his eyes. "I know you don't want me to have an abortion." I was speechless. I couldn't believe he was even thinking something like that. I couldn't endure that—again. I stood up. "Myles, that is not an option. I am thirty years old, and in case you haven't noticed, I am only getting older. So, I'm having this baby with or without you."

Myles hesitated before taking a deep breath and standing up. I thought he was about to come to his senses, but instead, he licked his lips and said, "A baby would mess up my plans. As that child's father, I do have some say-so. And I say I don't want to have a child right now. Do not bring an unwanted child into this world." Then he turned and walked out of the house, slamming the door on his way.

I didn't even know how long I sat on my sofa crying. How could Myles be so cold? I needed to get out of the house. I felt as if I were suffocating.

Fifteen minutes later, I found myself in front of Shereen's upscale townhome located on the outskirts of Third Ward. Although she and I were really good friends, Shereen had never seen me cry. She had never seen me hurting. That's because I seldom let anyone see me vulnerable. But I didn't know where else to go.

"It's gon' snow in hell," Shereen said as she opened the door. "Come in, girl. What are you doing over here slummin'?"

I walked inside, taking in the Afrocentric surroundings. Shereen was so at peace. I looked at a picture on her entertainment center of her at the beach, posing in the water. She looked so happy. I remembered that trip. She had gone to the Bahamas by herself. Who goes to the Bahamas by themselves? But it didn't seem to faze Shereen and she talked for months about what a wonderful time she had.

"So to what do I owe this pleasure? We've been friends—what?—three, four years and I think you've been over to my place three times."

I didn't say anything as I plopped down on her sofa. I guess she must've noticed I wasn't in a joking mood.

"Hey, what's going on?" she asked as she took a seat next to me.

"I'm pregnant."

"Get out of here! That is too cool."

"Myles doesn't think so."

"Screw Myles."

"I did. That's how I got in this predicament."

We both laughed. I was feeling better just being around Shereen.

"Seriously though," Shereen said as she got up and headed toward the kitchen, "this calls for some Boone's Farm. You want strawberry or peach?"

"Boone's Farm? You're kidding, right?"

Shereen opened the refrigerator. "Have you ever known me to kid about some good drinking?"

She had a point there. "Do you have some cabernet?"

"Girl, you in the hood. I'll get shot trying to go up in a store around here asking for some cabernet." She walked back in the living room and handed me a glass of strawberry wine. "Here. When in Rome, do as the Romans do. Besides," she said as she sat back down, "you need something strong."

I took the glass, then she jumped up and snatched it

right back. "What was I thinking? You just told me you're pregnant and here I am trying to get you drunk."

I looked at the glass. I hadn't even thought about that. "I guess I need to start thinking about someone other than myself now."

Shereen gulped my drink down. "So you won't get tempted," she said as she wiped her mouth. "Now, tell me this nonsense about Myles not wanting the baby."

"He says it's going to ruin his master plan."

"Life doesn't always go as planned."

"You can't tell Myles that."

"So what are you going to do?"

I rubbed my stomach. "I want my baby."

"Then have it. What's the big deal? You two are getting married anyway. Spiritually, that's probably not the right answer, but I'd rather you have a baby out of wedlock than have an abortion."

I cringed at that word. "Myles says it would look bad for me to be pregnant before we got married."

"Hello, does he think it's 1950? Give me a freaking break. I guess he thinks Wally and the Beev epitomize brotherhood, too?"

Shereen reached in her purse and pulled out a pack of cigarettes. I shot her a chastising look. "I thought you quit."

She shrugged. "I did. This is just my emergency stash, to calm my nerves." She popped out a cigarette, lit it, then took a long whiff. She closed her eyes, a look of pure ecstasy across her face. She gently blew out smoke. "You don't think this'll hurt the baby, huh?"

"Fine time to be asking now. But to answer your question, yes. Now put that mess out."

Shereen inhaled deeply again, closing her mouth and letting the smoke seep out of her nose. "Fine. I just needed a quick little puff. My nerves are bad. I just found out Franklin is gay." She smashed the cigarette out.

"Franklin? Is that your latest beau?"

"Yeah, chile, and I was really diggin' him." Shereen shook her head. "I should've known any man that could pass up all of this"—she squeezed her breasts—"would have to be gay."

I laughed. "You are too funny." You couldn't tell Shereen she didn't look good.

Shereen leaned back and surveyed me up and down. "So, are you all right for real?"

"I guess. Sometimes I wonder why I stay with Myles."

"'Cause he's fine as all get out and he gives you what you need. Or what you think you need."

I narrowed my eyes at Shereen. "What is that supposed to mean?"

Shereen brushed down her ankle-length skirt and repositioned herself on the sofa. "It means I don't think you know what you want."

"That's ridiculous. Of course I know what I want."

"You want a fairy-tale life and you think Myles can give it to you."

I debated protesting, but the more I thought about it, the more I realized Shereen was right on target. "So, what's wrong with that?"

"For starters, fairy tales only exist in storybooks, and I hate to break this to you, but as much as I like Myles, he ain't no Prince Charming."

I felt myself getting defensive. Shereen must've sensed it because her tone softened. She reached out and took my hand. "Look, I just want you to be happy, and I mean genuinely happy. And I don't think that's going to happen because, and don't get mad, but I don't think you're happy with yourself."

I snatched my hand away. "So now you're a psychiatrist?" I gathered my purse and stood to leave. I didn't like it when anyone, including Shereen, questioned my relationship with Myles.

"No, I'm just a friend. A very good friend who loves and cares for you and wants only the best for you."

I stared at her, waiting for her to say something silly or break out in her sister-girl role. She didn't. She just sat there, an intense look etched across her face. I felt my eyes watering up. I adjusted my purse strap on my shoulders, shifted my weight between feet, then decided to just go ahead and ask her what was on my mind.

"Shereen, why are you my friend?"

Shereen shook her head. "What kind of question is that?"

I shrugged. "I don't know. I was just wondering, that's all. As you may have noticed, I don't have a plethora of friends." I hesitated, feeling lonely for the first time in my life. "Not many people want to be around me. Even my own fiancé doesn't want to be around me."

Shereen twisted her lips upward. "Probably because it's not easy being in the presence of a diva such as yourself."

I forced a smile.

"But seriously," Shereen said as she got up and walked toward me. "I know you like to play hard, but I also know you got some inner demons you're trying to work through. I don't know exactly what they are, but they're there. And besides, I know beneath that tough exterior of yours is a beautiful spirit yearning to be loved. So that's why I'm your friend to the end."

My eyes were no longer watering. I was in full-fledged crying mode. This was the deepest conversation Shereen and I had ever had. Not only had she hit some nerves, she was giving me something I hadn't felt in a long time, unconditional love.

"Here, gimme a hug." She embraced me tightly. "Now, don't be looking for no more of this mushy stuff, a'ight? This here is enough to last a lifetime." She playfully flicked me off and walked back to her sofa. "Now go home. Take care of yourself and that baby. I need to finish my pity party."

I sniffed and smiled.

"Bye, girl." I laughed as I made my way out the door and back home to an empty house—yet again.

chapter 17

Despite my visit with Shereen, I was back depressed by the time I made it home. And I sat in my house all weekend, sulking because I wanted this baby and I wanted Myles to want this baby. He hadn't called, which to me wasn't a good sign. So that added to my depression. And making matters worse, I had morning, noon, and night sickness.

I'd called in sick this morning and had spent the day trying to come out of my funk. I felt like I'd been making some progress when my doorbell rang. I answered it to find Myles standing there, his face shielded by the most beautiful bouquet of flowers I'd ever seen. My eyes lit up as he peeked his head from behind the flowers. "Hello, my lovely fiancée. I just wanted to say I'm sorry for being a jerk, and I wanted to show you a small token of my appreciation for your being in my life."

I was still upset with him, but the fact that he was

here—finally—warmed my heart just a little. Still, I didn't crack a smile as I took the vase from him and stepped aside to let him in.

He leaned in and kissed me, then walked inside and sat down on the sofa.

"Come sit next to me, baby." Myles patted the spot next to him on the sofa.

I set the vase down on the coffee table and reluctantly sat beside him. I hoped he wasn't about to start in about how he didn't want this baby.

He reached out and started caressing my leg. "I missed you today. I had a horrible day at work and couldn't wait to see you. I've been thinking a lot about you and the baby . . . our baby."

I felt a small smile creep up on my face. "*Our* baby?"

"Yes, our baby." Myles grinned and kissed me. "I was worried about how it would look with us being unmarried and having a baby. So I think I've found the solution to that."

I looked at him, confused. I didn't know where he was going with this, but I sure hoped it wasn't down the abortion road. That wasn't even an option. Not this time.

"Let's get married now."

Now? I was stunned. Of course, I wanted to get married now so my baby could be brought into the world the way he or she deserved to be. But I'd also always dreamed of having a beautiful, exclusive wedding—one worthy of the society pages. Myles noticed the stressed look on my face.

"I thought this would make you happy."

"It does . . . it's just, well, I never saw myself getting married in someone's courthouse."

"Courthouse? You know I don't roll like that. We're still going to have a wedding; you just have to move fast. I was thinking the last weekend in August." He leaned back and crossed his legs, a confident look across his face.

"That's next month," I replied, facing a whirlwind of emotions. This was exactly what I'd dreamed of, but not like this.

"I know I didn't do that good in school, but last time I checked, August did come after July, and it is July, isn't it?" Myles grinned widely and caressed my hair.

"Myles, I can't plan a wedding in a month."

He lifted my chin with his hand. "You can do anything you set your mind to. Or hire a consultant."

I weighed my options. "Why the change of heart?"

Myles sighed like he couldn't understand why I wasn't jumping up and down. "Look, you're the one that wanted to get married, so I say let's get married. I need to do right by my little boy, or little girl." He rubbed my stomach.

I looked at him skeptically. This was all coming together too perfectly. Myles never gave in this easily. Something just wasn't right. Then it dawned on me. "This wouldn't have anything to do with you potentially running for mayor, would it?"

Myles didn't answer.

"Well, does it?"

"What difference does it make?" He got up, walked to my entertainment center, and began sifting through my CDs.

I stood up and followed him. "It makes a lot of difference. Are you trying to marry me only so it will look good in your political campaign?"

"Don't be ridiculous, Rae. I'm marrying you because I want to marry you and I don't want to have a child out of wedlock."

"Um-hmmm." Myles was lying. I could tell by how he kept diverting his eyes.

"Myles, is this about the campaign?"

He shrugged, his back still to me. "Well, so what if I want to set an example?"

"So you *are* going to run for mayor? When were you going to share that piece of information with me?" I should have known there was some ulterior motive behind his change of heart.

Myles turned toward me in frustration. "Look, Rae, you knew my political aspirations from day one. I didn't know I would run this soon, but I have several people backing me and they think I have a good shot. And they think my chances would be even better if I were a family man."

"So this proposal, this acceptance of our baby, it's all about your career?" I felt my legs getting weak.

"Rae, no. I probably would've waited a few more months if I weren't running for mayor, but only to give you more time to plan. Yes, it will help my campaign if I'm married to the beautiful, sexy, vivacious Rae Rollins. Married to the woman who is carrying my child. But more than anything, I love you." He leaned in and kissed me gently on the lips. As usual, I melted at his touch. He was right. It would be better for his campaign if he was married. Better for my career. Better for our baby.

"Okay?" he asked.

I weighed my options, then slowly smiled. "Okay, we can get married right away." I suddenly felt myself getting excited. "How in the world am I going to plan a wedding in a month?"

"I have faith in you." Myles stood up. "Now, I'm going to get going, so you can get to planning."

The smile left my face. "Going? You have to leave?"

"Yeah, babe. Gotta run. Got a meeting to be at this evening." He picked up his keys.

"I was hoping we could rent a movie or something."

He kissed me again. "With all the planning you have to do, I wouldn't think you'd have time to watch a movie."

"What about dinner? Have you eaten?" I asked as he headed to the door.

"I'll pick something up on my way to my meeting. Love you."

I stood there watching with mixed emotions as Myles walked out, again. On one hand I was ecstatic about my impending nuptials and the thought of us having a child. On the other hand, I could only hope that my marriage wouldn't end up with more nights like this.

chapter 18

Hey, big sis."

I smiled as I recognized Justin's voice. "Hey, little brother. What's up?" I propped the cell phone between my ear and shoulder as I turned down the fire under the shrimp Creole I was cooking. "I thought you'd lost my cell phone number, seeing how you never use it."

Justin laughed. "Seeing how you swore you'd put a hit out on me if I gave it to anyone, I was scared to use it."

"Whatever." I wiped my hands on a kitchen towel and made my way back into the living room, where I stretched out on my chocolate leather sectional.

"Just wondering why you haven't been to see me."

My smile faded. I hated having this conversation with my little brother. He brought it up every so often. I had written Justin a letter several years ago explaining why I could not come see him. I had told him he could come see me whenever he wanted, but he was always so sick, he was never able to visit. "I thought you understood why I can't come back."

"Yeah, but you know I can keep wishing you'll change your mind," he said wistfully.

I tried to change the subject. "How are you feeling, really?"

"Oh, same ol' same ol'. One cough away from death."

"Justin, don't say that." Although I loved my little brother, I got so down whenever I talked to him. Another reason I avoided talking to him.

"Sorry, when you're laying up in a hospital bed all day, pretty much all you do is think morbid thoughts." He sighed.

I didn't know what to say. I didn't even know he was back in the hospital.

"I thought Mama Tee said you were going home."

"I did. For about two weeks, then I came down with pneumonia, so I'm back."

I felt my heart getting heavy. The last time we'd talked, I'd cried for an hour afterward.

"Do you use the PlayStation I sent you?" I asked, trying to lighten the conversation. My little brother never asked me for anything so I made it a point to send him things whenever I could.

"Sometimes, but the nurses gave me some crap about it interfering with medical equipment. That's the dumbest thing I ever heard."

"I was wondering if you were too old for that."

"Are you crazy? You're never too old for PlayStation!"

I laughed. "What about the CDs? Did you get those?" I knew he was a big rap fan, so I'd sent him the latest rap CDs, with one signed by some local rapper who had appeared on my show.

"Yes, and thank you. But I told you to stop sending me stuff. Shondella is always bitching about how selfish you are. I don't understand why you want to keep all that you do for me a secret."

I didn't expect him to understand, but Shondella was the type who would throw my generosity toward Justin in my face. "I just do. And don't think I didn't catch you cursing."

"You keep forgetting, I am grown. Even though no one around here seems to think so."

"Ummm-hmmm. Anyway, it's just better that no one knows. Shondella is a trip and it would just cause more problems. Now, when do you get to leave the hospital?"

"Actually, I'm checking out this evening. Mama Tee is on her way to get me."

"That's great, Justin."

"Tell that to somebody else. Anyway, how's life as a big-time TV star? You had a chance to meet Shaquille O'Neal yet?"

"No, but I did interview Malcolm Long."

"Wow!" Justin got silent. "I wish I could leave Sweet Poke," he said softly.

I felt myself fighting back tears. My little brother had never had much of a life. Leukemia had kept him sidelined most of the time. In fact, doctors had said he wouldn't live past ten, then it was thirteen. And here he was, twenty-two years old and still hanging on. But it wasn't a normal, healthy life.

"I hate it here. I hate being constantly stuck in this hospital. Can't I come live with you? I'm grown, so it's not like I need anybody watching after me. Or better yet, I can convince Mama Tee to let me come to the family reunion next week. Then you can convince her to let me stay there," he said hopefully.

I would have let Justin come live with me in a heartbeat. I lost all selfishness when it came to my baby brother. But Mama Tee wasn't even trying to hear that. Justin could lapse into serious bouts of sickness. And I think even he knew that he needed someone who was skilled with him at all times.

"Justin, we've been through this before. You know Mama Tee wants you to be there so she can keep an eye on you."

"Please, Rae. Please, please, please," he begged. I almost smiled, because he sounded like my thirteen-year-old brother again.

"Justin, you know I can't do that."

Justin was quiet, and I thought I heard sniffling.

"Justin, don't be mad."

"Shondella was right," he snapped. "You are selfish. She said you want to forget we exist, that you just don't want to be bothered with none of us."

"Justin! That is not true and you know it."

"If it wasn't true, you would've come to see me by now. You don't even know what I look like now."

My heart sank because he was so right. I didn't even have any current pictures of him. Mama Tee had given me one the last time I'd gone to Sweet Poke, but he was fifteen in that picture. I don't know, I guess having pictures led to memories and questions—stuff I just didn't want to deal with. "Justin, it's not like that—"

"I gotta go. I don't feel so good." Before I could say another word, he hung up the phone.

chapter 19

It was Friday and I was spending another night alone. I was so sick of this. After Myles and I got married, things were gonna have to change. I refuse to sit at home all the time while he stays out in the streets. I don't care if he is working, as he always claims to be. He is going to have to make time for me and the baby.

I rubbed my stomach and thought about the life growing inside me. "I'm going to do right by you, little one," I muttered. It was a girl. Call me crazy, but I just knew in my heart that my baby was a girl. I'd already picked out a name, Angelique. I wanted something classy.

I kicked back in the love seat, grabbed the remote, and began flipping through the channels. Nothing was on so I left it on CNN. A few minutes later, my phone rang.

"Hello," I said, snatching it up.

"Hey, girl. What's up?"

"Hey, Shereen. What are you doing?"

"Just chillin'. You feel like company?"

"Sure."

"Then come open the door."

I looked toward the front door. "What?"

"Open the door; I'm outside."

I pushed the mute button on the television remote, got up, and went to open the door. "How'd you get in the gate?" I lived in a gated community. Not that I minded Shereen visiting, but I didn't like the thought that someone could get through without calling.

"I followed someone in," she said as she walked past me.

I closed the door. "Only one car is supposed to be able to go through that gate at a time."

"Hope you're not paying extra for that. If you are, you got gypped. I followed someone in and someone else followed me in." She dropped her purse on the sofa. She was clad in a long, flowing skirt, a baby blue blazer, a tight short-sleeved T-shirt that said FREE BOBBY BROWN, and some open-toe sandals. Several bangles adorned her arm and her neck was draped with three different necklaces.

I made a note to complain to the homeowners' association as I followed Shereen into the living room.

"I just left my date. He thinks I'm still in the restroom."

"What? Why'd you leave?"

"Girl, he's African, and he started talking that nonsense about how he believes a man should be allowed to have more than one wife." She shook her head. "You know I don't waste my time, so I left."

"Without even saying good-bye?"

"Without even saying good-bye."

"Dang, and I thought I was cold."

"Yeah, well, speaking of cold, what you got to drink?" She removed her jacket and threw it across my wing chair.

"There's some wine in the refrigerator. You want some?"

She nodded, then made her way to the kitchen. A few minutes later, she was back on the sofa, her wineglass filled to the brim.

"So where's Myles?"

"Where is he always?" I replied in disgust.

"Hey, ain't nothing wrong with a hardworking man."

"I know, but things are going to have to change after we get married." I sat down across from her.

"Girl, please. Don't you know you can't change a man? What you see is what you get." Shereen gulped down all of her wine. "Since you can't drink for a while, let me have that bottle." I shook my head as she got up, made her way back into the kitchen, and grabbed the bottle.

I leaned back and relaxed as she returned and sat back down on the sofa.

"So, how's work? Any more crazy calls?" Shereen asked. I had told her about the cryptic phone calls I'd been getting at work. I'd had two more in the last week. Each time it was a vaguely familiar voice spewing obscenities.

"No, but I let security know about it. Hopefully it's just some crank caller. Between that and Dina giving me a hard time, my job is starting to get on my last nerve."

"What? You have a dream job."

"I know. I just feel empty. I don't know what it is, but I'm just not getting as much fulfillment out of it anymore. I—"

"Hey, turn that up," Shereen cut me off, motioning toward the TV.

"Why, who is that?" I reached for the remote to turn up the volume.

"That's the governor of New Jersey. Did you hear what happened? He came out of the closet. He's married and everything. What is this world coming to?"

We both watched as the governor held a press conference announcing he had had an intimate relationship with another man. Throughout the whole press conference, his wife stood proudly by his side.

"That's a lot of love," Shereen said. "You know he's history. Secrets, I tell you, they can destroy a man's political career."

I cut my eyes at her, wondering if she was trying to throw me a hint. Shereen didn't respond to my funny look. Instead, she turned her attention to something else—the latest issue of *O* magazine on my coffee table. She picked it up and started flipping through it. "Ooooh, rate your relationship," she said, reading from one of the pages. "Gimme a pen."

I reached over, grabbed a pen off the end table, and handed it to her. "You don't have a relationship to rate." I laughed.

"I'm not rating my relationship. I'm rating yours."

I hesitated, but she had me intrigued. "Cool. I know we'll get a perfect score."

"We'll see. Number one. 'What's the biggest thing you argue about? Money, sex, family, or time?' "

I thought about it briefly. "Definitely not money. Surely not sex, because a sister be putting it on him." It couldn't be family because Myles didn't know about my family and I adored his family. But I didn't want to go there with Shereen. "I would have to say time."

She made a mark on the paper, then asked me several more questions. I answered them with ease, confident that I was scoring in the high percentile. Finally, she got to the last question. " 'How would you rank your honesty on a scale of one to ten?' "

That one had me stumped. I hadn't been honest with Myles about my family. Many people would consider that pretty big. "I would say five."

Shereen looked up from the magazine. "Five?"

I solemnly nodded. "Myles doesn't know about my family."

"And why not?" Shereen set the magazine down like she'd been waiting on this conversation.

I shrugged. I had opened up to Shereen but I just couldn't bring myself to do it with Myles.

"I don't know . . ."

We heard the garage door open and both of us turned our heads toward the door. Shereen spoke quickly. "Rae, I don't know why you don't want to be honest with Myles about your family. And Lord knows, I don't believe a man should know everything. But if you want to have a healthy marriage and do right by that baby, you need to come clean about your family because it's obvious it's eating you up."

The door leading out to the garage opened and Myles walked in. "Hello, ladies."

"Hey, baby," I muttered.

Shereen casually leaned back and flashed a smile at Myles. "What's up, Mr. Councilman?"

Myles dropped his keys on the bar and began loosening his tie. "Same ol', same ol'."

Shereen stood up to leave. "Well, I was just heading out."

"Don't leave on my account," Myles said.

"Naw, I was about to leave anyway. Your fiancée over here is trying to get me drunk."

Myles walked into the kitchen and opened the refrigerator door, no doubt looking for a beer. Shereen leaned over and hugged me. "Talk to him, tell him the truth," she whispered. "Because you flunked the quiz. Maybe opening up will be the start you need to get things right."

After Shereen left, I thought about what she had said. I would hate to destroy Myles's political future because of something with my family. But I didn't know how I could tell him, or if I even wanted to.

The reunion was tomorrow and I hadn't planned on going because I didn't know how I could explain my family to Myles. Maybe Shereen was right; I needed to be honest. We had too much at stake. I walked into the bedroom where Myles was relaxing on the bed watching *ESPN SportsCenter*.

"How was your day?" I asked.

"Tiring."

"Can I talk to you?"

"Can it wait? I'm exhausted."

"No, it's waited long enough."

"Rae, I don't feel like arguing with you. You know I work a lot."

"That's not what I want to talk about."

Myles looked at me in confusion.

"I have something I need to tell you. It's about my family." I sat down on the bed. "Myles, I'm from a small town called Sweet Poke, Arkansas."

"What? I thought you said you were from Little Rock."

"Please, just let me finish." I took a deep breath. "I didn't tell you where I was really from because I didn't want anybody to know my background. My family is not exactly something I'm proud of."

Myles flipped off the TV, giving me his undivided attention for a change. "Rae, you're not making any sense."

"Myles, my mother abandoned me when I was a little girl. I was raised by my grandmother. I have a sister with four kids by three different men and a brother who is sick with leukemia. My little sister died when she was just six years old. My father was shot to death over a game of craps. And my relatives make the Beverly Hillbillies look civilized. When I left Sweet Poke over ten years ago, I swore I was never going back. I wanted to erase that part of my life." I felt like I was rushing everything out.

Myles was silent for several minutes. "This isn't making any sense. Why did you feel you couldn't tell me that?" he finally asked.

"I felt like if I didn't acknowledge my past it would just disappear."

"That's crazy."

"I know."

"So why are you telling me now?"

"I didn't want to go into our marriage with any secrets. And my family is in town. They're having the family reunion here tomorrow."

Myles rubbed his head in astonishment. "This is unbelievable. What if this stuff had come out during the campaign?"

I should've known that would be his primary concern,

but I knew I couldn't get mad at him. It was a legitimate issue. "That's part of why I'm telling you as well. I just didn't want any surprises."

Myles leaned back against the bed. "Is it just crazy relatives, or are they into some illegal stuff?"

"I do have a couple of criminals in the family, but nothing really major. It's mainly just crazy relatives, not exactly political-family material," I responded.

Myles sat in silence for several minutes. I didn't know how he would react.

"So are you going?" he finally asked.

"Going where?"

"To the reunion?"

I shrugged, a wave of relief running through my body because he wasn't running for the hills. "My grandmother said that if I don't come, they'll all show up at my station."

Myles started laughing. "That would be funny."

I was a little uneasy. He seemed to be taking this a lot better than I thought. "No, it really wouldn't."

"Okay, how about I go with you tomorrow?"

I smiled. "Really?"

He leaned in and kissed me gently on the cheek. "Yes, really. I mean, good grief, most people have some crazy kinfolk. It's not that big of a deal. I don't understand why you felt you couldn't tell me about them."

"I'm sorry."

"I'll accept your apology if you promise to, one, never lie to me again."

I nodded. "I promise."

"And two . . . show me some love."

"You know I love you."

Myles lay back on the bed spread-eagle. "Show me."

I grinned and straddled him. "Your wish is my command."

As I began plastering his chest with kisses, I couldn't help but feel happy. This was the Myles I had fallen in love with. This was the man I wanted to spend the rest of my life with. And it felt so good to finally be honest.

chapter 20

I sat in the car, waiting. Waiting and contemplating whether I should just take my chances and blow this thing off. But images of the entire Rollins clan in the parking lot of Channel 2 convinced me that I had to get out.

"Are we just going to sit here all day?" Myles asked. He had been waiting patiently, knowing I was trying to work up the nerve to deal with my family.

"I don't want to do this." I sighed.

"What's the big deal? We get in, get out. It can't be that bad."

"You don't know my family."

"Come on. I'm going on up." Myles opened the door and stepped out.

I hesitated, then grabbed my purse and followed him.

My aunt Ola was the first to spot us walking up the sidewalk to the pavilion where everyone had gathered. "Well, well, well. Look what the cat done drug in."

"Lawd, have mercy. If it isn't Princess Diana back from the dead," my uncle Otis chimed in.

"Call *Ripley's Believe It or Not*," someone else shouted. "'Cause I can't believe this here."

I gave a meek wave. "Hey, everybody."

Myles lightly coughed. I motioned toward him. "This is Myles, my fiancé."

Uncle Otis walked over and peered at Myles's teeth. "Hey, boy, them all yo' teeth?"

Myles looked confused. I felt nauseous.

Uncle Otis cocked his head like it was the simplest question. "You deaf? I said, is them yo' teeth?"

Myles looked at me, then back at my uncle. "Ummm, yeah, they're mine."

Then Uncle Otis took his crusty hand and tried to lift Myles's lip. "Ola, come take a look at this boy's teeth."

Myles quickly jerked away and looked at Uncle Otis like he'd lost his mind.

"Otis, get out of that boy's mouth," Aunt Ola said.

Uncle Otis scrunched up his face, tilted his head, and peered into Myles's mouth again. "His teeth so straight and so white. How you get them so white?"

Mama Tee walked up, wiping her hands on her apron. "It's called brushing, Otis. Try it sometime, you might like it. Now, go'n."

Uncle Otis walked away shaking his head. "He must use that extra-strength Colgate."

Mama Tee extended her hand to Myles. "Don't pay that crazy brother of mine no never mind. He has a weird fascination with teeth. I'm Mama Tee." She turned toward me. "Glad you could join us."

"It's not like you gave me much of a choice," I mumbled with a slight smile. I was surprised at how good it felt to see Mama Tee.

"Well, you here now. So you thank you can give your grandma a hug? I ain't seen you since Jesus was a baby."

"Is Justin here?" I asked after pulling myself from her warm embrace.

"Justin just got out the hospital. I wasn't about to put him on the road." I felt my heart sink. I was really hoping he'd be here. "Mrs. Mary is staying at the house with him."

"Hmphh, if it isn't Miss Diva."

I turned around and glared at my big sister. "Hello, Shondella." She was forty pounds heavier, putting her at a good 270. She had finger waves covering her entire head, and something that looked like glitter was sprinkled throughout her hair. She was wearing a pair of bright pink capri pants and a black halter top.

My smile brightened when I saw the three kids gathered around her legs.

"And this must be Lexus, Mercedes, and Porsche."

Shondella shook her head. "No, that's Lexus." She pointed to the smallest one. "And that's Mercedes. This here is Cousin Essie Mae's daughter."

"That's a shame, gal don't even know her own nieces," Aunt Ola mumbled.

"Lawd, Lawd, Lawd, can somebody call 911!" Everyone turned toward my cousin Sugar, who was sashaying toward us.

"Why?" Aunt Ola asked.

Sugar, who had on a fluorescent green top that was unbuttoned and tied in the middle, along with a pair of black, boot-cut leggings, walked up and stood right in front of Myles. " 'Cuz my heart 'bout to stop beating at the sight of this fine specimen in front of me."

Myles's mouth dropped open. Sugar ignored his astonished look. "Hey, sweet thang. I'm Sugar."

Myles could barely get his words out. "Su . . . Sugar?"

"That's 'cuz he got a whole lot of sugar in his tank," Uncle Otis yelled.

Sugar dramatically rolled his eyes.

"That boy's name is Maurice," Mama Tee offered, shaking her head.

Sugar didn't take his eyes off Myles. "That's the name I was born with. My friends call me Reicy. My family calls me Sugar, but you"—Sugar leaned in seductively—"you can call me whatever you want."

Myles stepped away from Sugar and behind me. He looked flabbergasted.

"That's another one you can't pay no mind," Mama Tee said.

"My family has a hard time accepting who I am." Sugar dramatically flung his arms out and swung around. "But this is me. I been knowing I was gay ever since I was a little girl."

I decided it was time I stepped in. I had forgotten all about Sugar. He used to play with my dolls more than I did growing up. Even then, we all knew he was sweet.

"Sugar, can you please not scare off my fiancé?"

Sugar laughed before walking off. He mouthed, "Call me," to Myles.

I felt Myles shudder behind me. I turned and looked at him apologetically. But before I could say anything to him, Aunt Ola's only daughter, Nikki, had moved in next to Myles. She was rubbing Myles up and down his arm.

I quickly removed her hand. Nikki was the family freak. She didn't have any children, but it must be because she's barren, because she dang sure screws anything breathing. "That's my fiancé," I hissed.

"Dang, Cuz, you done good," she replied without taking her eyes off Myles. "Hey, sexy, I'm Nikki, like from the Prince song . . ." Nikki started grinding up and down Myles's leg while she sang, " 'I knew a girl named Nikki I guess u could say she was a sex fiend—' "

"Nikki!" Mama Tee shouted.

Nikki gave Myles a sly smile. "It's so nice to meet you. Umm, didn't catch your name."

I was going to cut this heifer if she made another pass at my man. "That's because he didn't throw it."

Nikki looked at me and did a fake shudder. "Ohhhhh, tough girl." She turned back to Myles and licked her lips before finally strutting off, making sure that big booty of hers jiggled from side to side as she walked away.

I caught Myles looking at her. He quickly diverted his eyes when he noticed my glare.

"I knew I shouldn't have come," I muttered.

"Chill, baby. She was just playing." I rolled my eyes at Myles. He appeared to have recovered from Sugar's encounter and was enjoying the attention from Nikki.

"Don't pay that fast child no never mind either," Mama Tee said. She took both my and Myles's hands and led us to a picnic table. "I'm just so thrilled that you decided to come."

"I'm starting to regret it," I mumbled again, trying to shake off the bad feeling that was building in my gut.

Mama Tee ignored me and turned to Myles. "I'd love

to say I've heard so much about you, but I haven't. Baby girl here don't come around like she should, but she know she still my heart."

I couldn't help but smile. Mama Tee amazed me. She could beat you one minute, then shower you with love the next. She was the backbone of our family, and no matter what anyone—including me—did, she still welcomed us with open arms.

My uncle Isaiah's deep baritone interrupted my pleasant thoughts. "Hey, Mr. Big City, you play bones?"

"Them old manicured hands probably don't know nothing 'bout no dominoes," one of my distant cousins interjected.

"Yeah, I've partaken in the game before. Probably could show you all a thing or two," Myles boasted.

I looked at Myles. In the two years I'd known him, he'd never indicated he knew how to play, let alone liked, dominoes.

"Did you hear that, Clydie? He's *partaken* in the game before," Uncle Isaiah said mockingly. He was sitting across from my cousin Clyde Jr. They were playing against June and some other man I didn't recognize. June looked up at me, scowled, then said sarcastically, "Kevin said to tell you what's up. He got life. Hope you happy."

I ignored June. As if I could really have made a difference. In Texas, Kevin was lucky he didn't get the death chamber.

"Ohhh, Raedella got her an Oreo," Clyde Jr. sang, quickly lightening the mood. I swear, to be dang near forty, he still acted like a little child.

"Or-e-or-e-oh," Clyde Jr. sang. Several people started

laughing. I glared at Clyde Jr. Why were my people so ignorant? Just because Myles was educated and spoke proper English, they wanted to say he sounded white.

"Brang it on, city boy. These here fools 'bout to get up 'cause we only need twenty-five to win," Uncle Isaiah called out as he viciously slammed a domino on the table. "And that there's ten!"

June and the man he was playing with groaned.

I followed Myles as he headed to the table. I just wasn't ready to let him at it alone.

"Gimme fourteen hookers and a pimp to run them hos," Clyde Jr. yelled as he slammed another domino on the table. "That's game! That's game! Get up and get to steppin'! Next!"

"How you gon' let him score on you?" June yelled to his partner.

"Me? Why didn't you set him up?" his partner screamed back. "Yo' slow behind don't know how to play no bones!"

"Don't tell me I can't play! Yo' mama can't play."

"I'm tired of your noise-talking."

"Sorry piece of sh—!"

"Yo' woman seems to like it," his partner interrupted.

Just then, June jumped across the table and grabbed the guy by the shirt. He threw him up against the wall of the pavilion as everyone scattered out of the way. Kids were screaming. Several of my uncles jumped in to pull June off the guy.

I sighed in frustration. Myles had a look of horror across his face. This was unbelievable.

"Cut it out!" Mama Tee screamed. "Y'all see we got

company here and y'all showing your tails. June, get up off that boy. Who is he anyway?"

"That's his best friend, Triggerman," Uncle Otis said as he pulled a frantically swinging June off his friend. Triggerman struggled to get up off the ground. He stood up and was getting ready to charge June again when Mama Tee stepped in front of him.

"Boy, don't you even think about it. Coming up here in other people's family reunion and starting some mess," she snapped.

"He started it," Triggerman said meekly. Mama Tee had a way of making even grown men feel five years old.

"I did not!" June yelled. "He said my woman slept with him."

"She probably did," Mama Tee said matter-of-factly. "You know that gal ain't worth a pinch of salt, so don't be getting mad at this here boy for telling the truth."

June pouted. Triggerman proudly stuck his chest out. Mama Tee turned and slapped Triggerman upside the head.

"And you, boy. What's your name? Because I know yo' mama ain't named you no damn Triggerman."

Triggerman lowered his eyes. "It's Solomon."

"Well, Solomon, who yo' people?"

"Bettie Graves is my grandma."

"You Bettie's boy? You the one been in prison?"

"Yes, ma'am."

"Well, you need to leave that jailbird stuff behind them bars. Civilized folks don't act like that, especially at other folks' functions. Your grandma would have your behind if she knew you was out here acting like that. Now, if y'all can't play that game like somebody with some sense, I'ma make y'all put those dominoes up. Now, pick them up!"

Several people were laughing and snickering as June and Triggerman picked up the dominoes.

Mama Tee turned to me. "Rae, come on over here and tell me what you been up to."

I looked at Myles. He had a please-don't-leave-me look on his face. But Mama Tee wasn't having it. She grabbed me by the arm and pulled me toward her. We headed back over to the table where she was cooking. Shondella was dumping baked beans on a little girl's plate.

"Who's dat?" the little girl asked, all wide-eyed and innocent.

"That's your auntie," Mama Tee said.

"Uh-uh. I don't know her."

Shondella walked over, glared at me, and said, "Neither do we, baby. Neither do we."

I ignored Shondella and looked over my shoulder to see how Myles was doing. I spotted him ogling Nikki's breasts.

Mama Tee saw it, too. "You'd better watch that one. He's a snake." She nodded toward Myles.

"You don't even know him," I snapped. I knew Mama Tee would have something to say about Myles. She had always been judgmental about any man in my or Shondella's life, even if it was just a casual date. Reno was the only exception. Mama Tee loved his dirty drawers.

"Don't have to bite me for me to know it's a snake," Mama Tee replied as she glanced at Myles again.

"You come bringing him round here like he's all that. He ain't nobody and neither are you," Shondella interjected.

That was it. Her big behind had just worked my last nerve. "Just because your trifling behind can't get a man, don't degrade mine. Myles is a good man. Can you say the same about Ezekiel Baxter?" I knew I had hit a sore spot. Ezekiel was Mercedes's and Camry's father and about the sorriest man you ever met. He and Shondella had dated off and on since she was in the ninth grade. He'd dropped out of high school, and from what I'd heard, did nothing but sleep all day and hang out in the streets all night. He occasionally lived with Shondella, until she got mad and put him out.

"You don't know nothing about Ezekiel," Shondella said.

"Just like you don't know nothing about Myles. You're just jealous." I flicked her off and turned away from her to let her know I was through talking.

"Hah! Honey, I'd rather be alone than have a slimy snake like that. Both of y'all go on back to your high-society world where you can pretend that you're all that, with the perfect job and the perfect man."

"You wish you had my life."

"Please, I wouldn't trade places with you for nothing, because one day your perfect house of cards will come tumbling down."

"Stop it!" Mama Tee snapped. "You two just don't change. Just like your mama and Ola, always fighting."

I sighed. I really wasn't in the mood to fight with Shondella. "Speaking of Rose, when's the last time you talked to her?" I asked Mama Tee.

"Oooowwee. I ain't talked to your mama in five years," Mama Tee replied.

Shondella rolled her eyes. "Why would you bring her

up?" She stopped talking and turned her attention to Lexus, who was climbing on top of the picnic table trying to reach for another hot dog. Shondella reached over and popped Lexus on her bottom. "Girl, get your tail down before I beat the hell out of you."

"You really shouldn't curse at the children."

Shondella cocked her head and squinted her eyes. "You really should mind your own business." She grabbed Lexus's arm and pulled her off the table. Lexus, who had managed to snag the hot dog, took a quick bite, then scurried off.

I decided against saying anything else to Shondella and turned back to Mama Tee. "Rose called me last week."

"Did she now?" Mama Tee didn't seem the least bit fazed. She kept spreading barbecue sauce over the meat.

"Well, not me, directly. She called in to my talk show, asking how she can get her daughter to forgive her for abandoning her."

"Well, what did you tell her?"

"There ain't no forgiving her."

"Umm-hmm" was all Mama Tee muttered.

"That's all you have to say?"

"Umm-hmm."

I fiddled with the napkins. "What was I supposed to say?" I finally asked.

Mama Tee flipped a slab of ribs over, brushing the thick sauce across the meat. "I guess you was supposed to say whatever your heart led you to say." She closed the top on the grill, allowing the meat to smoke some more. She wiped her hands again, then walked toward me. "Baby girl, I don't expect much from you. You barely talk to us. It don't surprise me one bit you won't talk to your mama. But I got a feeling one of these days you gon' figure it out. Sometimes family is all you got." She squeezed my chin, then walked off, leaving her words to simmer in my head.

chapter 21

I groaned as I walked out of the break room. Another day of being nauseous. "I'll be glad when this first trimester is over," I mumbled.

I woke up feeling like crap, but came on in to work because I wanted to save all my sick days for my maternity leave. Although I was dressed to the nines in a canary yellow Prada suit, I didn't have a drop of makeup on, which was unusual for me. I always wore at least a little makeup until I could get in to see Sasha, the station's makeup artist. But I was feeling so crappy this morning, I hadn't even bothered.

I'd eaten some crackers, hoping that would calm my stomach. I probably shouldn't have been drinking the coffee that was steaming in a paper cup in my hand, but my mornings just didn't get off to the right start without my daily cup of coffee. I had just taken another sip when

Tory, one of the photographers, bumped into me and made me almost spill the drink.

"Would you watch where you're going?" I snapped as I stuck the cup out, trying to keep it from wasting on my suit.

"Oh, Rae, I'm sorry. I was busy being nosy," Tory said as he slyly pointed toward Dina's office.

I was about to say something else when my eyes made their way toward the office. I frowned at what I saw. Simone was in Dina's office and they were laughing like old friends. I turned my nose up. Dina never laughed with anyone. What made Simone so special? Maybe she was brown-nosing Dina, something I was not about to do.

I lagged around the bulletin board, pretending to read the latest flyer about some party I wouldn't be attending. In actuality, I was trying to hear what Dina and Simone were talking about.

The sudden sound of sirens blasting across the scanner caught my attention.

"I need all crews to head to Sanchez Elementary School on Broadway. Key map 535J!" the assignment editor screamed into the two-way radio.

The commotion caused Dina to come running out of her office. Simone was right behind her. "What's going on?" Dina asked.

"We got a hostage situation at an elementary school. A teacher has gone berserk and taken a cafeteria full of students hostage!" yelled the assignment editor, Joe.

"We need to break into programming right now," Dina commanded. "Where's Keith?"

Keith was the anchor on the noon news.

"He's out sick. Rae is right there." Joe pointed to me standing by the bulletin board.

Dina spun toward me. "Rae, I need you on the set five minutes ago!" she snapped.

I looked at her as if she were crazy. "Sasha is just about to do my makeup and my hair hasn't been curled."

Dina shot me an incredulous look. "What?"

"Give me fifteen minutes." I started toward the dressing room. "I'll just slap some makeup on and throw a few curls in my hair, then I'll be good to go." If there was one thing I didn't do, it was go on the air looking like any old thing.

"Are you on drugs?" Dina raised her voice. "We have a teacher holding a cafeteria full of kids hostage and you want me to give you fifteen minutes so you can get pretty?" Dina shook her head like she couldn't fathom my request.

"Dina, surely you don't want me going on the air looking unprofessional," I tried to reason.

"You need to look professional when you walk through that door!" She looked like she was about to go off on me, then decided against it. "I don't have time for this; I will deal with you later." She turned to Simone. "Do you need time to get ready?"

"I came to work ready," Simone replied eagerly.

"Can you handle this?"

"Absolutely."

"Good. I want you on the air right now."

Simone had a huge grin on her face. "You got it." She raced to the news set.

I could not believe my eyes. I knew they were not about to put this little tramp on in my place.

"Fine! I will go on without my makeup," I said.

"Don't worry about it. You just go get pretty," Dina said, flicking me off as she turned back to Joe. "Get the helicopter up. I want Simone to toss to the chopper so the pilot can give us a bird's-eye view of what's going on."

"Dina, you can't be serious. I'm the anchor here," I protested.

She ignored me and just kept barking orders.

"Dina . . ." I stepped in front of her.

"Rae. I am dealing with a crisis here. You need to move out of my face," she said calmly.

I saw her look of anger and figured I would just let this slide. Fine. Let little Miss Simone mess it all up. It would serve them right. I stepped out of her way and headed to my office just as Simone popped up on the air.

"Hello, this is Simone Sanders and we have a breaking-news situation we want to tell you about . . ."

I plopped down on my sofa and waited for the ball to drop, for her to flub, stumble, anything. I was stunned when she didn't.

"I told you that girl is going places."

I looked up to see Shereen standing in my doorway. "What do you want, Shereen?"

As usual, she ignored my attitude. "Why are you in here and she's out there?"

I rolled my eyes. "Long story."

Shereen turned her attention back to the television. The helicopter was up and Simone was giving a play-by-play of the events as they unfolded. She wasn't missing a beat.

"You might need to watch out for that one." Shereen was shaking her head in awe.

"I don't need to watch anything." I stood up, stomped over to my computer, and began typing as if I weren't interested in Simone's report.

"Really, you do," Shereen said, not taking her eyes off the TV. "I thought she was just getting a chance because Dina is best friends with her sister—"

I spun around so fast I nearly fell over in my chair. "What did you say?"

"I said I thought Simone was just getting a chance because Dina and her sister are best friends, but I think she's earning her right to be here."

"Did you say Dina and Simone know each other?"

"Yeah, didn't you know that?"

"How would I know that?"

Shereen shrugged. "I don't know. I thought everybody knew."

"I can't believe you didn't tell me that. So that explains everything."

"Yeah, I think Dina and her sister are sorority sisters or something," Shereen added nonchalantly. "Oh, well. Gotta get back to work. I just came down to see why you weren't on the air."

"Call me tonight and I'll explain it all to you."

I grabbed the remote, muted the TV, then leaned back in my chair. That's why they were all chummy. I wondered if Stan knew that.

"I might just have to have a little talk with him," I muttered.

I turned my attention back to the TV. The sight of Simone was making me even sicker. I flipped the TV off, then tried to finish transcribing a tape from an interview I had done earlier.

I was halfway done with the transcription when my intercom buzzed. "Hi, Rae." It was Jamie, Dina's secretary. "Dina would like to see you in her office right now."

I rolled my eyes. "Fine."

"Oh, and Rae," she whispered, "if I were you, I wouldn't keep her waiting. She doesn't appear to be in a good mood."

I turned up my nose. Like I gave a fat rat about her mood. Still, I was in the doghouse, so why cause any more trouble? "I'm on my way."

I took my time, straightening items on my desk for a few minutes before heading to Dina's office.

"You wanted to see me."

"Close the door and have a seat."

Great. A closed-door meeting. Those were never good. I walked in casually, pushing the door shut behind me.

Dina purposely kept her eyes glued on the document she was reading for several minutes, no doubt trying to piss me off. It was working.

"We seem to have a fundamental problem," she said just as I was about to ask her why she was wasting my time. "You apparently are used to the way things *were*, and not how they *are*."

I was ready to interject. She must have noticed because she held up her hand. "There are no stars around here. I don't care what kind of ratings you bring in, or how valuable you *think* you are around here. You are dispensable. Do you understand that?"

I was really trying not to let my attitude show. "I am valuable," I replied with conviction.

"No, I repeat, you are *dispensable. The Rae Rollins Show* bears your name, but we can easily change that. I could find another just-as-talented six-o'clock news anchor. See, the bottom line is, I'm the head sista in charge. That means that if I tell you to get on the set, you get on the set. It's as simple as that. And if you have a problem with it, I would be more than willing to let you out of your contract so you can pursue other opportunities elsewhere."

I was fuming inside. "Other stations would love to have me."

"I'm sure they would. They'll just have to wait a year to get you. You have a noncompete clause in your contract, remember?"

Oh, yeah, that. That noncompete clause forbade me from working at another station in a one-hundred-mile radius within a year of leaving Channel 2.

"What's your problem with me? I would think we would try to stick together, *my sister*."

Dina laughed like that was the funniest thing she'd heard all week. "Rae, I don't play those games. I'm about business. I don't have a problem with you, but I know your type. You think the sun sets around you. But things don't work like that around here. Accept it or move on."

I wanted so badly to give her a piece of my mind. Two more minutes and I probably would have. But she didn't give me a chance. She shook her head in disgust and said, "That will be all. You're dismissed."

And then she turned her chair around and started typing on her computer. I wanted to take the paperweight that was sitting on the corner of her desk and smash her in the head with it. Instead, I rolled my eyes and stormed to the door.

"Oh, and, Rae?" she said just as I reached the door.

"Please stop back by before you leave today so you can sign your letter of reprimand for refusing to go on the air today. That will not be tolerated. So I am writing you up, and it will go in your file."

"What?"

"That will be all."

Okay, I had to get out of there before I said something to get me in even more trouble. But if Miss Dina thought she could just treat me like any old thing, she had another thing coming. This woman really and truly didn't know whom she was messing with.

chapter 22

"That woman is out to get me." I was sitting on my living room sofa with my legs draped across Myles's lap. He was engrossed in the paperwork for the new six-thousand-square-foot house we planned to buy and seemed oblivious to my sulking. "I said, Dina is out to get me." My mind had been swirling since I'd left the office. I had to figure out a way to get rid of Dina.

"Umm-huh," Myles responded without taking his eyes off the paperwork.

I pushed the paperwork down. "Myles, I need you to listen to me. This is serious."

"Isn't everything always serious with you?" He continued reading.

"What is that supposed to mean?" I pulled my legs down and sat up.

"Nothing, just drop it. I'm trying to make sure this contract for the house is right."

Now, not only was he ignoring me, but he was trying to blow me off. I snatched the paperwork from him. "I'm talking to you, Myles."

Myles huffed. "Rae, I'm not in the mood for this. I've had a very bad day. I want to review this contract, then watch TV in peace."

I was so sick of this. Myles never had time for me or my problems. I just needed someone to talk to, to vent to. And my own man acted like that was too much of an inconvenience.

"Well, excuse me for being a nuisance." I stood up and stormed into my exercise room. I half-expected him to stop me. I don't know why I was surprised when he didn't.

I stomped over to the treadmill and hopped on. I should have changed into my exercise clothes, but the T-shirt and shorts I was wearing would have to do. I had to blow off some steam—now.

After about twenty minutes on the treadmill, I'd managed to calm down and see the bigger picture. I saw the life Myles and I could have together. The picture-perfect life. The life I dreamed of growing up in Sweet Poke. Two professionals with 2.3 kids. Maybe even a little Pekingese dog. The dream home. The doting mother-in-law. We would have such a normal family. So, in my opinion, it was worth putting up with Myles's sometimes insensitive ways.

"Rae!"

I heard Myles calling my name, but I ignored him.

"Rae!"

I stopped the treadmill, got off, grabbed a towel, and wiped my face. I then headed to the bedroom without saying a word.

He walked into the bedroom behind me. "Oh, so you're ignoring me now?"

I cut my eyes at him. "Oh, so you have time for me now?"

Myles walked over and began massaging my neck. "Don't be like that, baby. I don't want to fight with you."

I felt myself melting at his touch. "I needed to talk to you. You never have time to talk to me," I whined.

Myles eased me down on the bed. "I'm sorry. I'm listening, baby."

"Never mind, now."

Myles took a deep breath. "Look, Rae, you wanted to talk, so talk."

I stared at him. We needed to get some things straight. "Look, Myles, I try to be there for you whenever you need me. But I can't say you give me that same thing."

"Rae, you know how I work."

"I also know that I need to be a priority in your life. I know we are set to be married in three weeks, but if this isn't right, we need to cut our losses now." I didn't know where all of this was coming from. If he had said fine to leaving me, I probably would've had a heart attack.

"Is that what you think I am, a loss?"

"I love you, Myles. I just don't want to feel like I'm in this thing alone."

"I love you and I want us to work, okay? Now, why don't you update me on the wedding progress? It seems all I've been doing is writing checks."

Now I couldn't help but break out in a big smile. Planning my wedding had been the only thing keeping me sane. I had hired one of the best wedding planners in the city. She was excellent at last-minute stuff and we got along wonderfully.

"We have the flowers picked out, Shereen's bridesmaid dress and my dress, which, by the way, you are going to love. We'll get married at First Baptist Church downtown and the reception will be held at the Westin in the Galleria. The only thing left to do is find the flower girls' dresses. Your nieces are still doing that, right?"

Myles nodded. His brother's twin daughters were going to serve as flower girls for the wedding. "Martin said the girls are excited. So just let him know what he needs to do. What about the invitations? Have those gone out yet?"

"I got your mother's list and those went out last week."

"Let me ask. Did you invite your family?"

He was ruining a great moment. "No. I don't want anyone messing up our day."

"Do you think you might regret that one day?" he asked, his voice full of concern.

"Please."

"So you don't want to invite anyone from your hometown?"

I sighed. "I really would love for Justin to be there. And maybe even Mama Tee. But you don't know my family. They're a package deal, and to invite one is to invite them all."

"If you say so. I just don't want my side of the church to be packed and yours empty." He grinned.

"Oh, I've taken care of that. There won't be any bride/groom sides. Everyone will sit wherever they want."

"So it looks like all I have to do is show up."

"That's it." I smiled.

"You're going to make a beautiful wife," he said as he stroked my hair.

I felt myself blushing. "We're going to be so happy."

"I will die trying." He pulled me to him. "I'm looking forward to the life we're going to have together."

"Me, too, baby." I kissed him passionately, happy that everything was going as planned.

chapter 23

I was two seconds away from quitting. Not really, but I sure felt like quitting. It had only been a short time since my reprimand, and my life at work had gotten progressively worse each day. Now here I was, about to go out on a stupid story about a cat that was hung. Who cares? I was so mad, I thought I was going to blow a gasket. Xavier, the photographer I was working with today, knew I was pissed, too. He hadn't said one word since we'd got in the news truck.

I had a right to be pissed. Dina had come to me personally and told me she needed me to go cover this story about three kids arrested for hanging and torturing a cat. "Who cares about that?" I'd asked her.

"Our viewers do," she'd snidely responded. "Pet stories bring in the ratings. And we do whatever brings in the ratings. After all, you're still here."

I wanted to slap her and made a mental note to complain to Stan about her ASAP. The last two times I'd tried to go talk to him, he'd been out of the office. I bit my tongue and told her, "Send someone else. I don't do pet stories."

She smirked and said, "You didn't *used* to do pet stories. Now you do whatever I tell you to." Then she turned and walked off.

She was messing with me, pure and simple.

I'd called my agent and he told me there was nothing in my contract to say I didn't have to cover certain stories. I'd screamed at him and slammed the phone down. What was the point of my giving him 10 percent of my salary if he couldn't keep me from doing stupid stories?

"Come on, we might as well get this over with," Xavier said.

I was so engrossed in thought I hadn't even noticed that we'd pulled up to the police station. When I didn't move, Xavier said, "Look, the sooner you get out, the sooner we get this over with. I'm just as mad as you. I didn't win all these photography awards to shoot dead-cat stories." He stepped out of the news truck, slamming the door.

He's right, I thought as Xavier opened the trunk and started unloading his gear. *I'm getting married in two days. Today's my last day at work for two weeks. Let this go.* I popped a Tylenol, pulled out my compact, and refreshed my lipstick. I took a deep breath, then stepped out of the car.

I numbly went through the interviews, asking two, maybe three questions to the parents of the kids that had tortured the cat. I couldn't really care less about their juvenile delinquents, and I'm sure they could tell that by my demeanor. I just wanted to get the story done and over with.

My cell phone rang just as we were getting back in the truck. The number came up unknown, but I answered it since few people had my cell phone number.

"Hello."

"What's up, Sis?"

"Justin! How's it going?"

"I'm still alive, so I guess it's going all right."

I hated when my little brother talked like that. "So to what do I owe the pleasure of this call?"

"You didn't tell nobody you were getting married."

I was silent. "How'd you know?"

He giggled. "They wrote about it in the paper, and you know how obsessive your sister is with the papers. She saw it and told everybody in Sweet Poke. Everybody all mad 'cause you didn't invite them. It's cool, though. You know Mama Tee wasn't gon' let me travel down there with her anyway."

With her? "So Mama Tee's coming?"

Justin burst out laughing. "Mama Tee and everybody else in Sweet Poke."

Could this day get any worse? I leaned back against the seat, closed my eyes, and bit my lip, trying to keep from screaming.

"If you didn't want anyone to know about the wedding, you shouldn't have had it in the paper. Mama Tee said her invitation must've gotten lost. I'm warning you now, you will hear about it when they get there."

"Why didn't she call me?"

"Please, so you can tell her not to come?" Justin was laughing like crazy.

"Oh, so you think this is funny?"

"It is. Boy, I wish I could be there to see Aunt Ola act a fool. She took some greens from her garden, talking about she gon' fix them for the reception."

I couldn't help but smile at my brother's incessant laughter. I could count on one hand the number of times he'd laughed like that.

"Okay, Mr. Funny Man, who's there with you?"

His laughter died down. "When are you guys going to realize I am a grown man? I don't need anyone to stay with me."

"Boy, please. I know Mama Tee didn't leave you by yourself."

I heard a long sigh before he spoke. "Mrs. Miller from down the street is here. I tried to tell Mama Tee I didn't need anyone here. She acts like I'm still ten years old. Besides, Uncle Frank is here."

"Isn't Uncle Frank comatose?"

"Sometimes. That's why I wouldn't have minded staying with him."

"Hush, boy." I giggled. "But you know, Mama Tee just feels better having someone there with you because she's scared you might have a seizure."

"Yeah, yeah, yeah. Whatever. When it's my time to go, it'll just be my time. I wish everyone would just let me live my life." Justin sighed heavily, then seemed to shake it off. "But I didn't call you to gripe. I just wanted to give you a heads-up."

"Well, thanks for calling me. You know I have to mentally prepare myself."

"Good luck. Well, I'll holla at you later. I'm about to go watch a nasty movie on pay-per-view. Mrs. Miller's downstairs sleep."

"I'm not even worried about that. Let Mama Tee see a bill for a nasty movie."

"You're right about that." He laughed. "Take care, Sis. I love you, even if you act like you don't love me."

I hesitated. "I do love you, Justin. No matter what you might think."

"I'm just joking, Raedella. I know you love me. Later." With that, he hung up.

I wiped away the single tear that was making its way down my cheek.

chapter 24

Today was my day. The day I had dreamed about. I was getting married. We were at Myles's mother's church, a huge cathedral nestled in the heart of downtown Houston. Shereen was running around the bride's dressing room trying to make sure everything was in order. She was the only bridesmaid I had in my wedding. Myles had been upset because he had a lot of friends he wanted as groomsmen, but since I only had one friend, there was nothing we could really do about it.

I was walking down the aisle by myself. I had no one to give me away. There was no way I would let one of my crazy uncles give me away. No, sir, I would just strut down that aisle by myself.

I surveyed myself in the mirror and smiled at my reflection, pleased at my appearance. Surprisingly, I wasn't nervous. I was just ready to become Mrs. Myles Jacobs and begin my fairy-tale life.

We had over three hundred people at our wedding. Two hundred and fifty of them were probably Myles's family, friends, and associates. Some of my coworkers had been invited, but other than that I was sure there weren't that many people here for me.

"Where she at? Where my niece?"

I grumbled when I heard Aunt Ola's voice bellowing down the hall. My family had actually shown up. I was hoping, no I'd prayed, that somehow none of them would show up. What was I thinking?

"Raedella?" Aunt Ola called out. "Baby girl, where are you?"

I was so not believing that she was standing in the church screaming my name like she was crazy. I buried my face in my hands. "Why, why, why?"

"Ola, shush all that noise," I heard Mama Tee say. "That lady up front said they were in here." Mama Tee knocked on the door. "Rae, you in there, baby?"

Shereen looked back and forth between me and the door. "Ummm, should I go tell them we're in here?"

"No, go tell them all to go away."

Shereen looked at me before spinning off. "I'll let them know we're in here."

A few minutes later, Mama Tee appeared in the doorway. She had on her Easter best, a lavender suit with a sequined collar, with the matching lavender hat, which had a banana, apples, grapes, and something I couldn't make out on top of it. I wanted to cry.

Mama Tee clapped her hands together. "Ohhhhh, my baby looks so precious."

"I don't know why you got on white; it ain't like you a virgin." I hadn't even noticed Shondella standing behind

Mama Tee. She had on a sequined dress that looked like it was buy-one/get-one-free at the flea market. It had diamond-shaped holes cut out of the side of it, and her rolls of fat were protruding from the openings. Her hair was whipped into an updo, and she had tiny rhinestones lined up along her hairline. I could only hope my disgust wasn't evident.

"Shondella, don't start with your sister," Mama Tee said. "I told you the only way we was coming was if you didn't cause no trouble."

Shondella sashayed in, leaned into the full-length mirror in the back of the room, and began adjusting one of the rhinestones that was coming loose in her hair. "I ain't the one you need to be worried about. Uncle Otis is already out in the lobby drunk. He tried to kiss the preacher's wife—on the lips."

I took a deep breath. I hadn't even spoken to my relatives and they were making my head hurt.

"I see you all made it." I was trying to muster up energy to deal with them.

"Chile, yes." Aunt Ola shook her head. "It look like the Democratic National Convention, all them people out there. How much y'all spend on this shindig?" She didn't give me time to answer, not that I would have. "Don't make no sense for y'all to spend all this money. You should've been getting married at Greater Gethsemane in Sweet Poke anyway. Me and the usher board coulda fixed you up a huge pot of collard greens and corn bread. Reverend Berry woulda been more than happy to marry you. Who's cooking for the reception anyway? Don't matter none, I brought my own seasoning." She held up a stained brown paper bag. "I know you got some white folks catering . . ." She turned to Shondella. "You know your sister thank she white anyway. But ain't nothing like some down-home cooking. So I brought some of my own concoctions to spice things up."

"Thanks, Aunt Ola, but the *African-American* caterers are more than prepared," I stressed. "And I'm sure their food will be delicious. As for why we're getting married here, this is where we want to get married." I sighed, then turned back to Mama Tee. "Why don't you all go on and take your seats."

"Why you ain't have Lexus or Mercedes as your flower girls?" Shondella stood with her hands on her hips. "You think they ain't good enough to be in your wedding? Or, let me guess, you would rather have them high-yella gals in your wedding. Umm-huh, I saw 'em when we was coming in. Little Puerto Rican-looking thangs."

"For your information, Shondella, they are half-Puerto Rican. They are Myles's nieces." I wouldn't have minded Shondella's kids in my wedding, but I knew that would've meant inviting Shondella. A moot point since I guess she was here anyway.

"Ladies, please. We need to get this show on the road, so if you can, go take your seats." Thank God for Shereen.

"And who are you?" Aunt Ola asked, her lip turned up.

"I'm the maid of honor, Rae's friend Shereen. We work together."

All three women looked her up and down like who was she to be telling them to leave.

"Please, go," I said. "We need to get started."

"Fine. Come on, y'all," Mama Tee said.

After they'd left, Shereen playfully shook her head. "Okay, now I see why you ran from your family."

I began massaging my temples. I wanted everything to be perfect today and it was getting off to a bad start.

"But, look, don't let them ruin your day," Shereen said as she walked over and adjusted my veil. "Don't let anyone ruin your day. The man of your dreams is waiting for you inside that sanctuary. Let's go." I managed a smile as I followed Shereen to the foyer.

My ceremony had to be the most beautiful in the world. But I guess I'm supposed to think that. I almost wanted to die when Aunt Ola began boo-hooing all loud, wailing, "My baby growing up!" I've been grown for years, so why she felt compelled to act a fool was beyond me, but that was my aunt Ola.

I fought back tears myself as Myles promised to love, honor, and cherish me until death did us part. I think I was in a trance for most of the wedding; I was just that happy.

At the end of the ceremony, Myles took my hand and turned me around toward the audience. The minister had just pronounced us man and wife. As Myles's cousin belted out the sounds of Natalie Cole's "Our Love," we began making our way down the center aisle. I gazed lovingly at Myles. He leaned in and whispered, "I will spend my life making you happy, Mrs. Jacobs."

I grinned like a Cheshire cat. "Mrs. Jacobs. I like the sound of that." I gently kissed my husband, then waved at everyone as we made our way out of the church and to our waiting horse-drawn carriage.

* * *

"Ladies and gentlemen, introducing Mr. and Mrs. Myles Jacobs."

The smile was still plastered on my face as the reception emcee announced our arrival. The horse ride over had been phenomenal and we were now standing in the doorway of the Westin Galleria's ballroom.

The wedding planner had done a magnificent job. The room was wonderfully decorated with fresh flowers. The twin swan ice sculptures sat on a long table against the wall. They were surrounded by every kind of food imaginable. Guests had already begun nibbling on fruit from the massive fruit display.

This was indeed a fairy-tale wedding.

"You okay, baby?" Myles asked.

"I couldn't be better." I draped my arm through his and walked into the ballroom.

Myles and I spent the reception mixing and mingling. We didn't even get a chance to enjoy the food, which I heard was phenomenal as well.

After our first dance to Etta James's "At Last," Myles grabbed my hand and headed to my family's table. I felt my stomach start turning flips. I just knew they were about to say or do something to ruin everything.

"How's everyone doing?" Myles asked.

"Fair to middling," Mama Tee replied. "Nice ceremony, real nice."

"Still don't make no sense, all this money y'all spent," Aunt Ola said as she surveyed the room.

Myles took her comment in stride. "Nothing is too good for my baby," he said, lifting my hand and gently kissing it.

"Ain't that sweet," Shondella said. I couldn't tell if she was being sarcastic, but at that moment I didn't really care.

"Boy, you sho' know how to do stuff," Uncle Otis said, interrupting my romantic moment. "This here is first-class. I done had seven glasses of this Moët stuff. Ain't never had none of that before, but it sho' beats my Ripple."

I inhaled deeply and Myles rubbed my back before leaning in and whispering, "We're happy today. Let it ride, baby. It's our night."

God, I loved this man. I smiled at Uncle Otis. "I'm glad you're enjoying yourself."

"Well, look here," Uncle Otis said. "Since y'all feeling all festive, I just wanted to tell you that I would love the honor and distinction of owing you a hundred dollars," Uncle Otis said.

Myles laughed. I couldn't help but laugh myself. "Uncle Otis, what do you need a hundred dollars for?"

"I'm trying to sue the state of Arkansas."

"For what?" Myles asked.

"That's right, you a lawyer." Uncle Otis stood up and pulled his champagne glass close to his chest. "I'm suing because the state sells alcohol, then wants to lock you up when you drink it."

We all busted out laughing at that.

Myles and I eventually finished making our rounds. At night's end, I was still floating on cloud nine. My husband had made that possible. He was not only attentive, but he helped me stay relaxed all night long. Things had even been peaceful with my family.

"See, that wasn't so painful," Myles said as we gathered

our things to head up to our honeymoon suite. "Maybe, you can find a way to permanently make peace with your family."

I smiled before noticing Shondella, Aunt Ola, and Nikki at the buffet table stuffing all the leftover food into plastic shopping bags. I sighed. "Then again, maybe not," I replied.

chapter 25

I couldn't help but smile as I thought of the wonderful night I'd had with my husband.

I was still basking in the afterglow of my wedding, magnificent reception, and spectacular night in the honeymoon suite. I couldn't have wished for a better start to my life with Myles. Today things felt complete. I had the best job and now the best husband. Myles had been shining as he flitted about among family and friends. He had even adapted well to my family. I was still kind of bothered about them just showing up uninvited, but I took Myles's advice and for once let it ride.

The day after the wedding we were gathered at my place. My thirty-five-hundred-square-foot home was cozy, yet big enough to host family and friends. His family, mine, several of Myles's friends, and some of my colleagues from work had all gathered for a postwedding brunch to watch us open our wedding gifts. We were heading out to Belize for a five-day honeymoon in the morning. We would've left right after the wedding but Myles's mother really wanted the brunch. I was just hoping it didn't turn disastrous. I hadn't really planned on my family coming over. I was hoping they'd be gone the first thing this morning, but luck was not on my side. In fact, I hadn't even told them about the brunch. Myles's brother had actually been the one to open his big mouth, and of course, Mama Tee just invited herself and the whole Rollins clan to the brunch. But again, I wasn't going to let their presence steal my joy.

I was in the kitchen, putting up some of the delicious food we'd enjoyed. I'd used the same caterers who'd prepared the food for the reception. After making sure everything was covered or put away, I made my way back into the living room.

"Come on, sweetie, why don't you start opening the gifts?" Myles's mother said. She was a small-statured woman, but she radiated elegance.

"Mrs. Jacobs, you know we can't open the gifts until Myles gets back," I replied.

"He's not back yet?"

"No, he had to drop Kenny off at the airport." Myles had been gone about an hour to take his college roommate to the airport.

"I still don't understand why he couldn't have had somebody else take that boy to the airport. This is his wedding, for Christ's sake," Shondella said.

"Nobody asked you to understand," I mumbled.

Mama Tee quickly jumped in. "Don't you two start. I'm sure he'll be back shortly. Why don't we watch the tape from the wedding?"

"What a good idea," Mrs. Jacobs said. She turned to her son, Myles's youngest brother, Martin. "Honey, go get the camcorder out of your truck." Turning back toward us, she said, "Martin thinks he's Spike Lee or something. He loves taping everything. I think he taped the entire wedding."

"Why don't I make us all mimosas while he's getting the tape," I said.

"What the hell is a Mosa?" Uncle Otis asked.

"It's a drank snooty folks have in the morning. It's orange juice and champagne," Aunt Ola replied.

"Hmmmph," Uncle Otis snorted. "Just make mine straight champagne. Ain't no sense in messing up a perfectly good drank by adding no damn orange juice."

I took a deep breath. *Let it ride,* I told myself. "Fine, Uncle Otis. I will leave off the orange juice in yours."

I made my way into the kitchen and began removing my crystal champagne flutes from the cabinet. I looked around for the Wal-Mart flutes I'd gotten years ago. Those would be for my family. No way was I chancing them breaking my expensive stuff.

A few minutes later, I was using my backside to push open the door that led from the kitchen into the den. "You all sure are quiet in here," I said when I stepped back in the den. Everyone was standing around the television. At the sound of my voice, in unison they turned to me, their expressions ranging from absolute horror to surprise to pity.

Then I heard it. The moans, the cries. Pleasurable cries. Then Myles's voice. "Who's your daddy?"

I was totally confused. "What's going on?"

Martin jumped to the television and pushed the off button.

"Awww, hell naw!" Shondella screamed. "Turn that back on and let her see it!"

I looked around the room. "Let me see what?"

No one said anything. Myles's mother was clutching her pearls, a stunned look etched across her face. Uncle Otis and Aunt Ola had their mouths wide open, as did several other people. Shondella was shaking her head. Mama Tee stepped toward me. "Baby, let's go in the back and talk."

I looked at her like she was crazy. Go talk? About what? What the hell were they watching? I set the tray of drinks down. I was definitely about to find out what was going on. I started toward the television.

Martin wouldn't move from in front of it. I glared at him so hard, he finally shrank out of the way.

"Rae, you don't want to do that," somebody, I don't even know who, called out. I ignored them and pushed the power button on the television. The voices came up before the pictures did.

"Ooooh, baby, right there."

I stared at the TV in disbelief. There on my big-screen TV was my husband, getting it on with some tramp. Make that tramps. He seemed to be having the time of his life. There was a lot of noise in the background. Men yelling.

"Work it, Myles!" somebody yelled.

"Can I get a turn?" someone else yelled.

"Naw, man, this is Myles's bachelor party. All these women are for him," the voice behind the camera said.

I sank to the floor as I noticed the date in the corner of the video: *Aug. 26.* Two days ago. The day before my wedding.

"Oh . . . my!" Myles screamed. "It's soooo good! I ain't never had no—"

"Enough!" Mama Tee slammed her hand against the power button, shutting off the television.

I sat there in utter disbelief. The man I had just promised to love, honor, and cherish until death did us part had screwed not one, but two women the night before our wedding. And he had had the audacity to allow it to be taped.

"Come on, Rae. Let's go to the back." Mama Tee tried to ease me up, but I couldn't move. This wasn't happening to me. This couldn't be happening to me. In a house full of my relatives. His relatives. My friends. His friends. My coworkers. Oh, my God. LaMonica was here. I hadn't personally invited her, but she had come with the assistant producer, Keria. LaMonica would tell everyone at work.

But all those thoughts quickly faded as I thought of how Myles had betrayed me.

Martin stepped forward. "Ummm, he didn't . . . he didn't know what he was doing."

"Look like he sho' knew what he was doing to me," Shondella snapped.

I heard the door to the garage suddenly open. Myles walked in, a huge smile across his face. "I'm back!" he called out.

I watched Martin ease toward him and try to nonchalantly whisper.

Myles looked at his brother strangely. I didn't give him time to ask any questions though. Suddenly, the strength I couldn't find to get off the floor just moments ago revealed itself and I lunged at Myles, my hands circling around his throat. "You bastard!" I screamed. "How could you do this to me!"

Myles toppled over backward and put his arm up to shield his face. "What—?"

I totally lost it. I was pounding his face, screaming obscenities. I heard Mama Tee and Mrs. Jacobs scream. Then several sets of hands started pulling me off Myles. He managed to get up.

"What is wrong with you?" he screamed as he nursed his bruised face.

"How could you do this to me?" All the resolve I had seemed to evaporate from my body and I dropped to the floor, sobbing uncontrollably.

"Would somebody tell me what's going on?" Myles stood there with a confused look on his face.

Nikki eased over to him. "She saw the tape, baby. Dang, I didn't know you had it going on like that. When do I get my turn?"

"Nikki!" Aunt Ola snapped.

"Well, if he's dishing it out . . ."

Myles ignored her. "What tape? What is she talking about?" Myles looked around the room. His mother was crying, Martin was in the corner pretending that the painting on the wall was interesting to him. Everyone else was looking at Myles with utter disgust.

I managed to stop sobbing long enough to say, "Play the tape."

"Don't do this, Rae," Shereen said. She had come over and was gently rubbing my back.

"Play the tape!" I screamed.

Not surprisingly, it was Shondella who walked over to the TV and cut it back on. The tape was still playing.

This time, I didn't turn my attention to it. I stood up and kept my eyes fixed on Myles. I heard his voice on the tape say, "My turn."

"Cut that trash off," Mrs. Jacobs finally said.

Myles looked at me. "Baby . . . that . . . that's old."

"Don't lie!" I screamed.

"Dog, the date was on the tape," one of his fraternity brothers muttered.

"Yeah, *dog*, the date was on the tape," I repeated. Okay, the pain was subsiding and I was getting severely pissed off. Especially because this fool was standing there lying to me.

"What I meant was . . . I was drunk."

"Drunk! Is that the best you can do?"

"Rae, can we go outside and talk about this please?"

"Talk to those whores on the tape!"

"I think it's time for us to go," I heard Mrs. Jacobs say.

Myles briefly turned his attention toward his mother. She couldn't even look him in the eye.

"It was a pleasure meeting you," Mrs. Jacobs said to Mama Tee, before scurrying out the door.

Mama Tee nodded solemnly.

Myles looked like he wanted to go after his mother, then decided all his attention should be focused on me.

"Please, Rae, let me explain. Those women meant nothing."

"So you threw away everything we have over women who meant nothing? Women who you don't even know?"

Martin stepped in. "He's telling the truth. He didn't even know them girls. They were just some strippers from the party."

Myles glared at his brother. "Shut up, Martin. It's

your fault. I told you not to even bring that camera!"

"No, *thank you*, Martin." I turned to him and bowed. "I'm glad you brought the camera. Otherwise I would've never known what a low-down dirty dog I married. And strippers? You had sex with some nasty strippers the night before our wedding?" My shoulders began to heave as the reality of what had happened began to set in.

"Let's not do this here," Myles pleaded.

I looked around the room. Mrs. Jacobs and her sister had left, but other than that, everyone was still there . . . staring intently at me, waiting like they were watching the cliff-hanger in a soap opera.

"Why should I pretend? They all saw it." I motioned wildly with my hands before turning to Myles's secretary. If I didn't know better, I would've thought she was as upset as I was. Maybe she was just as shocked. "You saw it, didn't you, Karen? And you, Sheila, you saw your cousin getting buck wild, didn't you?" I turned back to Myles. "Everyone saw it. Everyone saw it!" I sobbed and crumbled to the floor again. The joy of my wedding was gone. I felt pain, humiliation, and sadness that my dream had been shattered for a ménage à trois with strippers.

"Come on, baby." I hadn't noticed Mama Tee sit down next to me on the floor.

"Leave me alone! Everybody just leave me alone! Get out and leave me alone!"

Myles leaned down and tried to touch my shoulder. I slapped his hand away.

"I said go! Get away from me!" I jumped up and ran to my bedroom, making sure I slammed the door as hard as I could. I locked it, then threw myself across the bed, sobbing until sleep silenced my cries.

chapter 26

I don't know what time everyone left. I just knew the house was eerily quiet. I remember several people knocking on my bedroom door throughout the day, but I ignored them all. Finally, I guess they all got the picture that I wanted to be alone and left.

I glanced at the alarm clock on my nightstand: 6:30 p.m. I couldn't believe I had been out that long.

I looked at my Louis Vuitton luggage, packed and ready to be transported to Belize. A trip they wouldn't take. Tea. I needed some tea to calm my nerves.

I stumbled into the kitchen, still numb from the day's events. I half-expected all the remnants of breakfast to still be cluttering the counters, but Mama Tee had left everything spotless.

I cut on the teapot before flipping on the light. As I turned toward the pantry, I saw Myles sitting at the kitchen table.

"Why are you still here?" My voice was flat, exhausted. I was simply not in the mood to argue with the man who had shattered my world.

"You're my wife. Where else would I be?"

I laughed. A maniacal laugh. "Your wife? Not for long."

"So just like that, you're going to throw everything away?" Myles stared at me with a somber look in his eyes. It wasn't moving me.

"You threw it all away when you decided to sleep with two strippers on the eve of our wedding."

"I told you, I was drunk. They meant nothing."

"You might want to try another defense, because that one isn't going to fly." I snatched a teacup from the cabinet, making sure to let the cabinet doors slam.

"It's the only one I have. I was just being out. You know, enjoying my last night as a single man."

"Oh, you enjoyed it all right. Meanwhile, I was at home, getting a facial, a manicure, and a pedicure so that I could be beautiful for you the next day."

"I'm sorry, Rae. You have to know this wasn't about you. It was just me, sowing some wild oats. Every man does it the night before his wedding."

I tried to blow him off and continue making my tea. I didn't want to argue. After I filled the teapot with water, I set it down on the stove and turned toward him.

"How many other women have there been?"

"Rae . . ."

"Don't Rae me. You want me to believe you just slipped up that one time? No. How many other women have there been?"

Myles shook his head. "That was it. A bachelor party gone out of control."

I wanted so desperately to believe him. For the sake of our child, I needed to believe him. But still, that didn't excuse what I'd seen on that tape. What everyone had seen. I looked down at the diamond glistening on my finger. A symbol of the happily ever after I was supposed to have. Now my hopes of being a power couple were gone. My dream life had been shattered.

"How could you do this to me?"

"I'm sorry, okay, babe? I love you. Only you." He eased toward me. "We are so good together. You know can't nobody hold a candle to you. Why would I want anyone else?"

I couldn't believe I was allowing him to touch me, invade my space, justify his actions. He inched closer, trying to make sure it would be okay to keep touching me. He rubbed his hand up and down my arm. When I didn't move, he pulled me closer to him. I began sobbing into his chest. He gently rubbed my hair before lifting my face and softly kissing my tear-streaked cheeks. "I'm sorry, baby. I love you so much. I never meant to hurt you."

I wanted to curse him out, tell him it was over and to leave me alone. Tell him how he had ruined everything and how I never wanted to see him again. But my mouth could not form the words my heart didn't feel.

"I promise I'll never hurt you again," Myles said, his eyes watering up.

Seeing him on the verge of tears tore at my heart. At that moment I knew we had too much at stake to throw it all away over something many a man has probably done at his bachelor party.

I sighed. Call me stupid, but my life with Myles meant too much to give up over a bachelor party. I pulled out of his embrace, and took of couple of steps back, and rubbed my temple in frustration. "I don't know if I can get past this."

He gently eased toward me. "You can, doll. Think of our life. Think of what we're about to build. Think about that six-bedroom house we're buying. Of the impact we'll make on this town. Don't throw it all away. We are so good together. I messed up. But I am serious about my vows. From this day forward you never have to worry about me cheating again."

I wanted to hit him, scratch his eyes out, anything so he'd know my pain. But at the same time, I just wanted this nightmare to be over.

"I'm pissed at you, Myles."

"I know, baby. I'm sorry. For the millionth time, I'm sorry." He reached out for me again. At first my body tensed up, but when he caressed my arm, I felt my resolve weakening. "We're worth it. You know that," he whispered.

He pulled me to him and I inhaled his cologne and savored his smell. "I don't know how long it will take me to forget this. I don't know if I even can."

"I will do whatever it takes."

"If I stay, promise me you'll never hurt me like this again?" I sniffed. "Because I couldn't take it if you did."

He gazed into my eyes, his expression serious. "Cross my heart and hope to die." He kissed me passionately. At first I tried to resist, but my heart took over and I welcomed his touch.

"You did what?"

I groaned. What in the world was I thinking, telling

my sister anything? She'd caught me off guard when she asked if I'd put Myles out. Why hadn't I looked at the caller ID when the phone rang first thing this morning? That's what the device was for, to screen calls. "Shondella, I'm not getting into this with you. And come to think of it, how'd you get my home number anyway?"

"What difference does it make?" she snapped. "But if you must know, I called my cell phone from your house yesterday so the number would be stored. But the real question is, why would you take that dog back? The way he embarrassed you, cheated on you."

"Shondella, I wouldn't expect you to understand. You haven't had a meaningful relationship in years." I wanted to kick myself for sharing any of my personal information with her. But she sounded so self-assured when she called, like she could just picture me alone and miserable. When she'd told me I should just stop putting on airs, thinking I could be with a man like Myles, I'd lost it and told her not only were Myles and I working it out, but we were going to have a happiness she'd never know.

"Is that what you have? A meaningful relationship?" Shondella sneered.

I exhaled in frustration. I was tired of talking to her. "What do you want?"

"Look, I'm only calling because Mama Tee asked me to. We're leaving this morning and Mama Tee wanted to come by. I told her I would just call and check on you."

Finally, some good news. "Have a safe trip home. See you when I see you."

"Look, we came to Houston to be here for you on your funky wedding day—"

"I didn't ask you to be here."

"You know what? You're right. But Mama Tee gave that old 'she's family and family sticks together' speech. I told her we would be wasting our time coming here. After all, we remind you of a past you'd rather forget."

I absolutely, positively hated talking to my sister. But I was tired of arguing with her. Myles and I had a storybook future planned. When I'd left Sweet Poke, I'd promised myself that I would succeed personally and professionally. Breaking it off with Myles would prove I'd failed in my personal life, and I didn't want that.

Besides, having a man like Myles love me proved I was worthy and not some discarded little girl. "Look, you just don't understand. You never have."

"Oh, save that bull. You leave the country, shorten your name, and put on all these airs and you think that makes you better than us? Don't worry yourself, Raedella. I will do my best to make sure none of us bother you or your perfect little world ever again. Have a nice life."

She slammed the phone down. I was a little taken aback. Shondella had always been aggressive, but something about her words tore at my insides. It was the conviction with which she said them. I shrugged it off. Maybe my family would finally leave me alone and let me live my life. I smiled at the thought. It's not that I didn't appreciate all that Mama Tee had done for me; it's just that my family held me back, they reminded me of a past I'd rather forget. Plus, I had little patience for their country ways, and to be perfectly honest, they didn't fit into my life now. The sooner they realized that, the better off we'd all be.

chapter 27

I knew I should've stayed in bed. I was leaning out the passenger door of our news truck, throwing up again. It had been nearly a month since my wedding. Myles and I had taken a luxurious five-day honeymoon in Belize. We didn't have one single argument the whole time. With the exception of a few bouts with morning sickness, everything had gone extremely well. I hated to come back, but both of us had to get back to work. Since I'd been back, I was really just going through the motions. The job didn't excite me anymore.

I was in the station parking lot about to head out to interview Houston's mayor in twenty minutes. My photographer, Ray, and I were doing a profile on the mayor's final year in office. Myles was still trying to figure out if he'd get the mayor's endorsement, so I was hoping to ease that into the conversation. But now, I'd be lucky if I didn't throw up all over him. Not only did I feel nauseous, but I was exhausted and it was only ten in the morning.

"Are you going to be okay?" Ray asked. He was looking at me with a disgusted look across his face. I guess he was worried about me throwing up in his new Ford Expedition news truck.

"Yeah," I responded, wiping my mouth. "That Chinese food I had last night must've been bad. I've been throwing up all day." I hadn't told anyone at work yet I was pregnant. I was trying to wait until I was well into my second term.

"Maybe we should reschedule this interview."

"No, it took me too long to get this set up. If I cancel now, I can forget about doing this interview." Normally, I would've let the producer do the interview, but since I had a personal agenda, I'd decided to do this one myself.

"Okay, just let me know if I need to pull over."

I nodded as I leaned my head back against the seat. "I should be okay."

Ray backed the truck up and began making his way downtown. As we got closer to the mayor's office, I pulled out my makeup bag to freshen up. I might be sick, but I sure didn't need to look it.

"I'm going to pull into this gas station and get a Gatorade. Do you want anything?"

I shook my head. I just wanted to get back to the station so I could get home. I had a doctor's appointment later this afternoon, so they already had the fill-in anchor scheduled to do my newscast today. If we could wrap up this interview quickly, I could be back home in more than enough time to take a nice, long nap before my appointment. I closed my eyes as Ray navigated the

Expedition into the Shell station. I heard him get out of the truck and prayed that he would make it quick.

By the time we made it to the mayor's office and up to his fourth-floor office, we had ten minutes to spare before our interview. I felt awful and just wanted to go home and get some rest. So, I couldn't help but feel a sense of relief when the mayor's personal assistant told me we'd have to reschedule.

"I'm so sorry, Rae," she said, "the mayor's flight has been delayed and it looks like he won't make it back in until this evening."

I think I caught her by surprise when I perked up and said, "Oh, no problem. I'll just have my producer call and reschedule." I flashed a fake smile and spun around toward the door.

I had just laid my head back against the seat in the truck when my cell phone rang. I debated not answering it since digging for it in my overstuffed bag seemed like too much work, but I thought it might be Myles, so I pulled my bag up in my lap. I found my phone on the fourth ring and noticed Myles's mother's number on the screen. I quickly answered it.

"Hello."

"Rae, darling. How are you?"

"I've been better, Mrs. Jacobs."

"I've told you. It's *Mother* now."

That made me smile. I was finally going to call someone Mother, with pride. "I'm sorry, Mother." It felt so good to say that.

"Now, what's wrong? Morning sickness?" Mrs. Jacobs was one of the few people who knew about our pregnancy, only she thought I was about three weeks along. Myles didn't want her to know I had been pregnant *prior* to the wedding. He had it all figured out. When the baby came, he'd just convince his mother that I'd gone into labor early. It was a dumb idea to me, but I didn't fight him on it, especially when he told me it would hurt my standing with her if she thought I was pregnant before we got married.

"I don't know. I just know I feel horrible. As a matter of fact, I'm on my way back to the station, but I plan to leave immediately, go home, and get in the bed."

"Oh, sweetie, is there anything I can do? I can bring over some soup or something."

Why couldn't I have a mother like that? "No, thank you. I just need to get in the bed and rest."

"Well, okay, but you know you can't take any medication, so if you want me to come over and wait on you, I will."

"I know you will. But that's okay. Besides, I have a doctor's appointment at four thirty this afternoon. I will see if there's anything she can give me for this nausea. And I don't have to worry about driving. Myles promised he'd be home in time to take me."

Mrs. Jacobs drew in a long breath. "Actually, that's why I'm calling. I just got off the phone with Myles and he asked me to call and tell you that he wouldn't be able to make it to the appointment today. He had a very important meeting come up. So he called and asked me to go with you. I told him I'd be happy to oblige."

I felt my blood pressure rising. Myles was about to get on my last nerve. Not only was he backing out on coming to the doctor's appointment, but he wasn't even man enough to call me and tell me himself. Mrs. Jacobs must have sensed my anger.

"Rae, baby, he was on his way to a meeting when I talked to him. I knew he was in a hurry so I offered to call you for him."

"What is more important than his baby?" I hissed. I knew Ray could hear me, but at that point, I didn't really care.

"Now, Rae, don't be like that. You know my son has a very important job that keeps him very busy. He loves you and that baby, but he just couldn't get out of this last minute meeting."

Now, not only was I sick to my stomach, but my head had started pounding. There was no sense in debating this with her. Myles was the apple of her eye and could do no wrong, so arguing with her would be pointless.

"Fine. Thank you for calling me and letting me know. But I'll be okay at the doctor's by myself." As much as I loved Myles's mother, right now I just wanted to get off the phone with her.

"It's no problem," she insisted.

"No, I'll be fine. Thank you for the offer. I have to go; my photographer is waiting on me to shoot this story."

"Well, if you insist."

"Thank you for the offer, but really, I'll be fine. I'll talk to you later, okay?"

"Okay, sweetheart. Call me and let me know how things go at the doctor."

"I will. Good-bye." I pushed the end button on my cell phone, still trying to keep my fury from building.

Ray looked toward me. "You all right?"

"I'm fine. Perfectly, freakin' fine," I snapped as I tossed my cell phone back into my purse.

chapter 28

I stared at the image on the screen. My baby was beautiful. So what if I couldn't see anything but a blob. I still knew that was my child and I couldn't help but have my heart fill with warmth.

The ultrasound technician had smoothed cold jelly over my stomach and was now running this little device over my belly. I could barely contain my excitement. The anger I'd felt earlier about Myles's canceling out on my doctor's appointment for yet another meeting had subsided. He knew how important it was that he accompany me on my appointments. Especially today since they were doing an early ultrasound because my blood pressure was unusually high. I had called Myles on my way home from the station, screaming and crying, but nothing had worked. He'd claimed he couldn't get out of his meeting. I was still mad when I'd arrived at the doctor's office. But no way could I be mad after seeing my baby on the screen.

"Can you tell the sex of the baby yet?" I asked.

The technician shook her head without taking her eyes off the screen. "Not yet." She frowned.

"What?"

She took a deep breath and set the scanning device down. "Will you excuse me for just a moment?" She stood up and began making her way out of the room.

"Wait. What's going on?"

The technician ignored me and walked on out. I lay back down, my heart racing. Her mood had shifted. It wasn't two minutes later when the tech came back in with my doctor right behind her. A short, perky blond, Dr. Trahan was the best doctor any first-time mother could ask for.

"Dr. Trahan, what's going on? Is something wrong with my baby?"

Dr. Trahan caressed my arm. "Hello, Rae. Let me take a look at your precious little one. The technician just saw something that caught her eye and she wanted me to get a better look at it. You just lay back and let me do my job." She gently eased me back down. I felt a little more relaxed. Dr. Trahan had a calming effect.

The technician leaned over me, blocking my view while pointing to the screen and whispering to Dr. Trahan. I tried to stay calm but her whispering wasn't helping. Dr. Trahan ran the screening device over my belly, pushing down at certain angles. Then she took her stethoscope and listened to my heart, before moving the device down to my belly. She went back to the ultrasound machine and began typing in something. I could no longer hold my silence.

"Dr. Trahan, please tell me what is going on."

Dr. Trahan placed her stethoscope around her neck and turned to me. I could tell the news was not good by the look on her face. "Rae, I'm sorry."

"Sorry? Sorry about what?" I sat up, trying my best not to get hysterical.

"There is no easy way to say this, but the fetus is not viable."

"Not viable? Fetus? What are you talking about?"

Dr. Trahan gave me a sympathetic look. "Your baby has no heartbeat. We checked and can't find a heartbeat."

She couldn't be saying what I thought she was saying. "There must be something wrong with your machine." I hit the machine as if that would make it better. "Check again. That can't be right. I felt my baby move."

"What you felt could've been any number of things from heartburn on."

Dr. Trahan rubbed my arm again, her eyes full of sadness. "Your baby's heart never got a chance to develop, and he or she will not survive. I don't mean to sound clinical but—"

I cut her off before she could continue. "Dr. Trahan, there must be some mistake." I shook my head, hoping there was some way I was misunderstanding her.

"I wish there was a mistake and, of course, I encourage you to get a second opinion, but your baby will not be carried to term. Now, you can either have a D and C, where we will go in and remove the fetus and all signs of pregnancy, or the baby will expel itself in a few days."

I was speechless. Tears started welling up in my eyes. Selfishness had dashed my hopes of being a mother before. Now, my hopes were being dashed again. Maybe this was payback from God for having an abortion.

Maybe God was punishing me for all that I've done wrong in my life. I couldn't think straight.

"I'm sorry, Rae."

I fought back tears as I pulled myself up from the table and started putting my clothes back on. The reality of what she was saying slowly began seeping in. Dr. Trahan and the technician watched me struggle with my blouse, which was turned inside out. I snatched at the blouse as I tried to turn it on the right side, but it just wouldn't go.

"Here, let me help you," the technician said.

"I have it!" I snapped. She stepped back apologetically. *That's why you're being punished. Because you're so mean. She was only trying to help.* The voices in my head were getting louder. *Why would God let you be somebody's mother? You already killed one child. He didn't want to give you a chance to kill another. No one likes you. Your own family can't stand you.* "Shut up!" I screamed as I grabbed my head.

Dr. Trahan stepped toward me. "Rae, do you want me to call someone?"

I looked at her and realized I must've looked like a bumbling idiot standing there screaming to no one in particular. I tried my best to pull myself together. "I'm sorry. It's just . . . I really wanted this baby," I said, my voice cracking.

"I know, Rae." She paused, an uncomfortable silence hanging in the air.

"Umm . . . Dr. Trahan," I stammered. "Would this have anything to do with, you know, with the procedure I had when I was seventeen?" Dr. Trahan was the only person I had talked to about my abortion. We had spoken at length about it. I would never forgive myself if I had done some damage.

"No. If you were truthful with me and it was done how you said it was done, then there's no medical reason why you shouldn't be able to have more kids."

I nodded.

"I want you to go home and seriously consider if you want to have the D and C or if you want to wait and miscarry on your own. I would suggest a D and C because you have no idea when the miscarriage will occur, and the outpatient procedure is a lot less traumatic. I can get you in at the end of the week."

I nodded again.

"Call and let me know, okay? And are you sure you're okay to drive? I can call your husband."

I grabbed my purse. My hands were shaking. "No, I'm fine. I'll call you and let you know."

When I'd walked into that office, I was on top of the world. Now, I couldn't help but feel I had bottomed out.

chapter 29

Mama Tee used to always say, "God don't like ugly," and the fact that I had played God and taken my first child's life because it didn't fit in my life's plan was ugly. While it hurt me emotionally to have an abortion back then, the bottom line is that I still went through with it. Now I was being punished for that fateful day.

I wiped away my tears. I had been driving around Houston in a daze. My baby would never get a chance at life. I had been so happy thinking of the life growing inside me. And although Myles had not been as happy as I would've liked, he was coming around. Myles. I needed to see my husband. My heart was heavy and he was the only one who could make it right.

The blaring horn of the motorist next to me made me jump out of my trance. I hadn't noticed that I had started weaving into his lane and nearly run him off the road. I threw my hand up in an apologetic manner. He shot me the finger and sped on by. I started getting angry again. Not because of his road rage, but because my mind had drifted to Myles. He should have been there with me. I shouldn't have learned about my baby by myself. I was heading straight to his office to tell him.

I navigated my Mercedes onto the 610 Loop and began the fifteen-minute journey to Myles's Southside law office. Now that he was a city councilman, he didn't take on as many cases, but he still spent a great deal of time in his law office overseeing the business side.

On the way to Myles's office, I thought of all the plans I had made. I had already bought baby stuff and maternity clothes. I was going to have a local artist paint pink bunny ballerinas all over my baby's room.

I exited the freeway at Kirby and turned into Myles's office complex. I pulled around to the back parking lot, and as I turned into the reserved-parking area, I slowed down when I saw a man groping all over a rail-thin woman with long, flowing hair. She was holding balloons that looked like they said HAPPY BIRTHDAY. I peered through my window. Myles? It couldn't be Myles. He'd promised he would be faithful to me. He'd told me that incident with the strippers was a onetime thing. He wouldn't do this to me.

I inched the car closer. That was Myles! The woman was laughing and trying to pull herself from his embrace. He grabbed her arm and snatched her back toward him. He pushed her against the wall and began kissing her passionately and groping her breast. She threw her head back and moaned in delight. That's when I saw who she was. Karen. His secretary! They seemed oblivious to the fact that they were making out in a parking lot in the middle of the day.

Is this why Myles couldn't come with me to the doctor? He was so busy getting it on with his secretary that he couldn't be there for our baby? My mind started racing. I thought of our child. A child that would never be. I thought of what he was about to do with this woman and all the times she had smiled in my face. I thought of Delana, the crazy woman who had prompted Myles to propose to me in the first place. I thought of the two strippers and wondered if there were others. I thought of all his promises. His lies. One month. That's all we'd been married. One month, and he was in the parking lot of his office getting it on with his secretary. I felt a tightening in my chest, my anger building up from the pit of my stomach. Suddenly I lost it. I did the only thing I could do. I floored the accelerator and drove my car toward that bastard as fast as I could.

chapter 30

"You have the right to remain silent. Anything you say, can and will be held against you in a court of law."

I shook my head, dazed. *Where was I? Were those handcuffs around my wrists? Who were all these people?*

"Girl, that's the TV lady," someone whispered.

"It sure is. Rae Rollins," someone else responded. "She must've finally caught that dog husband of hers cheating."

"Yeah, I work on the floor below him. I swear he's with a different woman each day," someone said.

"Honey, I don't blame you. You should've ran over his cheating tail!" another woman screamed.

"Let her go! That dog deserved to be hit!"

Why were all these people yelling? What were they talking about? Ran over? Deserved to be hit? I shook my head, trying to get some clarity. I looked around. I was in the parking lot of my husband's law office, surrounded by gawkers. Suddenly, everything started coming back to me. Oh, my God. What had I done?

"Is my husband going to be all right?" I asked the officer who was leading me to his car.

"I think it's a little late to be concerned about his well-being," the officer snapped. "But you better hope he lives or you can be facing some serious time for murder."

Did he say murder? This can't be happening. I fought back tears and violently shook my head. Just when I thought things couldn't get any worse, two news trucks came speeding toward us. Both were from competing stations. The photographers jumped out, grabbed their cameras, and started shooting. Their cameras were pointed directly at me. If I could've died right then and there, I would have.

I tried to cover my face but I knew from years of being on the opposite end that that looked horrible to viewers. *Have some dignity!* I snapped to myself. But where was the dignity in trying to run down your man? How had my life been reduced to this?

"Rae, what happened?" A redheaded reporter thrust a microphone in my face. She had a sympathetic look on her face, but I knew that was all an act to try to get me to talk. She couldn't care less about my well-being. "We want to give you a chance to tell your side."

Whatever. She wanted a story. And I was a big story. Oh, God, what did this mean to my job?

Suddenly, another reporter pushed his microphone into my face.

"Rae, how do you feel?"

Why do reporters ask stupid questions like that? I

wanted to say I'd just found out I'm losing my baby. I'd just caught my husband of one month cheating, then I'd tried to kill him and his bimbo girlfriend, and I'm probably going to lose my job. *How the hell do you think I feel?* I wanted to scream.

"Why'd you try to run over your husband?" the reporter asked when I didn't respond.

Just then, our news crew—Simone and a photographer named Charles—pulled up. I felt the tears about to fall. I swear I saw a smile on Simone's face as she got out of the truck. She was probably eating this up.

This had to be the single worst moment of my life. I didn't know what to do. This would be all over the news, all over the country. They'd probably make a movie of the week out of it. Yes, I wanted fame, but not like this. The only option now would be to try to garner sympathy. And I knew just how to do it. I took a deep breath, closed my eyes, and let my body slink to the ground.

"Hey! Can we get a paramedic here!" the cop screamed. "She fainted."

I lay on the ground, fighting back tears with all my might, struggling to keep my breathing steady. I refused to open my eyes until we were far away from that place. If I kept them closed long enough, maybe, just maybe, when I opened them, I would realize this was all a dream. A really, really bad dream.

chapter 31

So much for dreaming. The assistant district attorney that stood in front of me was very real.

It had been less than a week since I'd tried to run over my husband, and as I'd suspected, it had been all over the news.

After I was released on $60,000 bail, I stayed holed up in my house. I unplugged my phone because it was ringing off the hook from reporters who wanted an "exclusive." Thankfully, Shereen had stepped in, arranged my leave of absence from work, and called my attorney, Carl Goldberg.

Now, Carl, a short, balding Jewish man, sat next to me as we met with the assistant district attorney. We'd been going around and around with the ADA for over an hour. They had been tossing around phrases like "crime of passion," "impeccable record," and "credit to society." I couldn't make out what they were talking about. I was numb. I felt transplanted from another time, another place. My life had unraveled before my eyes. Now, here I was sitting in the very courthouse I had covered so many times.

"We can't just let her off. What kind of message would that send?" the assistant DA said.

"Come on, Sid. You know she just got caught up in the moment. She's pregnant and had just caught her husband cheating. She simply had a nervous breakdown," Carl said.

A nervous breakdown? Is that what it was? We had never discussed that. But at that point, I couldn't care less. I just prayed the ADA wouldn't take this to court.

Sid shook his head like he was weighing the issue. "I just don't know. I can't do any special treatment."

"Come on, Sid; it's an election year. Women's groups will be all over this case. She's big-time and it will become a media circus. Don't waste the taxpayers' money. Myles is going to be fine. Slap her with a hefty fine and some community service. Don't take this case to court," my attorney pleaded.

"I'll think about it. That's all I can promise."

My attorney looked relieved. "That's all we ask."

He looked at me, urging me with his eyes to say something to Sid. I don't know where I got the energy, but I mustered up the effort. "Thank you very much."

Sid looked at me pitifully before standing up and shaking my hand. "Take care of yourself, Mrs. Jacobs. I'll be in touch with your attorney."

I nodded and let Carl lead me out the door and down the back steps of the courthouse. Carl was excellent at what he did. He'd had someone make an anonymous call to all the TV stations that I would be appearing in court tomorrow so we could escape a media circus. Still, I didn't want to take any chances that my colleagues were lying in wait. The news had been my whole world, but this last week, I had learned to hate it.

From one meeting to another. Why we had to do this today was beyond me, but here I was sitting in Stan's, my general manager's, office. Dina was sitting next to me. She barely looked my way and acted as if she were engrossed in her notes.

I'd known this meeting was coming. Dina had called me at home the night I was released and told me to take some time to get my head together. She had sounded surprisingly sympathetic. Now, here we were in Stan's office and she looked anything but sympathetic. Although I knew Stan liked me, he had to take a stand for the record, so I was sure they were about to berate me for making the station look bad.

I wasn't in the mood to hear that, but I knew I had to take their tongue-thrashing. I knew that was all it was because the bottom line was my show made money. They wouldn't fire me. After all, they had sent the weatherman to drug rehab three times.

Dina began talking. "You know we have been the talk of the town, right?"

I shrugged. I didn't mean to belittle my actions, but I just was not in the mood for a lecture from the Queen Bee. My indifference seemed to piss her off.

"I'm glad you can have such a nonchalant attitude about this," she hissed.

I softened. I certainly did not want to make the situation any worse. I leaned toward her. "Dina, I didn't mean to cast a negative light on you or the station. But I had a little slipup."

"A little slipup! You tried to kill one of Houston's top politicians!" Dina screamed.

"He is also my husband who is cheating on me."

"I don't care. That doesn't give you carte blanche to try and kill him!"

Stan jumped in. "Now, ladies, calm down."

I leaned back in my chair, crossing my arms. "I am calm. It's her who seems to be losing it."

Dina huffed, stood up, and stomped over to the window. "I can't take this, Stan. You brought me in here to take this station to new levels. How am I supposed to do that, dealing with this mess?"

Stan sighed and the look in his eyes ate at my soul. I had never seen a look like that. Suddenly, my job confidence began to waver. It was time to go to bat and defend my position.

"Look, Stan, I know I messed up. I was going through some things and I . . . I just snapped. But my attorney doesn't think the DA is going to press charges since Myles is going to be fine." That was the irony of all of this. Myles suffered a broken bone in his arm and a contusion, but the impact had knocked him onto the hood of my car and he'd bounced off without suffering serious injury. Karen had suffered minor injuries and I had no doubt she would be trying to sue me at some point. But I just couldn't concern myself with that now.

Stan lowered his eyes and shook his head.

"Tell her," Dina hissed.

"Tell me what?" I looked back and forth between the two of them. The look on Stan's face told me enough.

"Oh, my God, no! You're not letting me go."

"I'm sorry," Stan whispered, "we don't have a choice."

Dina, a proud and defiant look on her face, walked over behind Stan and picked up a thick document. She flipped over several pages. "Page seven of your contract. 'Employee will be subject to immediate termination in the violation of any of the above listed morals clauses'," she read. Dina looked up and glared at me. "While attempted murder isn't specifically listed in the morals clause, I think it's safe to say that's considered a moral violation."

I offered a pleading look to Stan. "Please, don't let her do this. She's just doing it because she hates me. She's jealous, that's all. She probably could never get an on-air job and is just jealous because I have."

Dina laughed like that was the most absurd thing she'd ever heard. "First of all, sweetheart, I don't have, nor have I ever had, a desire to be in front of the camera. I have always wanted to be behind the scenes where the power is, the one making the decisions, like who stays and who goes. And you, Rae Rollins, have got to go."

I was furious. "You can't just toss me out! I have a contract. I have a year and a half left on that contract! If you get rid of me, I'll sue and make sure you not only pay out the remainder of my contract, but I'll also make sure the entire black community knows how you treated me."

Dina laughed again. She was making me even angrier. "Let's see, you told members of the National Association of Black Journalists you would not join because there was, and I quote, 'nothing you can do for me'. You aren't active in the black community, except when it serves your needs. And what else? Oh, yeah, you tried to run over your husband. You think the black community will rally around you? Hah! And lastly"—she began flipping through the contract again—"page eight of your contract reads as follows: 'Violation of the morals clause nullifies this entire contract. This contract will be void immediately and the employee will not be entitled to any outstanding compensation. Employee also waives the right to litigation involving dismissal based on the morals clause.' " Dina snapped the document closed.

Was I hearing things? They were going to fire me *and* not give me any money? And why would I have signed anything giving up my right to sue? I kicked myself. I couldn't believe this. "*The Rae Rollins Show* is the highest-rated show in this market! I am this station!" I yelled.

"No, Rae. You *were* this station. Now you're simply a mess we have to clean up." She tossed the contract back on Stan's desk. "Security is waiting outside to escort you back to the newsroom so you can clear out your desk."

With that, she walked out of the office. I was about to plead with Stan when I noticed two of our security guards—I had never even bothered to learn their names—motioning for me to come with them.

"Stan . . . ," I pleaded as I slowly stood up.

"I'm sorry." Then the man I thought would always be in my corner turned his back to me and began typing on his computer.

"Don't do this, please. Can I at least come back tonight and get my things?"

Stan didn't turn around. "Security will escort you to your desk right now. You will not be allowed back on the property."

I wanted so desperately to break down crying, but my body was numb. After all my years dedicated to this station, after all that I had done to make this station number one, this was how I would go out. Escorted to my desk by security. All eyes would be on me.

"Come on, Ms. Rollins," one of the guards said. "You only have fifteen minutes to clear everything out."

I contemplated having someone just box up all my belongings, but I had so many personal things and I didn't want just anyone handling them.

I inhaled deeply. I had been stripped of my dignity, but I could not let anyone in that newsroom see me cry.

"Fine." I glared at Stan one last time, willing him to turn around and look at me. He wouldn't. I wanted to hurl insults at him, tell him how this station would plummet without me, but I no longer had the energy. "Fine," I told the security guard again. "Let's go get my stuff."

chapter 32

Here I was, sitting in my house, in the dark. I shook my head, trying to get my bearings. How long had I been here? And what was that pounding in my head? I remembered all the stares and whispers as I'd packed up my stuff in my desk. A couple of people tried to talk to me, but security had kept them at bay. It was one of the most humiliating moments of my life.

After I'd left work, I'd stopped at the liquor store and the pharmacy, where I picked up two bottles of tequila and three boxes of Tylenol PM. While thoughts of suicide never crossed my mind, I did want to do whatever it took to erase the past week from my memory.

At home, I had downed glass after glass of Jose Cuervo and popped pill after pill. I'd repeated this off and on all week, until I felt numb to all the pain.

I glanced around my home. Boxes were everywhere. We were supposed to be moving at the end of the month.

Closing on our dream home on the thirty-first. Now, I wouldn't have that dream home and I didn't have Myles. I didn't have anyone. I was all alone. I caught my reflection in my china cabinet as I tried to stand. It seemed to bellow at me, "You have no one to blame but yourself." My world had come to an end. I'd lost my baby, my man, my job, and my dignity.

I tried to move toward the kitchen. Every ounce of my body ached. It felt like I *had* tried to kill myself. I sank to the floor in tears.

I was still sobbing when I heard banging on the front door. Who could that possibly be? Maybe it was Shereen. Besides my attorney, she was the only person I'd talked to. Then again, maybe it was Myles. I shook off that thought. I knew he would not be bold enough to show his face here. I figured that if I ignored whoever it was, they'd go away. I was wrong. The pounding continued. I eased up and made my way back into the living room.

"Raedella Rollins, open this door or I'm calling the cops and having them bust the door down!"

Mama Tee! What in the world was she doing here? I had to be imagining things.

"I'm calling the cops! Shondella, go call the cops," she bellowed.

Shondella was with her? They were the last two people I felt like dealing with, but I definitely didn't need any more cops around.

"Yeah," I managed to mutter. "I'm coming."

I glanced in the hall mirror and frowned. My eyes were red and puffy. My hair was matted to my head. My lips were cracked and ashen. I sniffed under my arms and nearly doubled over. I hadn't had a bath in a week. I thought about trying to quickly fix myself up, but I just didn't have the energy.

I dragged myself into the living room and opened the door.

"Holy mother of Mary," Mama Tee proclaimed. She clutched her chest and her eyes widened.

"Dang, girl," Shondella chimed in. "You look like crap."

Mama Tee stared at me, a look of horror across her face. Her eyes watered up, which was astonishing because I could count on one hand the number of times I'd seen Mama Tee cry.

"My baby. My poor, poor baby." Mama Tee stretched out her arms toward me.

I felt awkward seeing my grandmother standing there ready to comfort me. It had been so long since anyone had really comforted me, let alone Mama Tee. I contemplated putting on my strong, invincible air, but I didn't have the strength to pretend. Truth be told, I wanted my grandmother to comfort me. I wanted her to hold me and tell me everything would be all right. I wanted her to help me escape this nightmare that had become my life.

I slowly stepped toward Mama Tee, and before I knew it, I had flung myself into her arms.

"Oh, Mama Tee," I sobbed.

"Shhhh," she said, stroking my hair. "Mama Tee's here. It's gon' be all right."

I didn't know how all right things were going to be, but I did know, right now, buried in Mama Tee's arms was the safest I'd felt in a long time.

* * *

Mama Tee made her way about my massive kitchen like she had been there a hundred times. She was rummaging through the cabinet now, looking for more coffee to brew. I sat at the kitchen table.

"Mama Tee, I don't want any more coffee." My grandmother had been at my house for almost two hours and I'd yet to find out why she'd come. Maybe because I had been so busy bawling since she'd walked through the door. Even Shondella amazed me, sitting in the living room quietly watching television.

"You need to drink some of this so you can get some pep back in your step."

But I didn't think I'd ever get my pep back.

Thoughts of my precious baby made me want to sink back into my depression. And images of Myles and the hoochie-ho constantly flashed in my mind. "I just want to die," I said, as I buried my head in my arms on the kitchen table.

"Gal, quit being dramatic. You ain't got no reason to wanna die," Mama Tee said as she put another pot of coffee on.

"I have no reason to want to live."

"Hush all that nonsense."

"You just don't understand."

"I understand a lot better than you think." Mama Tee pulled out a chair and sat across from me at the table. "Just 'cause you caught your man with another woman ain't no reason for you to be talking about dying."

I gasped, even though it shouldn't have come as any surprise that Mama Tee knew what had happened. "So word has gotten around, huh?" I asked her.

"It's the talk of the town," Shondella called out from

the living room. Surprisingly, her voice didn't have the condescending tone I would've expected.

Mama Tee nodded. "Sadie Merriweather's niece lives here in Houston. She called Sadie the day after it happened and told her all about it. She said they had it in the newspapers and on TV. You know Sadie 'bout the biggest gossip in town. She told Mr. Lawrence and God only knows who else. Next thing I know, someone come up to me at usher board meeting and told me about it."

Shondella appeared in the kitchen entrance. "I read about it in the papers myself. Yep, looks like you messed your life up, little sis. But I told you that would happen. It just took a little longer than I expected."

I cut my eyes at her. There was the Shondella I knew and despised.

"Shondella, go on back in there and mind your business. Ain't nobody asked you nothing," Mama Tee snapped.

Shondella snickered and walked off. "Whatever."

I couldn't bring myself to get upset with her. I was emotionally exhausted. I lowered my head in shame. "I'm sorry I embarrassed you, Mama Tee."

"Hush talking that foolishness. It takes a lot more than attempted murder to embarrass Mama Tee." She leaned in and smiled. "Don't tell nobody I told you this, but you come by it honestly. You remember that big, long scar your Grandpa Walter had along his arm?"

Who couldn't remember that scar? It snaked around his arm. It had keloided up, and when we were little, all the kids used to dare each other to go touch it.

"Yeah, what about it?"

Mama Tee looked around the room like we were in

the middle of a crowded restaurant. "I did that," she whispered.

"Huh?"

"I sliced him up. Filleted that fool. From his shoulder to his little pinkie. Tried to plunge that knife right into his chest. Caught him with another woman and damn near killed him. Would have, too, but I needed him to take care of them eight chil'ren." Mama Tee laughed at the memory.

I was dumbfounded. My grandmother, a crazed woman scorned? It just didn't fit.

"It's not just that, Mama Tee. I lost my job. I was arrested and . . ." I just couldn't bring myself to tell her the *and* part.

"So? You'll find another job and you ain't the first person ever to be arrested."

"Mama Tee, you don't understand. I'm probably blackballed. I'll never work in the business again."

"Good. You can come on back home and teach or something."

I looked at her like she had lost her mind. I know she couldn't possibly think I was going back to Sweet Poke with my tail tucked between my legs.

"Mama Tee, I can't go back."

"Why not?"

"This is my home now."

"This ain't your home. This ain't never been your home. Sweet Poke is your home," she responded matter-of-factly as she took my empty coffee cup, refilled it, then placed it back in front of me.

I had never entertained the idea of returning home. My pride wouldn't let me go back home. *Your pride went out the window when you tried to run down your husband,* I heard a little voice in my head say.

"Mama Tee . . . I can't do—"

"Hush up, now."

"Mama Tee, I'm pregnant. They told me my baby wouldn't make it."

Mama Tee didn't miss a beat as she walked over and began taking dishes out of the dishwasher. "That's just God's will, baby. But we Rollins women are fertile. Just look at your sister. You'll have another baby."

"The doctor said I have to have something called a D and C, or just wait for the baby to miscarry. I don't know what to do."

Mama Tee stopped removing the dishes and shook her finger at me. "Don't let them doctors get to fooling around with your insides. You know they want us all to be barren anyway. They be done took your uterus out. You just wait. When that baby's ready to come out, she'll come out on her own and we'll have a proper home-going celebration."

"Why do you think it was a girl?"

Mama Tee closed the dishwasher and smiled. "Don't rightly know. Just a gut feeling, I guess."

I lowered my eyes. "I would have loved to have a little girl."

Mama Tee nodded knowingly as she walked over, sat down across from me again, and took my hands in hers. "You know what you need?"

I shook my head.

"You need us. Family. You been running from us because of your mama. The root of all your problems stems from your mama. But it's time to let that go."

Once again, Mama Tee just didn't get it. Yes, I wanted my life with Myles, and maybe a little of it was to prove I was worthy of having a man like him love me. But the bottom line remained—I was bigger than Sweet Poke. I wiped my nose as I prepared to try to rationalize with Mama Tee.

"So that settles it. You coming back with us," she said.

"Go back to Sweet Poke? I can't do that. What will everyone say?"

Mama Tee exhaled in frustration. "Now, you know we couldn't care less what people say about us. Besides, what are your options? Stay here and wallow in sorrow by yourself?"

I didn't know what my options were. But I knew returning to Sweet Poke was not on the list.

"Plus, baby girl," Mama Tee continued, "I just don't think you're strong enough to do this by yourself. Nobody would be. Come home and let Mama Tee make you strong."

I was just about to protest some more when Shondella spoke up. "Raedella, Mama Tee is right. Ain't nothing here for you no more. You need to come home, where you can be around"—she hesitated as if it were hard for her to get it out—"where you can be around people who love you. Around family."

I was absolutely speechless. Truer words had never been spoken—there was nothing here for me now. But to hear those words come from my sister spoke volumes. I don't think I could ever recall a time she had ever said anything remotely close to that in her life. This time, there was no holding back the tears that starting pouring down. Shondella walked over to me and eased me into her arms. She hugged me tightly as she said, "Sugar Smack, it's time to stop running and just come home."

I decided right then and there that was the only choice I had.

"But she ain't gon' nowhere 'till she take a bath," Mama Tee interjected. "Good Lawd, don't make no sense for nobody to smell like that." She shook her head and walked out of the kitchen. For the first time since I could remember, my sister and I roared with laughter—together.

chapter 33

I felt myself getting tense. I was back. Back in the place I'd said I'd never set foot in again.

We were pulling up to the house Mama Tee's had for over fifty years. I looked at the sagging roof, the front porch that looked like it was about to cave in, and the blue paint chipping off the sides of the house. The screen on the front door was peeled back in one corner. The house was literally falling apart. Why hadn't Mama Tee asked me for money to get this repaired? Why didn't I just send it? It was bad when I'd left; why didn't I know it would only get worse and do something about it?

I glanced over at Shondella's double-wide trailer, which sat in the back of Mama Tee's acre-and-a-half lot. She'd put that trailer there right after she had had Mercedes and thought she and Ezekiel were going to get married. It, too, was falling apart. I thought of all the money I had given Shondella. It was obvious none of it had gone toward the upkeep of her trailer.

I tried to shake off the guilt that was eating away at my conscience. It had been a quiet ride back to Arkansas. Even Shondella was unusually quiet.

"Shondella, grab your sister's luggage," Mama Tee said as she popped the trunk, then stepped out of the car.

I half-expected Shondella to complain and was shocked when she didn't. She grabbed my two large suitcases and began lugging them toward the house.

I slowly stepped out of the car. As I made my way up the walk to the house, I cringed at the sight of the old toilet sitting on the front porch. A leafy plant—it looked like a eucalyptus—was growing wildly from the bowl. A beat-up old sofa sat next to the toilet.

Inside, the stench of mothballs permeated the living room. Plastic slipcovers draped the sofa and love seat. Years' worth of pictures of children and grandchildren hung along the living room wall. I felt a flutter in my heart as I gently touched a picture of Jasmine. I caught myself imagining what she'd look like if she were still alive.

I continued to survey the room. A huge, frayed burgundy rug covered the rough wooden floor. Everything was pretty much the same as when I'd left, except for the full-size bed sitting in the corner. And the crusty old man lying in it, hooked to an oxygen tank.

"Uncle Frank!" I was surprised at how happy I was to see Mama Tee's oldest brother. He used to give me quarters and tell funny jokes when I was a little girl.

Uncle Frank struggled to sit up, then narrowed his eyes, focusing in on me. "Who you is, gal?"

Mama Tee moved over to the bed and fluffed Uncle Frank's pillows. "Frank, you remember my granddaughter Raedella?"

Uncle Frank coughed violently for about two minutes straight. I thought he was going to keel over and die right then and there. Finally, the coughing subsided. "I thought you was dead." With that he plopped back down in the bed and closed his eyes.

"Don't listen to that old fool. He ain't playing with a full deck these days."

Uncle Frank never opened his eyes. "All my facilities is working just fine. Just don't know why you bringing strangers in the house, is all."

"I'm no stranger, Uncle Frank. It's me, Rae."

He still didn't bother to open his eyes. "You might as well be a stranger. Now, leave me be."

I tried not to let it show, but Uncle Frank's words pierced my heart. I looked around the room. It had been so long since I'd been here. Uncle Frank was right. I was a stranger. And it had been my own choice.

"If I didn't know better, I would think that's my big sister standing in the living room."

I turned toward the one voice that could still put a huge smile on my face, Justin.

"Hey, you." I stretched out my arms so he could give me a big hug. I squeezed him tightly in return. "You've grown so much," I said after I pulled back and stared him up and down. His cotton robe hung on his frail frame. His eyes looked hollow, and despite his attempt to smile, a sadness seemed ingrained across his face.

"Four years will do that to you." He smirked.

"Don't you start, too."

"I'm just messing with you, girl." He laughed. I couldn't help but stare at him. He had truly grown into a handsome young man. Unfortunately, he looked tired, like life had dealt him more than his fair share of blows. "I'm so glad you're back. I missed you," Justin said as he playfully threw a punch my way. It was a weak attempt that seemed to require a lot of energy. I felt my heart get heavy. Justin must have noticed my mood change because he quickly stood up tall. "Rule number one. No feeling sorry for Justin, okay?"

I forced a smile and nodded.

"I'm sorry I haven't been there for you," I said as I reached out to hug him again.

"Can y'all take that damn family reunion outside," Uncle Frank barked. "I'm trying to sleep."

"Frank, shut up, it's five o'clock in the evening," Mama Tee snapped.

"Well, I told you if you build me my own . . ." He paused to cough for about three minutes before he continued. "I told you that if you build me my own room and get my bed out the dadgum living room, I wouldn't have to bother nobody and wouldn't nobody have to bother me!"

"And I told you I can barely pay for your medicine. I can't build you your own room, so we just have to make do," Mama Tee said.

Uncle Frank sighed wistfully. "Well, don't worry; I ain't gon' be here much longer. I feel it. I'm probably gon' die tonight anyway."

"Frank, hush. You been telling that lie for the last three years and your ancient tail still hanging on."

Uncle Frank wiggled his long, bony finger at Mama

Tee. "You'll be sorry when you come in here and find me dead!" he threatened. Uncle Frank pulled his covers over his head.

Justin laughed. "You'd better get used to that. They do it all the time."

"You hush, too, boy. Now, I thought I told you I didn't want you out of the bed either," Mama Tee chastised. "The doctor said he didn't want you up and about for two weeks."

"Awwww, come on, Mama Tee. Raedella just got here," Justin whined.

"And she gon' be here a while. Now, git." Mama Tee shooed Justin away.

"I'll holla at you later, Sis. I have to go back on lockdown 'cause Mama Tee thinks I'll pass out and die if I walk to the bathroom." He smiled.

I returned his smile. He managed to have such a good attitude for someone so sick.

"Come on, baby girl," Mama Tee said. "You can put your stuff in your old room upstairs."

I stared blankly at Mama Tee. How could she show me so much love after the way I'd treated her all this time? She smiled warmly, then took one of my bags and led me up the stairs, then down the long hall to the back room that I had grown up in. The room was still the way I had left it. My Prince poster still hung on the wall, even though the ends were brown and tattered. My celebrity pictures from *Right On!* magazine also adorned the wall.

"You lucky your uncle Frank can't climb those stairs, because I sho' would have put him in here and got him out of my living room." Mama Tee walked over and opened the small window. "Here, this will let some fresh air in. You want to lie down while I fix you something to eat? I know that drive got you tired."

"Mama Tee, I slept most of the way here, so I'm fine." Shondella had driven the entire six hours without complaining. "I need to call Shereen and let her know I made it and tell her where I left the key to my house. She'll be handling my bills and everything for me. After that I think I just want to go for a walk, see the old neighborhood."

"Chile, ain't nothing changed round here. But you go on."

I smiled as Mama Tee left the room. I glanced at my bags, contemplated unpacking them, then decided against it. I don't think I had been on a walk since I'd left Sweet Poke. I was looking forward to strolling down the street, nowhere to go, no one to see. I hadn't known such calm in years.

I changed into my tennis shoes and slipped out the back door, laughing at Mama Tee's chicken coop. She still had several hens and a rooster roaming about the pen. I forgot about all the fun we used to have as kids chasing her chickens around that coop. I paused and reflected on that memory—a memory I hadn't had in years.

I started walking toward town, remembering the many journeys I had taken this way growing up. I rubbed my stomach, hoping against hope that somehow, someway, Dr. Trahan was wrong and my baby would make it. Especially since now it had been two weeks since they'd told me my baby wasn't "viable." With everything going on with the case, I'd tried to keep thoughts of losing my baby out of my mind. I had ruled out the D&C, and although I wasn't a religious person, I was praying God would have mercy on me and spare my child.

I don't know how long I had been walking, but I found myself in front of the high school. I hadn't been in too many organizations in school because my only goal had been to get out of Sweet Poke. It was a small school—there were only about a hundred people in my graduating class, so most of us knew each other.

It was just after four, so most of the students were already gone. I glanced over on the football field. The team was gathered there practicing. Reno. My mind raced back to Reno. He was probably out there. Other than in the newspaper articles Shondella had sent me, I hadn't seen him since I'd left Sweet Poke. I debated whether I should go over and say something, but before I could make up my mind, I felt a sharp pain in my abdomen. That pain was quickly followed by another. I doubled over and screamed. My heart dropped when I felt the blood creeping down my leg. My baby. I sank to the ground and began sobbing.

"Ma'am, are you all right?" I looked up at a student standing in front of me. The tall, slender girl looked genuinely concerned. When she noticed the blood that had begun seeping through my pants, her eyes bulged. "Oh, no!"

"C . . . can you call for help for me please?" I managed to say. I grabbed my stomach again as the girl took off running. I couldn't believe I was about to lose my baby on the sidewalk in Sweet Poke, Arkansas.

I watched her run to the football field and scream something, then point at me. Several people took off running toward me. I prayed that Reno was not one of them.

The last thing I wanted was for us to see each other for the first time in years like this.

But of course, why would luck be on my side?

"Oh my God. Rae?" Reno dropped to the ground beside me. "What are you doing here? What's wrong?" He looked down at the puddle of blood that was growing bigger by the minute. "What's going on? Just hold on. I sent someone to call for help."

I wanted to fix my hair, wipe up the blood, anything so that this wouldn't be Reno's first impression of what I'd turned into. But the pain ripping through my abdomen wouldn't let me think of anything, or anyone else. I screamed again after yet another pain kicked in. It felt like someone was ripping my insides out.

"Reno . . . ," I stammered. I felt weak.

"Shhhhh." He pulled me to him. "Help is on the way. It's on the way."

I felt groggy. My eyes fluttered before opening. I tried to take in my surroundings. I was lying in a hospital bed. Mama Tee and Reno were whispering in the corner. I felt sadness set in when I recalled why I was there. I slowly rubbed my hand over my stomach as a tear ran down my cheek.

"Is my baby gone?" I asked.

Both Mama Tee and Reno turned to me. Mama Tee quickly eased over to me and began stroking my hair. "Yes, sweetie. But you're gon' to be just fine." She took Reno's hand. "Thanks to Reno here, you got to the hospital before you lost too much blood."

I looked at Reno. "Thank you," I softly responded. "I'm sorry we had to meet up like this."

"Please," he responded. "You're as pretty as you were the day you left."

I tried to force a laugh. "Yeah, right."

His comment made me rub my hair down. I was sure I looked a mess and contemplated asking for a mirror. But as my thoughts returned to my baby, I didn't have the energy to request one.

"Do they know if it was a boy or a girl?"

Mama Tee shook her head. "I'm sorry, sugar. It was a girl."

I turned my head so neither Mama Tee or Reno would see me cry.

Reno stepped closer to me. "Rae, do you mind if I pray with you?"

I sighed, but kept my head turned. "I'm sorry. I just don't feel prayerful right now."

"You need to always stay in prayer," Mama Tee chastised.

I took a deep breath. I wanted to tell Mama Tee I wasn't strong like her. I couldn't stand in the face of adversity yet still praise God.

"How do you keep the faith?" I asked no one in particular. "I'm so mad at God right now. How am I supposed to be faithful and prayerful through my anger?"

"God don't care 'bout you being mad." Mama Tee was getting worked up. I knew I was treading on thin ice with her because she has never liked for anyone to question God. But at that moment, I didn't really care.

"What kind of God inflicts so much pain?" I asked.

"A gracious one! You—"

"Ms. Rollins, no disrespect, but may I talk to Rae?" Reno interjected.

Mama Tee huffed. "Fine. You know I try to be understanding, but I just can't have that gal being blasphemous."

Reno sat down next to my bed and gently took my hand. "I don't think she's being blasphemous, Ms. Rollins," he said without taking his eyes off me. "I just think Raedella is in pain. But God understands that pain. Just like God is real, so is the devil. And the devil is hard at work on Raedella right now."

"Amen to that," Mama Tee replied, nodding feverishly.

"But the devil is a liar," Reno softly said. "And God will see you through this, Raedella. You might not be able to see that right now, but He has a plan, and as crazy as this may sound, this," he said, pointing to my stomach, "this is all in His plan."

Reno reached up and wiped away my tears. He then took my hand and gently closed my eyes. "Let us pray . . ."

chapter 34

I flinched as Mama Tee flicked on the light in my bedroom.

"Okay, I gave you two days to sit in this bed and mourn. Now, enough of that. It's time to get up." Mama Tee walked to the window and pulled back the drapes.

I moaned as I pulled the covers over my face. I should've known that wouldn't stop my grandmother. She grabbed my blanket and the top sheet and pulled them completely off the bed. I shivered as the cool breeze shot up my spine.

"Mama Tee, please, I don't feel like getting up," I whined.

"I ain't felt like doing a lot of things but I had to do them nonetheless. So get on up."

"Why won't you just let me get over my depression? I just lost my baby."

"And I'm not downplayin' that. But you knew you was

gon' lose the baby. God don't give us more than we can handle. Now get up."

"Maybe my losing the baby was God's payback," I said somberly as I sat up.

Mama Tee shook her head. "Gal, don't talk that nonsense. My Lord don't work like that. I know. I got a personal relationship. I have him over to dinner every night." Mama Tee smiled as she adjusted the drapes. Suddenly she started banging on the window. "Mercedes, get your little fast behind down outta that tree before I come out there and beat you into next week," she screamed. I peered out the window just in time to see Shondella's oldest daughter scurry down out of the tree. "Them damn chil'ren get on my nerve. Why they all up in my peach tree? Know I done told they little tails about that. Now, as I was saying," Mama Tee continued, turning back to face me, "me and the Lord, we got a personal relationship. And even though He said vengeance is mine, He don't work like that. So you just get that foolishness out your mind and get on up outta that bed. We gotta go to June Bug's wedding today."

I looked at her like she was crazy, not just for her cursing and praising the Lord in the same breath, but because she actually thought I was going to somebody's wedding. "I don't feel like going to a wedding."

"And I repeat, I do a lot of things I don't feel like doing." Mama Tee headed toward the door. "Be ready to go in thirty minutes," she said without looking back.

I silently cursed as I dragged myself out of the bed. It had been two days since I'd come home from the hospital and I hadn't moved. I made my way to the bathroom and began running bathwater. "Why doesn't Mama Tee get a shower?" I mumbled as I tried to adjust the steaming-hot water. I looked around for some bubble bath. Growing up, we never used the stuff. Mama Tee believed a bar of soap and some hot water were all you needed. But times had changed so I knew she had to have had some somewhere.

"Mama Tee, do you have some bubble bath?" I called out.

"Hold on," she responded. I had started taking off my gown when she entered the bathroom, walked straight to the tub, and started pouring in a green liquid.

"What is that?" I peered at the set of hands on the front of the bottle.

"Palmolive."

"Dishwashing liquid?"

"And?" Mama Tee looked at me as if it were perfectly normal to use dishwashing liquid for bubble bath.

"Mama Tee, that's for dishes."

"Girl, you wanted bubbles, you got bubbles." She turned and walked out of the bathroom before I could say anything else.

I thought about draining the water and just taking a bath without the bubbles, but I decided a little Palmolive wouldn't kill me. I sank into the tub and enjoyed the hot water as it surrounded my skin.

After my brief, yet relaxing bath, I dressed and met Mama Tee downstairs and we headed to the wedding.

Ten minutes later we were standing in front of Greater Gethsemane. I stared up at the huge cross that sat on top of the building. It looked like it was about to topple over at any moment.

"Why don't they fix that?" I asked Mama Tee, who was fumbling through her purse.

"We fixed it once and it fell right back over. So we left

it alone." Mama Tee found the handkerchief she must've been looking for and used it to dab the beads of sweat off her forehead. "That cross done withstood all kinds of storms. Pastor says it's a sign that you may bend, but with the Lord on your side, you won't break."

I stared at her. "What are you trying to say, Mama Tee?"

"It ain't what I'm *trying* to say, it's what I'm saying." She put the handkerchief back in her purse. "Maybe if you'd had the Lord on your side all along, nothing coulda broke you. Not no man, no job, not even your mama." Mama Tee walked on in.

I was still thinking about what Mama Tee had said as I followed her in. We took our seats on June's side of the church. I was surprised at all the emotions I felt as I sat in the third row of the church I had grown up in.

The vestibule was nicely decorated, which was a total shock to me. June had absolutely no class, so I was expecting a ghetto-fabulous wedding. And if the wedding programs were any indication, I was going to have to bite my tongue to keep from cracking up. The homemade programs looked like they were printed on a home computer with an ink-jet printer. There was a picture of June and Shoshanna on the front. Not even a nice picture. One of those you take at the mall and put on buttons. Then inside there was a collage of them and their three children. I vaguely remembered the girl he was marrying. A cocoa-brown girl, she was two years behind me in high school. I knew she had twins by June. They were five years old now and she'd had a baby a year ago. I guess June decided to finally marry her. I'm sure it was because she was pressuring him.

"Lawd, have mercy," Mama Tee mumbled, as she fanned herself with the Martin Luther King Jr. funeral-home fan.

I leaned in and whispered, "What?"

Mama Tee kept her eyes focused straight ahead. "Look at Shoshanna's mama. She look like a two-dollar hooker who needs to give you some change back."

I turned my attention to the tall, busty woman making her way down the aisle. She had on a bright yellow, sequined suit with a matching hat. Her skirt was so tight she could only take small steps or else all her goods would bust out.

"She look like a straight hussy. Shame on her. Probably came straight from the club," Mama Tee muttered as Shoshanna's mother made her way toward them. "Well, hello, Sister Banks. You sho' is looking lovely today. I just love that bright yellow on you. Everybody ain't brave enough to wear something so . . . so colorful."

My mouth dropped at the sudden change in Mama Tee's tone.

"Thank you, Ms. Rollins. You know I had to look my best for my baby girl. You know we's about to be family now so that means you gon' have to share your recipe for sweet potato pie with me."

"Call me, sugar," Mama Tee said, flashing Ms. Banks a fake smile. She squeezed Mama Tee's hand and sashayed to her seat. Mama Tee turned to see me staring at her. "What? I can't just be mean to the woman, now can I?"

I just shook my head and tried not to laugh. Maybe coming to this wedding was just what I needed to get me out of my slump. I had already laughed more in the last hour than I had in the last few months.

I felt my heart flutter when I noticed Reno coming into the church. My smile quickly faded when I noticed his wife and kids were right behind him. He waved at me, then took his wife's hand and slid into a back pew. His wave didn't go unnoticed, and his wife shot me a look that I couldn't quite make out.

The pianist started playing, signaling that the wedding was about to start.

"Get ready for a show," Mama Tee mumbled.

I leaned in and whispered, "It doesn't look like it's going to be that bad." I think I spoke too soon, because the pianist stopped playing and someone turned on a cassette that began playing "I Wanna Be Your Man" by Roger Troutman. Then June came pimpin' down the aisle to that song. He had on an all-white tux, a top hat, and a cane.

Mama Tee threw me an I-told-you-so look. That was just the beginning of the spectacle. The bridesmaids and groomsmen began making their way in. I guess making sure your hair was at least two feet high was a requirement, because every one of the bridesmaids had her hair swooped up into a French twist. And each of them had deep burgundy hair with glitter sprinkled throughout. Shoshanna's wedding colors were burgundy and gold, but good grief. And then the groomsmen weren't any better. Two had cornrows, three had Jheri curls, and the others all had huge unkempt Afros.

After all twelve bridesmaids and groomsmen made their way to the front to "Computer Love," a little boy came running down the aisle, blaring a trumpet. He stopped at the front of the church and screamed, *"The bride is coming! The bride is coming!"*

The audience stood up and the church's back doors

opened to reveal the bride. She actually looked quite nice in a strapless wedding gown. The train was probably a mile and a half long, but other than that, the off-white dress was pretty. She was escorted by a man with a Jheri curl so wet that the tuxedo rental place was sure to be furious when he returned it.

The wedding itself actually turned out to be uneventful, with the exception of Aunt Ola wailing as usual.

We were all standing outside the church when I saw Rose. She had on a pair of sunglasses and a large-brimmed hat. But there was no disguise that could keep me from recognizing my own mother. She was leaning up against a tree outside the church, puffing on a cigarette and rolling it nervously between her fingers.

I tugged on Shondella's arm. "Look." I nodded my head toward Rose, and Shondella's gaze followed. The smile immediately left her face, and after staring for a few minutes, she turned back toward me.

"Should we go say something?" I asked.

"You can do whatever you want. Me and my kids are leaving." Shondella grabbed her girls' hands and dragged them toward her car.

I stood there staring at Rose. She looked like she wanted to say something. I contemplated following Shondella's lead and turning away and acting like I'd never seen my mother. But Mama Tee's words rang in my head. "The source of all your problems stems from your mama."

No, it was past time for us to talk. I slowly walked toward her. I heard Shondella call my name, but I ignored her and kept walking.

"Still puffing those cancer sticks, I see."

Rose looked at the cigarette, then threw it to the ground before grinding it with her foot. "Old habits die hard."

"Ummm-hmmm."

We stood there in awkward silence for a few minutes.

"So, how you doing?"

"I've been better. I thought you'd moved to Houston."

"I left. There was nothing there for me anymore . . . since you left."

She looked like she was struggling for something to say. I couldn't feel any sympathy for her. It wasn't my fault she didn't know what to say to her own daughter. "I heard about all that stuff that happened to you. I kept up with you. How successful you was and all," Rose softly said.

I looked at her and had no idea what to say. Was I supposed to be grateful that she had been following my life?

"I also heard you lost your baby the other day. I'm sorry."

I stood there speechless. I didn't need or want her sympathy.

"Sugar Smack—"

I shot her a mean look. As far as I was concerned, she had lost the right to call me that. I guess she realized that because she corrected herself. "I mean, Raedella—you gon' be all right. You were raised to be a strong—how you say it?—resilient woman. So you gon' make it."

I shot her an incredulous look. "How do you know how I was raised?"

She lowered her head. "I guess I deserved that one."

"I guess you did."

Rose removed her sunglasses. "Raedella, I need to make amends."

"You've got to be kidding me, right?"

"No, I'm saved now. I want to get things right with my family. With God."

I cocked my head in confusion. Was I supposed to feel anything but contempt for the woman who had abandoned me at a gas station? Was I supposed to take her into my arms and act like all was well with the world because she had claimed to find Jesus? I didn't think so.

"I know there's no hope for me and your sister. Believe me, I've tried. But she hates me."

"Can you blame her?"

She ignored me and kept talking. "But I'm hoping I can reach you. You always was the one with the big heart."

I laughed when I thought of all the people who would think she was crazy to say something like that. "Correction, Rose. I lost any semblance of a heart the day you walked out of my life."

"You can't mean that."

"Oh, I mean it. Just ask anyone who knows me. You abandoned me and I spent all my life looking for a love to replace yours."

"You had Mama."

"*Your* mama. I wanted mine. And when I couldn't have you, I learned the only way to never be in that position again was to always look out for myself. Nobody else mattered but me. I had no friends, a cheating man, and it was all because of you."

I was shocking myself. Where was all of this coming from? I had never equated my mother's abandonment with the way I was. But the more I thought about it, the more sense it made. Not having my mother had made me bitter.

"Do you remember how sweet I was as a little girl?" I continued. "Well, I'm the total opposite now. Or I was. I wanted to forget you existed. I wanted to forget this side of my life existed. But Mama Tee wouldn't let me. I pushed and pushed and pushed her away and she kept coming back. Where were you? Why did you never come back? You lived forty miles away! Why did you never come back?" I was screaming and crying now and hadn't even realized it. Rose looked like she didn't know what to do. I was releasing years of pent-up anger and I didn't care about her feelings. I was just about to let into her some more when I felt someone grab my arm.

"Come on, Rae. She ain't worth it." Shondella was pulling me. She wouldn't even look at Rose. "You don't need the stress."

I jerked my arm away. "No, she has a lot of nerve, showing up here now, talking about she saved and expecting somebody to feel sorry for her."

"If it makes you feel any better, I've been miserable all my life," Rose said softly.

I glared at Rose. "You've been miserable? You hear that, Shondella? *She's* been miserable. Do you think we care about your misery? Do you think we care that all of a sudden you are saved and sanctified? As far as we're concerned, you died the day you drove off and left us."

Rose pleadingly looked at Shondella. "I know you hate me, but I'm still your mother. Will you please talk to your sister?"

Shondella turned and walked off.

By this time, Mama Tee and several other people had

noticed the commotion and began making their way over toward the tree where we were standing. Mama Tee rushed to me. "Rose, what are you doing?"

"Hey, Mama," Rose said.

"Don't come here starting no trouble, Rose. This girl been through enough."

"I know that, Mama. I just want to make peace."

I stared at her with tear-filled eyes. "It's too late for peace. Just go back to wherever you've been all these years and leave me alone!" I turned and walked away, calling out to my sister, "Shondella, wait for me!"

Rose may have found Jesus, but it was going to take even more than His help for me to let her back into my heart.

chapter 35

"Somebody get me an ax," I muttered. I knew I was talking to myself, but that rooster was driving me crazy. It was barely daylight and he was crowing like there was no tomorrow. I couldn't for the life of me understand why Mama Tee kept that rooster around. She got up at the break of dawn anyway, so it's not like she needed it to wake her up. My mind flashed back to how Mama Tee used to slaughter her chickens, grabbing one by the neck, swinging the animal around in the air, then laying it across the tree stump before chopping its head off. I remembered how terrified I used to be when that headless chicken would get up and run around for five minutes before flopping over and dying. Then Mama Tee would wonder why I'd rather starve than eat her fried chicken.

Uncle Frank was having another coughing fit, and I swear it sounded like he was about to cough up a lung.

I moaned as I rolled out of bed. Forget about going

back to sleep, my head was throbbing. That rooster would be crowing the rest of the morning. I stumbled into the kitchen, where Mama Tee was already up and making coffee. Shondella was sitting at the table reading the paper.

"Does everyone around here get up early?"

"Early to bed, early to rise, makes a woman healthy, wealthy, and wise," Mama Tee sang.

I rolled my eyes. "May I please have a cup?" I motioned to the coffeepot as I plopped down in a chair at the kitchen table.

Mama Tee poured me a cup, then handed it to me. "You wanna talk about it?" she asked.

I knew it was just a matter of time before she brought up Rose. Shondella must have known it was coming, too, because she immediately closed the paper, set it down, stood up, and left the kitchen.

After following Shondella with her eyes, Mama Tee turned back to me. "How you feeling?"

"Why do you keep Uncle Frank around? Don't you think he'd be better off in a home?" I listened to him wheeze and cough in the living room.

"He don't want to be in a home. And I keep telling you, he's family. Family is always first." Mama Tee shook her head as she chastised me. "Besides, he won't be here much longer."

My eyes grew wide.

"No, I'm not predicting his death." Mama Tee laughed. "He does that enough. You remember his daughter, Christina? Well, she doing mighty well in California and she wants to bring him out there with her. Seems to think that California smog will make him better." Mama Tee shook her head like it was the most absurd thing she'd ever heard. "But who am I to argue with that chile about her own daddy? He'll be gone by the end of the week." Mama Tee shook her finger at me. "But see, that's what I'm talking about. That's what family does. Family is supposed to be there for you through thick and thin. I don't think you've ever quite gotten that."

"Is family supposed to leave you stranded at a gas station in the dead of night?" My voice dripped with sarcasm.

"No, but *I* didn't leave you. That was your mama all by herself. But you ran from all of us here. All of us who love and care about you." Mama Tee sat down at the table across from me.

"Mama Tee, you just don't understand." I felt myself struggling not to cry.

"Baby girl, I know my existence here has been meager. But it's what the good Lord gave to me. And I'm grateful for it. Besides, all that glitters ain't gold, as you very well know by now."

I shrugged and gulped down my coffee, letting the steaming liquid glide down my throat.

"You still haven't answered my question."

"What question?" I asked.

"How are you feeling? About yesterday?"

"I'm fine. Dang, I wish you would quit fussing over me."

"I'm your grandma. I'm supposed to fuss over you. And you should know by now, Raedella, that you can't run me off with that nasty attitude of yours."

"Mama Tee, my name is Rae."

"Gal, hush yo' mouth! I was right there when yo' mama named you, and she didn't say nothing 'bout no damn Rae." Mama Tee reached out and grabbed my hand, her look turning serious. "Baby girl, why you gotta try and pretend you something you not?"

"'Cause she think she was s'posed to be born to royalty or something, not to this poor little family," Shondella chimed in. I hadn't even noticed her come back in the room.

"Shut up. Didn't nobody ask for your two cents."

Shondella put her hand to her chest and feigned astonishment. "What? Miss Proper TV Personality is using improper grammar? Oh, my God. But then I guess since you're now a washed-up, former TV star, you can go back to using Ebonics."

"Shut up before I . . ."

"Before you what? Run me over with your car?"

"Shondella," Mama Tee snapped.

"No, Mama Tee. I'm sick of her walking around like somebody owe her something. Like she's ashamed of us. She's so daggone self-righteous. Like she's better than somebody. Now, she's around here wallowing in self-pity like somebody should feel sorry for her because her dream life fell apart. Well, Miss TV Star, I been through the same things as you. I was right there when Mama ran off and left us. You don't see me walking around here whining about it all my life."

"I wouldn't expect you to understand either," I said, rolling my eyes.

"Not understand? Oh, I understand all too well. Poor Raedella. She grew up without her mommy. Her life is so miserable because she didn't have her mommy. She was poor and country. Woe is Raedella. Get over it! Justin needed his mother more than anyone else and you don't hear him whining," Shondella snapped.

"Hey," said a small voice from the doorway.

Shondella and I kept arguing, not paying much attention to Justin leaning against the doorway to the kitchen.

"Hey," he muttered again, this time a little louder. All of us turned to him. His face was ashen and he looked like he was struggling to breathe. His arms were wrapped around his stomach and he had tears in his eyes.

"Justin!" we all called out.

"What's wrong?" Mama Tee cried as she raced to him.

"It hurts. It hurts . . . so . . . bad."

I felt a scream building in my throat as my little brother closed his eyes and collapsed to the floor.

chapter 36

We had been sitting in the waiting room for over three hours with no word from Justin's doctor. It was driving me absolutely insane. And I wasn't the only one.

"I don't understand what is taking so long!" Shondella snapped as she paced back and forth for the 27 millionth time.

"Chile, just sit down. When the doctor got some news for us, he'll be out," Mama Tee said gently.

"But in three hours, you'd think they know something."

"Shondella, would you sit down?" I said.

Shondella spun on me. "I don't recall talking to you."

Mama Tee sighed heavily. "Oh, Lord, would you two just stop all that arguing? You getting on my last nerve. Your brother is laying in there fighting for his life and you two goin' at each other's throats."

"Mama Tee, I'm just—"

Mama Tee cut me off, throwing up her hands in frustration. "Just shush! I'm tired of y'all. For years you two have been fighting."

"That's because she thinks she's so much better than everybody else," Shondella pouted.

"No, that's because your ghetto behind just mad because you haven't done anything with your life and you're jealous because I have!" I didn't care if we were in a hospital. I was about to give my sister a piece of my mind.

"Jealous of what? A washed-up, wannabe, attempted murderer!"

"It's better than being a washed-up, never-has-been, can't-keep-a-man-so-I'll-just-get-pregnant, overweight—"

"I said stop it!" Mama Tee stood up and yelled, snapping us out of our shouting match.

I glared at my sister, willing back the tears that were forming under my eyelids.

Shondella rolled her eyes and walked away, plopping down on one of the hard emergency-room sofas.

We sat in silence for the next hour until Justin's longtime doctor, Dr. Wang, finally came in. All three of us jumped up and raced toward him.

"Please tell me my baby's gonna be fine," Mama Tee pleaded.

Dr. Wang pushed his glasses up on his nose and took a deep breath. "I wish that I could tell you that. Justin's kidneys have failed. Because the leukemia has left him anemic and he has chronic kidney failure, he's not a candidate for dialysis. Unless we can get him a kidney quickly, his chances of survival are slim."

"A kidney? Is that all he needs?" Shondella piped in. "Where do I check in so you can take one of mine. I mean, I heard people can live fine off of one kidney, so he can have one of mine."

I stared at Shondella in amazement. The ease with which she had jumped up to offer a vital organ was amazing. As hateful as she could be, there was no denying her love for family.

The doctor looked at Shondella. "Ma'am, I wish it were that easy." He opened his folder and started perusing the records. "What is your name?"

"Shondella Rollins."

He glanced at the chart for a few minutes. "I see that you have been tested before and your blood type is AB positive. That's incompatible with your brother's O negative. Plus we have to take into consideration tissue type for an organ transplant."

Shondella's eyes watered up and her shoulders slumped. She turned to me. I didn't know what to say. Of course I loved my brother, but giving up my kidney?

"What about me?" Mama Tee said.

"Unfortunately, and not to be disrespectful, but with your age, you're not compatible either," Dr. Wang replied.

"What about Raedella?" Shondella asked without even looking at me.

The doctor turned toward me, oblivious to the look of horror across my face. "Do you know your blood type?"

"It's O positive."

The doctor wearily shook his head. "Sorry, that won't work either."

I felt bad about the sense of relief that swept through my body.

Shondella began crying. "What does this mean? Don't you have an organ donor list? Didn't someone just die in a car wreck or something?" She seemed to be grasping at straws.

"Unfortunately, all we can do is put him on an organ donor list, and we have no idea how long it will be before we can get a kidney for him. It's best that you all just go on home. We've stabilized Justin, but there's nothing more we can do until we find a donor. If we find a donor. We'll be in touch if we find out anything new." Dr. Wang gave us a sorrowful look, then walked out of the waiting room.

We had been moping around the hospital in silence for the last two days, each of us, I imagine, trying to envision life without Justin. It had been the hardest two days of our lives. The hospital had made desperate calls as far away as Minnesota, but still no luck.

Me, Shondella, and Mama Tee were back at home after waiting at the hospital all day. We'd tried to get some sleep, to no avail, and were now sitting in the living room. Shondella was braiding Lexus's hair. Mama Tee was knitting, and I was just staring blankly at the TV.

"You know what? I want us to pray," Mama Tee announced.

I looked at her like she was crazy. "No disrespect, Mama Tee, but I'm so not feeling God right now. How can I? What kind of God would bring Justin so much pain?"

"I done told you, an awesome God," she replied forcefully.

I stared at her, trying to understand how she could sit there and say that to me. "Awesome? He took everything I ever wanted. My brother is knocking on death's door, and you want me to say, 'Thank you, Jesus'?"

"I sure do," Mama Tee said. "Yes, I'm worried about Justin, but the Lord will take care of my baby."

I wasn't convinced. Still, it was useless to try to talk to Mama Tee about this. I'd tried to see her point after my miscarriage, but now this with Justin. Nope, I just couldn't agree with her.

"Maybe the Lord took away what you really wanted to make room for what you really needed," Mama Tee gingerly added.

I was just about to say something when the telephone rang.

Mama Tee rose and walked into the hallway to answer it. "Hello."

She was silent for a minute, but the expression on her face began to change, the weary look turning bright.

"Thank you, Lord Jesus. I knew He would work this out! We're on our way." Mama Tee slammed the phone down and excitedly began jumping up and down. "They found a donor. The doctor said it's nothing short of a miracle! Somebody needs to take me over there right now."

We dropped Shondella's kids off at Mrs. Miller's and thirty minutes later we were pulling into the Arkansas Medical Center and racing up to Justin's fifth-floor room. Watching him lying there hooked to a machine was heartbreaking. He seemed to be sleeping peacefully, though. The nurse was monitoring his vital signs.

"How's he doing?" Mama Tee whispered.

"He's sedated," the nurse replied.

Just then, Dr. Wang walked in, a smile across his face. "You all must have been praying really hard because we found someone who is compatible and willing to give him a kidney. This is almost unheard of to get such a quick donation."

All three of us hugged in excitement, Shondella and I briefly calling a truce.

Shondella pulled away, still smiling. "How'd you get him moved up the list so fast?"

"We actually found a compatible donor who wanted to specifically give him a kidney," Dr. Wang said as he stuck a funny-looking contraption into Justin's ear.

"What? Who?" Shondella asked.

"You know, I don't know. She's been hanging around the hospital quite a bit . . . well, speak of the devil," Dr. Wang said as the door to Justin's hospital room eased open.

We all turned to the door and all of our mouths dropped wide open.

Shondella was the first to speak. "What is she doing here?"

"I'm his mother; I have a right to be here."

Shondella glared at Rose. The doctor, who seemed oblivious to the tension in the room, ran over and eagerly grasped Rose's hand. "A perfect match! I'm so excited!"

Rose stood there like she didn't know what to say. A small smile crept across her face.

"I'm just thankful that it worked out," she said.

"Well, my brother doesn't need her crappy, drug-infested kidney," Shondella said.

The doctor looked astonished.

"Shondella, despite what hatred you harbor for me or how you feel about me, right now our attention needs to be focused on Justin," Rose said.

Shondella glared at Rose with extreme hatred. "Oh, so

now you want to be concerned about Justin? Where was that concern all the other times he was in the hospital. Were you concerned about Justin when he had violent coughing fits at night and cried himself to sleep because he was in so much pain? Were you concerned all the nights he asked me did you leave us because he was sick? All the nights I comforted him. Me! Where were you then? Where were you when I had to explain to him why his twin sister wasn't coming back?" Tears were streaming down Shondella's face. I was shocked.

"Enough!" Mama Tee yelled. The force in her voice caught everyone by surprise.

"Mama Tee, make her leave," Shondella sniffled.

"Shondella, I can't make her do nothing. That's her boy. Like it or not. Besides, do you have a better idea? Right now, she's all we got."

I stepped in. "Mama Tee's right. Rose gave birth to Justin and hasn't given him anything since. A kidney is the least she can do."

Shondella stood glaring at Rose, tears slowly falling from her eyes. She walked over to Justin, leaned down, and kissed him on the head, then turned and stomped out of the room, nearly knocking Rose over.

"Mama . . ." Rose pleaded.

"This ain't about you, Rose. I don't want to hear nothing you got to say. This is about saving Justin." Mama Tee turned to the doctor. "Now, Doctor, as bad as I want my grandson to make it, my daughter here did drugs for several years. Don't even know if she still do 'em."

"I'm clean, Mama. I have been for the last five years."

"Of course we'll have to run some tests and see how everything progresses, but if she has indeed been clean for five years, it shouldn't be any problem," Dr. Wang interjected. He still looked shaken up by all the drama that had just unfolded.

"So what will that do to her?" Mama Tee asked.

"I've been taking care of myself. I'll be all right."

"Ms. Rollins, if you'll follow me back here, we'll do the necessary paperwork and get you suited up. We don't have much time."

Rose looked at me. "Raedella . . ."

I didn't want to hear anything she had to say. I turned my back to her and gazed out the window. I heard her let out a deep sigh, then she turned and walked out the door.

Mama Tee began fluffing up Justin's pillow. "You can't even rest in the hospital, all this madness going on up in here. But don't you worry, baby. You gon' be all right. Your mama is finally going to do right by you."

Suddenly the door swung open and Aunt Ola came racing in. "Ohhhh, Lord! No, Lord, noooooooo!" she screamed as she threw herself across Justin. "Don't take him, Lord. Take me! Take me!"

Mama Tee closed her eyes, inhaled deeply, and shook her head. "Jesus, be my guide," she whispered.

"Lord, he just a baby! Take me!" Aunt Ola continued wailing. Luckily, Justin was asleep and oblivious to Aunt Ola's ranting.

"Ola, get yo' behind up off that boy before you suffocate him," Mama Tee snapped.

"But I just can't believe he's gone."

"He's gone—to sleep, Ola. And all that ruckus is gon' wake him up."

"Sleep?" Aunt Ola stood up and cocked her head in

confusion. "But Lula said Mary told her that Vera told her that Justin had died of lung failure."

Mama Tee shook her head again. "It's the boy's kidneys, not his lungs. And you know better than to believe anything that lying Lula Mae says in the first place. If she said it was raining outside, I wouldn't believe it until I was soaking wet."

Aunt Ola looked back and forth between Justin and Mama Tee. "So he ain't dead?"

"No, he's not," I interjected.

"Oh." She stood there awkwardly for a few moments. "Oh, well, I'm going outside to smoke. Y'all call me if anything changes."

Aunt Ola sashayed out the door like nothing was wrong. I shook my head in disbelief. "Them yo' people," I joked to Mama Tee.

Mama Tee rubbed Justin's head. "Naw, baby girl, them *our* people. And ain't nothing we can do about it," she said without cracking a smile.

chapter 37

It had been a long week. I sighed as I navigated Mama Tee's 1990 Eldorado onto her street. The police were still holding my car as evidence, but when they did release it, I planned to sell it and buy another one. But for now, I had to piddle around town in Mama Tee's car, which didn't have any air-conditioning. I was about to burn up.

I was leaving the hospital in a good mood because Rose's kidney had been compatible and things were looking up for Justin. He would still be hospitalized for a couple more weeks, but at least he was not in pain. He was even talking, although it wasn't easy.

I nearly choked as I pulled up in front of Mama Tee's house. My eyes had to be deceiving me. I stepped out of the car, staring at the figure in front of me.

"Hey, sweet thang."

"Myles? What are you doing here?"

He was leaning against his Navigator, looking good as

usual. His left arm was wrapped up in a cast, but other than that, he showed no signs that he'd suffered any injuries.

"Is that any way to greet your husband? Especially after I drove all the way up to this hick town?"

"I will ask you again. What do you want?"

Myles laughed. "You tried to kill me and you have the nerve to act like you're mad at me."

I was silent.

"I came to tell you that I pulled some strings and got all the charges against you dropped. You don't have to come back to Houston for a trial. They'll even release your car to you at the end of the week."

I should've been relieved, but watching him standing there, gloating like I should forever be indebted to him, made me want to get back in the car and run him over again. I took a deep breath and pushed the evil thoughts away.

"Thank you, Myles. Bye." I stepped around him and headed to the house.

"I also came all this way to tell you I forgive you."

I stopped in my tracks and turned back toward him, an astonished look on my face. "*You* forgive *me*? Gee, thanks."

"Of course, I needed to check on my blossoming baby, as well. You sure aren't growing much." He walked over and placed a hand on my stomach. I slapped it away. I'd never told him I had lost the baby. I was wearing a big shirt, but even still, I didn't look anywhere near five months pregnant.

Myles laughed, infuriating me.

"Girl, you need to be at my beck and call. I saved you

from the slammer. You have nothing and you're back here in this dump. I see why you'd lie about this place." He looked up and down the street, then turned his nose up in disgust at Mama Tee's house. "I wouldn't want anyone to know I was from some place like this either. The Rae Rollins I knew could never thrive in a place like this."

"Myles, I will ask you again. Why are you here?" I didn't know it was possible to hate someone so much, but that's exactly what I felt for Myles right then.

"I had to pull some strings to get the DA to give me your address. You need to consider yourself lucky that I'm willing to give you a second chance." His look softened. "I could be real upset, but I know how seeing me with Karen must have looked to you, so I understand your anger.

"But, still, the way I see it," he said as a sly smile crossed his face, "you tried to kill me. See, my public relations people can put a spin on it where you misconstrued my conversation with Karen and simply lost it. But it'll look real good for my campaign if I play the remorseful, yet forgiving, spouse. We are a power couple, remember? It will speak volumes for us to work through this tragedy. Imagine all the women voters I can win over if you come back being remorseful and me forgiving." He grinned like he had it all figured out. "Besides, I still love you, especially since you're carrying my baby." He kissed me. I jerked my head violently.

"Get off of me!" I shouted.

He laughed and pulled me to him, his hand gripped firmly around my arm. "Oh, so it's like that? How's my baby doing?" He tried to rub my stomach again.

"Myles, just go." I was trying not to cry. His touching

me reminded me of my loss. I couldn't believe he had come here. "Just please go."

"If I was you, I'd listen to the little lady. I wouldn't want to make her mad."

Myles slowly released his grip on my arm and scanned all six feet five inches of Reno. He was probably surveying whether he could take him on. I guess he decided he couldn't because he smiled. "Look, big man, this is between me and my woman."

"Seems to me like your woman don't want to be your woman no more," Reno said.

I guess Myles got a little juice in him because he stepped toward Reno. "Sounds like your big country ass don't know how to mind your own business." Myles poked Reno in the chest with his finger.

Bad move.

Reno kept his gaze steady as he quickly reached down, grabbed Myles's crotch, and twisted it. Myles yelled out in pain.

"As I was saying, you needs to be moving on, *little* man."

Reno released his grip and Myles fell to the ground, holding his crotch and moaning.

Reno stepped over Myles's writhing body and extended his hand toward me. I glanced at Myles, then took Reno's hand and let him lead me up the walkway to Mama Tee's house.

"You can't keep me from my child."

I calmly turned around. "There is no child, Myles. I lost my baby the day I tried to kill you, as you put it. That's why I came to the office in the first place, to tell you I lost the baby."

Myles paused like he was shocked. I could tell he hadn't anticipated that response.

"Have a good life, Myles." Reno opened the front door for me and I stepped inside the house.

"You can't leave me. I decide when this relationship is over!" Myles called out after us. Reno let the door slam on his shouts.

"Didn't I hear that he was supposed to be some kind of politician?" Reno asked once we were inside.

"Yeah, he puts on a huge act." I felt exhausted. "Do you want something to drink?"

"Some iced tea would be nice."

I smiled, then made my way into the kitchen. I looked around—Mama Tee always had some fresh-brewed tea somewhere. It was her trademark. I noticed the tea sitting on the windowsill, percolating in the sun. I grabbed the jar, poured Reno and myself a glass, then filled it with ice.

I returned to the living room and handed Reno a glass. He downed his drink in one long gulp.

"Thank you," he said, handing the glass back to me. He looked around. "Where's Mr. Frank?" he asked, motioning to the empty bed.

I took his glass. "His daughter came and got him, took him back with her to California. Mama Tee is at the hospital with Justin."

"How's he doing?" Reno asked.

"Much better, thank God."

Reno looked taken aback. I knew exactly what he was thinking. "Yes, I thanked God. It's amazing how a little adversity can make you start to look at things differently." I smiled.

"Wow. I'm glad to hear that. With God on your side, you can make it through anything. I was just talking with Mrs. Mary about Second Corinthians—"

"Hold on a minute. It's a slow walk for me. I don't know if I'm ready to start listening to Bible verses."

We both laughed. "I can respect that," Reno said. "I'm just happy to hear you're letting Him in your life, period, because you know that was always a source of contention with us."

Did I know. Even as teenagers, Reno was always up in the church. It got on my nerves. I think that's why Mama Tee liked him so much. When he got with Ann Paxton, it proved my point that there wasn't nothing but hypocrites in the church.

"I'll keep you in my prayers, Raedella."

I gently smiled at him. After all the years I'd spent trying to keep people from calling me by my full name, I welcomed it coming from Reno. "Yes, do that. Keep me in your prayers," I softly replied. Our gaze met and we stood in awkward silence for a few minutes.

"So, what were you doing up this way?" I finally said.

"Actually, I come and cut Mrs. Mary's grass next door every other week. I'd just finished when I saw your ex there grab you. You have to pardon my getting involved, but it ain't right for no man to be putting his hands on a woman."

I looked at Reno. He looked so mature, so handsome. I felt myself longing for his touch.

"Well, I'd better be getting on home," he said.

I don't know why, but I didn't want him to leave. Maybe I was just lonely, but I was really enjoying being around him again. "Can you stay and talk a bit?"

He hesitated before replying, "I guess I can stay a little while."

We sat down on Mama Tee's sofa and Reno filled me in on who had done what and with whom in the last seven years. He had me cracking up at some of the stories of our old classmates. He also informed me that Felton, the crazy boy who'd given me money for the abortion, had stalked him for nearly a year after I'd left, claiming Reno had run me off. In all, we talked for nearly two hours.

"So, tell me, why did you never try and leave here?" I asked.

Reno leaned back like he was thinking about it. "Not everyone wants big-city living. Some of us like our little country existence. Besides, I visited Miami a couple of years ago and had someone ask me if I wanted a burned CD, and I looked at him like he was crazy. I asked him, why would anyone want a CD that was burned up?"

I doubled over in laughter. That sounded so like something Reno would say. "You're still funny as all get out, Reno."

"I know. I'm expecting Hollywood to come calling any moment now." He grinned.

I hadn't realized how much I missed my conversations with Reno. I had forgotten how warm and loved he made me feel.

"What happened to us?" I said, my expression turning serious.

Reno shrugged. "Your big dreams." He smiled. "What do you think happened?"

I smiled back. "Ann Paxton."

"There you go with that." He playfully rolled his eyes. "No, I definitely think it was you and all your big dreams.

I'm not making excuses, but you were always degrading me. I think I just messed with Ann because she made me feel worthy."

"Oh, so you're admitting it now?" I joked.

Reno smiled mischievously. "I know you don't believe me, but I really did go in that motel room just to help her get her earring out the sink. But once we were inside, she started talking about how I deserved a woman who appreciated me. She made me feel good about myself and I guess I was just weak."

I lowered my eyes. "I'm sorry, Reno."

"No need to be sorry, Raedella. That was a lifetime ago. But you know you were my first true love."

I couldn't help but blush. After the way I'd treated him, this man was sitting here telling me how much he had loved me. Had I been so anxious to become the next big star that I was willing to throw that all away? I guess I was.

I looked in Reno's eyes, and I swear, I saw some of that love still there. I don't know what came over me, but the next thing I knew, I was leaning over and my lips had found their way to his. I kissed him and I could feel his resolve weakening.

But then just as quickly as he'd let himself kiss me back, he pulled away and stood up.

"Raedella," he said with his back to me.

I stood up, too, wrapping my arms around his waist. I knew he still loved me. He had never been able to resist me. I could see it in his eyes, feel it in his kiss.

"Do you still love me?" I whispered.

He turned toward me. "I will always love you."

I leaned in and tried to kiss him again.

He pushed me back with a force that caught me off guard. "But I love my wife more."

It felt like someone had slapped me with a brick.

"Raedella, I don't mean to hurt you. But you chose your life and forced me to choose mine. And although you feel like yours is crumbling, mine is still strong. And the glue that holds it together is my wife. I won't disrespect her, my marriage, or myself."

I stared at him and wanted to burst into tears. I had run from this? A man who respected his vows. A man who loved his wife so unconditionally that he wouldn't want to do anything to jeopardize it. I had run from that and to a man like Myles, who didn't know what the word *faithful* meant?

"I . . . I thought you said you loved me."

"I did, once upon a time." Reno wiped at the tears that were trickling down my cheeks. "Come on, Rae. You don't want me. I'm just a country boy who could never live up to your expectations. You're just feeling vulnerable right now. You know, all them hormones at work." He laughed, obviously trying to cheer me up.

"I'm sorry."

"Don't apologize. Just take this time for yourself. You thought being a star was what you wanted out of life. Now that you know it's not, take this time to find out what is."

Reno kissed me gently on the forehead and left me standing in the middle of the living room.

chapter 38

I leaned against the doorway and stared at my little brother as he lay across the sofa laughing at an episode of *The Steve Harvey Show.* My heart warmed at the sight of him laughing like a normal young man. It was hard to believe that it had been almost a month since he'd been released from the hospital. Although he was still moving about slowly, he was doing remarkably well.

"Hey, Sis," he said when he noticed me standing there. "Why are you staring at me like you're scared I'm gon' die any minute now?"

I walked into the room and sat down across from him. "I'm just worried about you, that's all."

"Well, I took a licking and kept on ticking. I fell down, but I got up." He smirked.

I threw a pillow at him. "You've been watching too much TV."

He laughed. I noticed a stack of comic books lying on

the coffee table. "Wow! The original *Incredible Hulk* comics. I haven't seen those in years."

"Yeah, Ma . . . I mean Rose bought them for me. They're collector's items." He turned back toward the television. "She's recovering well, too. She dropped the comic books off yesterday. She also left you a letter. It's in the kitchen by the phone."

"I'm not interested in her letters," I mumbled.

"Raedella, she's really sorry," Justin said, still not looking at me. "I just think you should know that."

I debated whether I should say something to him. He knew about Rose's desertion, but he was too young to really be affected by it. Unless, of course, you count not having your mother around. But his hatred for Rose was nowhere near as strong as mine and Shondella's. Rose had also just saved his life. Of course, he would feel a little sympathy for her.

"Let's not talk about Rose, okay?"

He shrugged. "Whatever."

"Where's Mama Tee?"

"In the kitchen." He glanced toward the kitchen, his demeanor quickly changing. "Look here, can you convince her to let me go to Freaknik this weekend? Tyrone an' 'nem are going and they asked me if I wanted to go." He sighed heavily as he shook his head. "It's a shame. I'm a grown man and I have to ask my grandmother if I can go somewhere." Justin frowned.

"You know why that is." In addition to the complications from leukemia, Justin was prone to seizures that to this day none of the doctors had been able to explain. Justin had almost died when he was fourteen and Mama Tee let him go fishing with some of his cousins. He'd had a seizure and they'd had no idea what to do. Luckily, a doctor was fishing nearby and was able to help them out. But from that day, Mama Tee hardly let Justin out of her sight.

"Anyway, do you want me to get in the middle of that? Why don't you ask Mama Tee yourself?"

"Ask me what?"

We both looked up at Mama Tee, standing in the living room doorway. Justin looked like he was debating whether to say anything. Finally, he spoke up. "I was just telling Raedella that I'm rolling out to Freaknik this weekend," Justin boldly proclaimed. He defiantly pursed his lips before turning back to the TV.

"You gon' to what 'nik?" Mama Tee asked, confusion etched across her brow.

"Freaknik. In Atlanta. I'm going with my boys," Justin replied with a little more bass in his voice than usual.

"Oh, you are, are you? And what happens when you break out in a seizure or you fall deathly ill? Your boys gon' stop their skirt-chasing long enough to see after you?" Mama Tee was looking at Justin like he was crazy.

"I'll cross that bridge when I come to it. But I'm going." Justin stood up. I was dumbfounded, watching him be so defiant. "I'm sick of y'all treating me like some invalid little boy. I'm twenty-three years old. I'm grown, despite what everyone around here thinks."

The room fell silent as Justin glared at Mama Tee. Mama Tee glared right back, her chest slowly rising and falling. I'm sure she was just as shocked as me. This was totally out of character for Justin.

"You must be high on painkillers, 'cuz you done lost your mind!" Mama Tee huffed.

Justin didn't back down. "I'm going and ain't nothing nobody can do to stop me."

I stood up because I just knew Mama Tee was about to bust him in his jaw.

"Boy, don't let your mouth write a check your ass can't cash," she hissed.

"Whatever." Justin flicked Mama Tee off, and I swear I felt the fury rise from her body.

"Did this little fool just flick me off?" she screamed to no one in particular. "I know he did not just flick me off." She looked around like she was trying to find something to knock Justin upside the head with. I decided it was about time for me to jump in.

"Mama Tee, calm down. Justin is just trippin'."

"Oh, he gon' be trippin' all right. Trippin' all over the furniture while I tear his behind up." Mama Tee, I guess deciding she didn't need an object, lunged toward Justin. I jumped in front of her just as she was about to make contact with his head.

Justin scurried out of the way, his confidence gone, replaced by a look of terror. Mama Tee caught herself, I guess realizing she couldn't outrun Justin. "That boy done gone plumb crazy. He smelling his own piss," she yelled at me. "Gon' try and flick me off, like he all big and bad." She waved her finger at Justin, who was cowering behind the sofa. "Don't you forget, I used to wash that funky little behind of yours, boy." Mama Tee took another deep breath in an effort to calm herself down. "I'm goin' outside to work in my garden before I hurt somebody. Send that boy back to the hospital." Mama Tee walked off muttering, "It's them damn videos. Watching that Two Quarters boy all the time got him thinking he tough." I couldn't make out the rest of what she was saying as she slammed the door behind her.

I turned back to Justin, who was easing out from behind the sofa. "What is she talking about, Two Quarters boy?" I asked.

"50 Cent, the rapper. That's what she calls him, Two Quarters." Justin sank back on the sofa.

I couldn't help but laugh as I sat down next to him. "Only Mama Tee would come up with something like that." My laughter faded as I noticed the scowl still plastered across Justin's face. "You want to tell me what that was about?"

Justin shrugged. "I'm just tired of everybody treating me like a kid, that's all. I'm a man. I'm ready for people to start treating me like one."

I stared at my little brother. He had grown into a handsome young man. His butterscotch complexion was smooth. His eyes were a beautiful shade of hazel. I could only imagine what he was feeling. But I also understood Mama Tee's point as well. Taking care of Justin had been a full-time job and one she'd done without complaint. A job she should've never been saddled with in the first place. At that point, I felt even more contempt for Rose and knew that no matter how many kidneys she tried to give up, there was no turning back. As far as I was concerned, our family was irreparably damaged and there was no one to blame but my mother.

chapter 39

I stared at my little windup clock. I couldn't believe I had been asleep two whole hours. Maybe everything had calmed down after Mama Tee's blowup. I peeked out the window to see if she was still working off steam in her garden. She wasn't.

I got up, went into the bathroom, and splashed some cold water on my face. I made my way into the kitchen, where I noticed the letter from Rose still lying on the counter. She had had the audacity to draw a rose on the envelope. That woman wouldn't give up. Where was all this dedication when I was growing up?

Mama Tee was sitting at the kitchen table shelling peas. Shondella was sitting next to her helping. She watched me as I picked the letter up, walked over, and dropped it in the trash. "So you not gon' read it?" Mama Tee asked.

"Why bother? You calmed down?"

"I'm fine. It's that brother of yours you need to be worried about," Mama Tee responded. "Now, I'll ask you again, you don't plan on reading the letter?"

"No, I don't, and I'd appreciate it if you'd just drop it."

Mama Tee dropped the peas she had just shelled into a large tin bowl. She motioned to the chair across from her. "Sit down, gal."

"Mama Tee, I really don't have—"

"Did that sound like a request? If it did, I need to say it again, because it wasn't a request. Now, sit your tail down."

Shondella snickered. I wanted to say something. Like Justin, tell Mama Tee I was a grown woman. But it wouldn't be beneath Mama Tee to take her shoe off and knock me upside my head. When I was fifteen, I watched her take her Sunday pump off and toss it at Uncle Clyde, hitting him square in the center of his head. I don't even remember what it was he said, but it was enough to make Mama Tee's nostrils flare up before she took off her shoe and threw it. I sat down without uttering a word.

"Before you start, let me tell you, there's nothing you can say to get me to change my mind about Rose," I said.

Mama Tee shook her head, then looked at Shondella.

"Don't even look at me. Because you know I ain't got no love for her. That's why she don't even bother me." Shondella scooted her chair back to get up from the table.

"Sit down!" Mama Tee snapped. "You two gon' drive me to an early grave. Now, hush up. I got something I want to say 'bout yo mama."

"Rose," I said. "She ain't my mama."

"Like it or not, she gon' always be your mama. Contrary to some convoluted—yeah, I said *convoluted*—I know some big words, too. Contrary to your convoluted belief, you can't just decide someone ain't gon' be your family no more. This is the family God gave you and ain't nothing you can do to change that. And that family includes your mama."

"But Mama Tee, she left us. She never tried to get back in contact with us. I can't get over that," I said.

"Well, you need to get over it. Besides, it wasn't all your mama."

"What is that supposed to mean?" I asked.

Mama Tee's look softened. "I swore I'd never tell you girls this, but I need to. Your mother did try to see you kids. I wouldn't let her."

We looked at Mama Tee in disbelief.

"There. I said it. She tried many, many times to see you all. Even tried to get you all back at one point. Threatened to call the police and tell them I kidnapped her kids."

"Mama Tee, you don't have to make up stories to try and get us to forgive Rose," Shondella said.

Mama Tee clenched her teeth and bawled up her fist. "Girl, if I wasn't saved, I'd bust you in yo' jaw."

Shondella leaned back, rolling her eyes.

"And don't think you too old for me to snatch them eyes right out of your head. Everybody losing their damn minds!" Mama Tee released her fist and exhaled. "Anyway, as I was saying, your mama tried to call you all, but I wouldn't let her. She wasn't clean."

"What does that mean, wasn't clean?" I asked.

"I know you're not that dang naive," Shondella said. "She was a junkie."

I was dumbfounded. I mean, I knew that she dabbled

in drugs, but a junkie? Why did I not remember that? I know I was little, but it seems I would recall something like that. I turned to Shondella. "Did you know she was a junkie?"

"Yeah, I knew. I think after she sold the TV I kinda figured it all out."

"But . . . how . . ." I was at a loss for words.

"It was that boyfriend of hers. Sam. He got her hooked," Mama Tee said. "She was high and not thinking straight the night she brought y'all here. I told her that if she ever stayed clean for more than six months, I'd gladly give y'all back to her. But I wasn't about to let y'all go back to her until she had her act together. So if you want to hate somebody, hate me."

Shondella and I were both quiet. Okay, so the news had us speechless. But as far as I was concerned, it didn't change anything.

"The bottom line is, she chose Sam over us. And when Sam didn't want her anymore, she came trying to reclaim us." Shondella said exactly what I was thinking.

"I understand that, and I'm not saying you have to ever forget that. Just maybe you ought to think about forgiving her." Mama Tee rocked back and forth while we let her words sink in. "The Bible said—"

Shondella stood up, disgusted. "Pardon my French, Mama Tee, but it will be a cold day in hell before I let that woman back into my life." She banged on the kitchen window. "Lexus, Mercedes! Get your sisters and come on."

"So that's your answer, Shondella? Just run away. That's always been your answer, just leave," Mama Tee said.

Shondella glared at Mama Tee as her kids came running inside. I could've sworn I saw her fighting back tears.

"Yeah, that's how I deal with my problems, Mama Tee. I just leave. But I come by it honestly, don't you think?"

With that, Shondella grabbed Camry's hand, spun, and stomped out of the kitchen with all of her children close on her heels.

Mama Tee didn't say anything for several minutes after Shondella left, then finally said, "That gal's anger gon' be the death of her."

"But, Mama Tee, can you blame her?" I couldn't believe I was coming to my sister's aid, but I definitely felt her on this one.

"You think y'all the only people ever been abandoned by their parents? You wasn't the first and you ain't gon' be the last."

"It's not just that, Mama Tee, she's the reason . . . she's the reason . . . Jasmine . . ." Suddenly, images of Jasmine started flashing through my mind. I put my hands over my eyes and tried to keep from sobbing. I couldn't even get my sentence out, I had gotten so worked up.

"The reason Jasmine what? Died? I told you that God was just ready to take Jasmine home. Ain't no sense in rehashing Jasmine's death, because if it was her time, it was just her time. And ain't nothing you, Rose, or anyone else could've done about it. So don't even go down that road again."

It was too late. The memories had already come rushing back.

I threw the sheet over the clothesline, cursing as I squeezed the clothespin and locked the sheet down. I was mad because not only was I having to hang the clothes up, but I was being forced to watch Jasmine again. Shondella had gone with Mama Tee to take Justin to Little Rock for some medical treatment. I was thirteen years old. Who makes a thirteen-year-old watch a six-year-old all day long? I had to stay home from school and everything, and today was the day Jimmy Lee had told my friend Shana that he planned to kiss me after school.

I looked over at Jasmine playing with King, Mama Tee's seven-year-old mutt. She made me sick. I wasn't her mama, so why did I have to be stuck with her all day? But then again, everybody always acted like I was her mama, making me do everything for her. Shondella had a part-time job to help Mama Tee with the bills, so everything at the house fell on my shoulders. Cook, clean, take care of Jasmine and Justin. I hated my life.

"Dang, girl, you sho' looking good hanging up them clothes."

The sound of Jimmy Lee's voice brought me out of my funk. "Hey, Jimmy Lee, what you doing here?" I said, dropping the basket of clothes and plastering on a huge smile.

"Didn't Shana tell you what I wanted to do to you after school today?"

I blushed and started fidgeting with my charm bracelet. Jimmy Lee was fifteen years old and one of the best-looking boys in Sweet Poke. He had wavy, good hair, deep brown eyes, and sandpaper-colored skin. He was already six feet tall and had bowlegs that just drove all the girls crazy. My heart was beating so fast, I thought it was going to pop right out of my chest. "Yeah, she told me."

"So, why you didn't come to school then? You made

me come all the way over here." He leaned against Mama Tee's old woodshed.

"I'm sorry. I had to stay home and watch my little sister today."

"Dang, you're just a little girl yourself."

I was offended that he saw me as a little girl. "No, I'm not."

He leaned in closer. "Oh, really? Show me then that you ain't no little girl."

"What does that mean?" I said, trying to stick my little, barely A-cup breasts out.

Jimmy Lee looked around. "Let's go in the woodshed so you can show me just how much of a woman you are."

I blushed again. This time a nervous charge shot up my body. I had kissed a couple of boys already, but no one as fine as Jimmy Lee.

"Jimmy Lee, I . . . I just don't know. I'm supposed to be watching my sister."

He moved in and whispered in my ear. "Come on, baby."

I inhaled deeply. Mama Tee would skin me alive if she caught me in the woodshed with Jimmy Lee. But then again, she did tell me they wouldn't be back until well after dark.

My hesitation must've been frustrating him because he threw up his hands. "You know what? Forget it. I told you, you were a little girl. Now, your cousin Nikki, she's only twelve, and she's already trying to get with me," he said, stroking his hairless chin.

Nikki? That skank knew I liked Jimmy Lee. That was just like her, to try to get with him. "But—"

"But nothing," Jimmy responded. "I just want to kiss

you, that's all. It won't take but a minute. Your sister will be all right."

I glanced over at Jasmine again, running around and around in circles with King.

"Besides, you ain't her mama. Why you gotta be responsible for her? All you ever do is babysit and take care of the house like somebody mama."

Jimmy Lee must have been reading my mind. If there was anything I needed to convince me to follow my heart, that was it. "Come on," I said, as I pulled him into the shed.

I don't know how long we were in the shed. I just knew I was feeling good when I heard King's incessant barking. I tried to block it out as Jimmy Lee sucked on my neck, but then I heard King's paws on the woodshed.

"Hold on, Jimmy. Let me see what's going on."

"Unh-unh," Jimmy moaned. "In a minute."

It was feeling good, but I was starting to get scared. Besides, King's barking and scratching at the door was distracting me. "Wait, wait."

That's when I heard it. A bloodcurdling scream that sent me racing out of the shed and into the backyard. I don't remember much after that. Just the screams coming from my auntie Mel, and Jasmine's lifeless body floating in Mama Tee's pond.

"You're not to blame for Jasmine's death and neither is your mama." Mama Tee's voice snapped me out of my thoughts. I didn't realize I was crying.

"It is my fault."

"You did have your fast little tail in there with that no good Jimmy Lee, who, by the way, is in prison now.

Did I tell you that? Anyway, no, you didn't have any business in there, but it wasn't your fault. It was just her time, that's all."

As best as could be determined, Jasmine had wandered over to the pond trying to chase her ball. She must've gotten too close and fallen in. King was soaking wet, so it was believed he had jumped in to try to save her. But in the end, the medical examiner said her lungs had quickly filled with water and she died in a matter of seconds.

I was devastated by what happened. Shondella had called me a dirty whore and every other name under the sun. Even at Jasmine's funeral, which I hadn't wanted to attend, people were staring at me, whispering. I think that's when I really and truly began to have a deep hatred for Sweet Poke.

"Why did you all leave her with me? I was only a child," I sobbed. We had never talked about that day. After Jasmine's death, I shut down for a while. Especially when Rose didn't even show up for the funeral. Nobody even knew how to get in touch with her to tell her Jasmine had died.

"Baby, we have to pull together in this family. And that means sometimes children got to do adult things. I'm sorry if you didn't have the Girl Scout, slumber-party childhood you think you was entitled to, but this is the life you was given, so this is the life you had to deal with."

I tried to picture Jasmine's angelic face. I couldn't. I had blocked images of her out of my mind for so long, they were no longer even there.

"First, you blamed yourself," Mama Tee continued, "then you blamed your mama because she wasn't here. Then you figured you'd just run away and forget us all, forget your life here, and that would make everything okay. I guess you see by now it don't work like that."

I wiped my tears away. I didn't care what Mama Tee said, I would always feel responsible for Jasmine's death. And part of me would always blame Rose. "Maybe if Rose had been there, I would've had more respect than to be in that shed with Jimmy. Maybe if she had been there, she could've been watching Jasmine instead of me."

"If, if was a fifth, we'd all be rich," Mama Tee said.

I looked at her in confusion. "What does that mean?" I sniffed.

"It means you'll get nowhere talking about, if only this, if only that." Mama Tee sighed. "Baby girl, it's time to move on. It's time to let go of the past, let go of the hatred and the pain and try to forgive yourself. Stop running from the past, face it, conquer it, and look to the future. Let go and let God."

I weighed her words. What she was asking seemed impossible, but I wanted to try anything to heal my heart. "Mama Tee, I'm sorry." I scooted closer to her and laid my head in her lap. "I'm so sorry.

She gently stroked my hair. "I know, baby. I know."

chapter 40

I could not believe I was doing this. Sneaking around Piggly Wiggly, following Reno's wife as she shopped for groceries. I had to see what it was about her that made Reno so committed to her. From her outside appearance, there was not much to her. So she had to have a dynamic personality or something. I watched her as she compared Bisquick pancake mix with the generic brand. She opted for the generic.

She turned toward me. I pretended to be looking at the various brands of flour.

"Hello, Raedella."

I stood up tall, trying to save face. "Umm, hello." I faked confusion. "Do I know you?"

She snickered. "Not really, but you know my husband."

I diverted my gaze down. I couldn't help it; she made me feel so uncomfortable.

"It's all right." She touched my arm. "Reno told me all about you. He told me about how he cheated on you and lost you. He also told me about your baby. I'm really sorry."

Why was this woman being so nice to me? I wondered if she would be as cordial if she knew I had tried to seduce her husband.

"I also know your history with my husband," she continued.

I didn't know if she was about to go off on me or what.

"What Reno and I had was a long time ago," I said, looking her straight in her eyes.

"I know that. You're his past. I'm his present and his future," she said, a huge smile across her face. "Don't get me wrong. I know he still cares for you. He told me about the other day at your grandmother's house."

I half-expected her to change her demeanor and curse me or something. I was amazed when she continued talking calmly.

"I don't have to issue any threats, get mad, or anything of that nature. I trust my husband with all of my heart. God has cemented our relationship, and not you, or any other woman, can break that bond." She smiled again and walked off with such confidence that I was speechless. I felt a huge lump forming in my throat. She was a heavyset woman who wore no makeup. Although she was plain looking, she had a sort of natural beauty. But the most striking thing about her was that she seemed so at peace. I guess you can be that way when you have faith in your marriage, faith in God. That's something I knew nothing about.

As I stood in the checkout line, Reno's wife's words

kept ringing in my head. *God has cemented our relationship.* How could anyone feel that passionately about someone?

"She can't hold a candle to you, baby."

I turned around to face Rose, who was standing right behind me in the line.

"How you doing?" she asked when I didn't say anything.

"What, are you following me now?"

Rose laughed. "No, I haven't resorted to that yet. I was just doing some grocery shopping myself."

"Humph."

"I wouldn't be ashamed to tell you if I were following you." She looked at me somberly. We stood in awkward silence.

"You feeling okay?" I finally asked.

"I'm doing fine. I'm just glad Justin took the transplant with no problems."

"Yeah, well, we'll see if it takes." I fidgeted with my purse. Why was I even standing there talking to her?

"Justin doing okay? I want to stop by and see him, but I don't want to cause any trouble."

"He's doing well." I hesitated. "That was a good thing you did for him."

"It was the least I could do."

"You got that right." I didn't want her to think she was getting to me.

Rose sighed. "Can we go talk? We can walk across the street to Murphy's Deli."

"Rose, I really don't have anything to say to you."

"Please. Just hear me out. If you give me fifteen minutes, I'll leave you alone after that."

I contemplated it. Fifteen minutes to get rid of her forever. Besides, maybe if I could get some answers, I could move on myself.

"Fine." I set the bread and juice I was holding on a shelf.

"I can get that for you."

I glared at her. "I'm more than capable of paying for my own groceries." My voice softened when I noticed how she shrank back. "I'll just come back for them later."

At Murphy's, we both ordered coffee and bagels. After the waitress left, I looked into Rose's eyes. They were the eyes of a woman who had been to hell and back. I shook my head, trying to get rid of any sympathy that might have been creeping into my body.

"I don't know where to begin."

"How about D-day."

"D-day? What's that?"

"That's what we've always called the day you abandoned us. Drop-off day. So tell me, what kind of mother would drop off her kids in a strange place so she could run off with her boyfriend?"

"A confused one."

"Confused? Is that the best you can do?"

"Sugar Smack, I made a lot of mistakes in my life, getting involved with Sam, drugs, not finishing high school. But my biggest was letting go of my kids. But you gotta understand, times were hard."

"No, I don't have to understand. I can't and never will understand."

She kept on speaking in the same calm manner, as if I hadn't said anything. "I couldn't find a job. Sam wasn't working. I let him convince me that things would be so much easier for us if we didn't have any kids to worry about. I know it's dumb now. But the heroin was clouding my judgment. I just wanted the pain of being unhappy to go away."

Rose fiddled with her bracelet before continuing. "When I left Sweet Poke with Sam, I knew I was wrong. I mean, he was your daddy's friend, a friend who had taken the life of the only man who ever really loved me. I knew Sam never meant to kill your daddy. They were both drunk and out of control that night. So three years after your daddy died, when the twin's daddy ran out on me, I found myself alone and broke with four kids. I was desperate.

"You know how much you wanted to get out of this place? That was me ten times over. I wanted out of here. I felt like I was suffocating here. I had dreams. I didn't want to be poor and destined to a life in this town. But I had baby after baby and that's just what happened."

"We didn't ask to be born," I interrupted.

"I know that," Rose responded. "I loved you all, I did, but I just knew my dreams would never be fulfilled. Then Sam asked me to leave Sweet Poke with him. I thought that would be my chance to finally realize my dream of a better life. But we moved to Lake Charles and things went from bad to worse. Pretty soon we were both so strung out on drugs that life was even worse than it was when we were in Sweet Poke."

I listening intently, shocked at her desire to get out of Sweet Poke. It had mirrored mine. Would I have ended up like her if I had stayed? Could I have followed in her footsteps? I shook off those thoughts. No, I never would've abandoned my children.

"I wanted you all to have a better life," she continued. "I ran from the life God had given me in hopes that I could find one better."

"Well, did you?"

She shook her head. "Never." Her eyes filled with tears. "My babies haunted me night and day. I fell asleep and woke up with you all on my mind. I had nightmares. I was depressed and couldn't function. So much so that I couldn't even be a good woman to Sam. That's why he got involved with another woman. Our life had become so miserable. Then I had nothing but the drugs, so I got in deeper and deeper. I tried to let them go and get you back, but it was hard, so hard."

"I don't have a child, but I believe I could give up *anything* for him."

"That's easy to say, but when you're in that situation, it's just not so easy to do, especially when the only solace I ever found was in drugs." Rose wiped at the tears trickling down her cheeks.

"Am I supposed to feel sorry for you?" I asked with disdain.

"I don't want your sympathy. Just your understanding, that's all. And I want my family back. God knows I want my family back."

I stood up. I was tired of talking to her. "Both Shondella and I had to grow up too fast. Mama Tee was too old to raise four kids. Justin needed your care. And Jasmine . . . you didn't even come say good-bye to Jasmine. No, Rose. That I'll never understand." I turned and walked off, part of me not caring if I ever saw my mother again, the other desperate to leave before I burst into tears myself.

chapter 41

I never did make it back inside to pick up the groceries I was buying before I ran into Rose. When I left her, I was so flustered that I just wanted to drive around for a while. I hopped into the used Maxima I had purchased last week after selling my car to one of Shereen's friends. I didn't know where I was headed; I just lowered the window and took in the fresh air as I drove around town.

I couldn't believe all the memories that came flooding back as I drove around Sweet Poke. Surprisingly, besides the images of Jasmine, the memories swirling through my mind were all good. All these years and I'd only recalled the negative things about my life in Sweet Poke.

I slowed down as I neared Dr. Warrington's office. He was the main doctor in Sweet Poke and the man who had calmed my fears when I'd got my finger stuck in Mama Tee's spare tire when I was ten years old. We were supposed to be raking up leaves, but I had gotten bored and started fooling around in Mama Tee's trunk. Don't ask me why, but I just decided to stick my finger in one of the holes on the rim of the spare tire. But then it wouldn't come out. I sat back there for twenty minutes trying to get it out. By the time Mama Tee discovered me, my finger had swollen so much that the only option was to take me to Dr. Warrington. I remember being so embarrassed when I had to ride in the trunk down to the doctor's office. His whole staff had laughed at me as they called the people from Firestone to come cut my finger out. But Dr. Warrington acted like it was no big deal, even telling me he had just removed a kid's arm from a gas tank the week before. He probably just made that up, but it made me relax nonetheless.

I smiled at the memory as I slowly headed toward the dike. That was another place we used to play. Aunt Ola lived right next to the dike, and growing up we used to spend countless hours at her house, throwing rocks off the small cliff, and the brave ones jumping off the cliff into the lake below. I parked, got out, and went looking for a rock to throw for old times' sake. I tossed a couple of rocks, then leaned back against the car, enjoying the scenery.

I guess I was so engrossed in my thoughts that I didn't see the heavyset man until he was right up on me. His hair was matted, his teeth a horrid brownish yellow, and he had a crazed look about him. It took a moment before I realized who it was.

"Felton?" I said as I looked him up and down.

"Hey there, Rae baby. Long time no see," he slurred.

I was amazed at how unkempt he looked. Even though we were the same age, he looked like he was pushing fifty years old. "What are you doing out here?" I asked.

"I've been wondering when you was gon' give me a call."

I looked at him like he was crazy. "Why in the world would I call you?"

"Oh, so it's like that, huh?" He moved closer to me. I took two steps back. The stench of liquor permeated his clothes. I felt repulsed.

"Felton, what are you talking about?"

"I miss you so much, baby," he said as he reached out to me. "It's been a long time since I seen you. Can I at least get a hug?"

I was getting an uneasy feeling in my stomach. Something about the look in his eyes didn't set right with me.

"I'll ask you again," I said, backing up even more. "What are you doing out here?"

"What, you think you own this place or something? For your information, I been keeping up with you. I called you all the time at your fancy TV station just to hear your voice on the answering machine. I'll admit, I would get angry from time to time and say some pretty hateful things, but I never really meant them." He wiped at some drool that was trickling down his chin.

I knew I recognized that voice. "You're the one who has been leaving me those messages? Why?"

Felton started nervously rubbing his pants legs. "You make me so mad, Rae. I have loved you since we were kids, and you never gave me a second look." He started pacing back and forth. "Then I thought, maybe if I try to be her friend, she'll give me a chance, but noooo. I was never good enough for you."

He was definitely scaring me now.

"Then, you came to me after that big, Amazon-looking boyfriend of yours knocked you up. He wouldn't help you, but I did. Me! I stole my mama's rainy-day money for you and you didn't even appreciate it!"

"Felton, I did appreciate it." I moved toward my car, trying to talk as calmly as possible.

"Liar!" he screamed just as he reached out and snatched my car keys from my hands. He threw them over the cliff before turning back to me. "My mama beat me silly for taking her money, but I didn't care because it was for you. And you didn't even say thank you!"

Felton was shaking now and I was ready to make a run for it because he seemed like he was losing control. "I drove down to Houston many, many times and would just follow you around. I was hoping that one day you'd come around and come back to me."

"Felton, I don't know what ever gave you the idea you and I were anything more than friends." I tried to discreetly survey the area and see which way I could make a quick getaway.

"You did, you little tease," he snarled. "But, I know you probably laughed at me the whole time: 'Ha-ha, I took the slow boy's money.' "

"Felton, I never called you slow."

"Shut up lying!" His chest was heaving up and down. Just when I thought he was calming down, he said, "You owe me. Not just for the money I stole, but for leading me on and making me wait this long."

I knew he was delusional, but at that point I could tell there would be no reasoning with him. I knew there wasn't but one thing I could do—run for my life. I darted around Felton and took off. I didn't make it two feet before he had me by my hair. He threw me against the hood of my car.

"You little tramp. I'ma teach you to lead people on."

Felton had me pinned to the car with one hand while the other worked feverishly to unbuckle his pants.

I was in shock. I couldn't understand where all of this was coming from. Yes, I took Felton's money, but I never led him on. "No! Please don't," I cried as I tried to break free from his grip.

"Oh, don't act like you don't want it." He tried to kiss me on my neck. Slobber ran down the side of my neck.

"Felton, get off of me!" I screamed.

"Come on, baby. Don't fight it. I missed you so much."

I felt sick to the stomach. I was not about to be raped on the hood of my car.

"Please, God, don't let this happen," I softly prayed. "I know I haven't been a good servant, but please don't let him do this to me."

"Shut up," he said as he tore at my skirt. "Can't nobody hear you. Not even God."

God can always hear you, even when we don't think He's listening, Mama Tee's voice echoed in my head. *He'll give you strength to make it through anything.*

Mama Tee's words snapped me out of my daze. I was strong enough to make it through. I had to think fast.

Felton eased up off me to pull his pants down, and I used that moment to make a break for it. I kicked him in between his legs with all my might and took off running. He doubled over and screamed in agony. I desperately ran toward Aunt Ola's house.

"Help!" I said, banging on the door. "Aunt Ola!"

I couldn't tell if someone was home. Four cars were sitting in the driveway, but knowing Aunt Ola's sons, none of the cars were working.

"Help me, somebody, please!" I continued to scream.

Just when I was about to turn away and keep running, I heard the lock click. The door swung open and Scooter stood there in a pair of boxer shorts. He looked like he had been sleeping.

"What the hell you want? Banging all on the door, waking people up," he asked, staring me up and down.

"Scooter, help me, please. Felton"—I pointed to the dike—"Felton just tried to rape me."

Scooter peered toward the dike. "Who?"

"Felton. Felton Peterson."

"That slow boy who lives across the tracks?"

I nodded.

"What you doing at the dike with him?"

"Scooter, please, can you just let me in so I can call the police?"

Scooter moved to open the screen door, then stopped. "Wait a minute. When we came to you for help, you blew us off."

"Scooter, please. That was different. There wasn't anything I could do."

"You wouldn't even try. Now Kevin is locked up forever."

I started crying. "Please, just call the police for me."

Scooter scratched his head. "Ummm, let me see what were your words? Oh, yeah." He snapped his fingers. "'There's nothing I can ever do for you. So get off my property before I call security.'" With, that Scooter slammed the door in my face.

chapter 42

I was leaning up against my car, giving the police officer a full description of what had happened with Felton. They had arrested him as he'd walked back to his house, and I could only pray that they would lock him up for a long time.

After I had left Scooter, I walked nearly a mile to find a phone to call the police. The officer actually passed me on my way to the phone. I guess my torn skirt and ragged expression made him stop.

Turns out, Scooter had called the police after all. I guess I deserved what he had done. Despite how I'd acted, he still couldn't turn his back on me.

"Even though I can't stand your bougie butt, you still family," he'd said when I'd called him back on the officer's cell phone to thank him for calling the police.

Why was it that everyone got the concept of family but me?

"So, do you have any idea why Felton would try and attack you?" the officer asked.

"He seemed . . . he seemed deranged." That was the only word I could use to describe him. The officer scribbled something down on a piece of paper, then tore it off and handed it to me. "This is your case number. He's already done time for rape and is on probation. So he should get some hard time." I nodded numbly as I took the piece of paper. I was just about to ask him for a ride home when a red Taurus came speeding up. Rose parked the car and jumped out.

"Are you okay?" She looked like she had been crying.

"I'm fine. What are you doing here?"

"Scooter called me and said you'd been attacked." Rose grabbed me and hugged me. "Oh, God, I'm so glad you're okay. I was scared to death that something had happened to you. I prayed all the way over here." She was holding me so tight I could hardly breathe.

"Rose, I'm fine," I said, trying to wriggle from her grasp. I was stunned at how frantic she looked and shocked at how touched I felt by her concern.

Rose released her grip and smoothed down my hair. "Oh, baby. I know you hate me, but I would just die if something happened to you."

I stared at my mother. Her words seemed so genuine. She was making me uncomfortable.

"Don't worry about me. I was able to get away before Felton did anything."

"Felton? You knew the person who attacked you?"

That reminded me of how little my mother knew about me. Every one of my family members knew Felton. "Yeah, he's an old classmate. Anyway, I don't want to talk about that. I just want to go home and lie down."

"Is there anything I can do?"

Rose was getting on my nerves with all this motherly concern. I didn't know if I was more frustrated because she was bothering me, or because she was actually getting to me. "Rose, I will say it again. The only thing you can do for me is leave me alone."

Rose stared at me, a determined look across her face. "I left you alone once. As God is my witness, I'll never do it again."

I stared at her as Mama Tee's words rang in my head. Did I need to forgive her and move on? *Could* I forgive her and move on?

We stood in silence for a few minutes. Finally it dawned on me: I didn't have my keys, and since Felton had tossed them off the cliff, the chances of my finding them were slim to none. No one was at the house to bring me my spare keys. Mama Tee had taken Justin in for a checkup and Shondella was at work.

"Look, can you give me a ride to the house? I need to get my spare keys," I said finally.

Rose tried to ward off a smile. "It would be my pleasure."

We hadn't been in the car five minutes before she spoke. "I'm sorry. I know I promised to leave you alone at the grocery store today, but honestly, I can't."

I sighed, too tired to argue with her.

"You really are a beautiful woman. I am so proud of you."

I cut my eyes at her. I wanted to say something smart, but I just couldn't form the words. I don't know if it was because I was just that exhausted or because I liked hearing her compliment me.

"You know, Mama Tee used to say, 'Anything worth having is worth working for,' " Rose said as she pulled into Mama Tee's driveway. "I'm willing to do whatever it takes, for however long it takes, to make things right. Not only with you, but Shondella and Justin, too. I know it won't be easy, but I won't give up. I've prayed on it and asked God to give me the strength to see this through, and He has."

I stared at her as I prepared to get out of the car. I didn't know what to say. "Thanks for the ride."

"Rae," she said, placing her hand on my arm, "I love you."

I simply did not know how to respond, but *I love you, too* was definitely not an option. Something else that was not an option was letting her know that she was finally getting to me, and a piece of me—albeit a little piece—really wanted to forgive and forget. Unfortunately, as Rose said, that was so much easier said than done.

chapter 43

"Today is the first day of the rest of your life."

Why did it seem like Oprah was talking directly to me when she said that? I was lying across the sofa in Mama Tee's living room. Pretty much the same thing I'd been doing for the last few weeks. I don't know if it was watching *Oprah* and *Dr. Phil* daily, but I was starting to feel empowered. Like I wanted to do something productive once again.

"Why you sitting there smiling like a sissy with a bag full—"

"Mama Tee!" I cut her off. She had just walked in the room and I hadn't even noticed her standing there staring at me.

"What?"

"You sure have a filthy mouth to be such a Christian." I laughed.

"The Lord knows I try to be a good servant, but He

also know I got a crazy family. So He gives me a pass from time to time. Now, what you watching that got you smiling like you done hit the lotto?" Mama Tee plopped down on the sofa next to me.

"Oh, I was just thinking about what Oprah said. Today is the first day of the rest of my life," I said dreamily.

"I been telling you that since you was ten years old. But I guess I ain't got a gazillion dollars, so I'm no expert."

I leaned in and hugged Mama Tee, nuzzling my head against her neck. "No, Mama Tee, you know I was just hardheaded and wouldn't listen."

"Umm-hmmm."

We sat in comfortable silence before Mama Tee finally said, "I got something better than Oprah." She stood up and walked over to her television stand. She sifted through a box before pulling out a tape. "Now, this is who you need to be listening to." Mama Tee popped the tape in. A pretty, chocolate-skinned woman came up on the screen. She was in the pulpit of a massive church, preaching to what looked like ten thousand people.

"Who is that?"

"Her name is Juanita Bynum," Mama Tee said with admiration. "They call her a prophetess."

"I've heard of her. I've just never heard her preach."

"You know I ain't into these new-school preachers, and Lord knows I ain't never heard of no woman preacher in my day, but that woman sho' can preach."

Mama Tee returned to the sofa and we watched Juanita deliver a rousing sermon.

I was amazed. It was like Juanita was speaking directly to me. I don't think I'd ever had anyone move me like she did.

"Wow," I said when the tape finally finished.

"Wow is right," Mama Tee said as she got up and popped the tape out. "Told you that gal is good." She turned to me. "I hope you was listening."

I nodded. "I was."

Mama Tee nodded as well, a pleased look across her face. She grabbed a clothes basket from the corner. "I'm gon' to take the clothes off the line. You think about what that lady preacher said."

I sat and reflected on everything I'd just heard. I'd kept cursing God for all the bad I felt He had done to me, but I'd never looked at the good.

Mama Tee returned and sat back down next to me. "I just want to say I'm sorry," I told her.

"Sorry for what?" Shondella had appeared in the doorway, all of her kids in tow. "Y'all go outside and play," she said, shooing them away.

"But, Mama, we wanna watch TV," Lexus whined.

"Go play, or go get my belt. The choice is yours." Shondella stood firm. I guess the choice wasn't too hard, because all four kids took off outside. I smiled. Sure, my nieces were country-ghetto just like their mama, but there was no doubt, my sister had done a good job with her kids.

Shondella turned back to me. "Sorry about what?"

I debated whether I should tell her none of her business. But like it or not, Shondella had been there for me as well. And it was time to try to move forward with her as well.

"I'm sorry I've been such a witch these last few years."

"You ain't been a witch," Shondella said.

"No, I really have—"

"You been a *bitch,*" Shondella quickly turned to Mama Tee. "Sorry, Mama Tee, but she has."

Mama Tee shot Shondella an evil look, then slowly smiled. "She has, hasn't she?"

"Well, I want to make things right."

"Humph, now you sound like Rose."

I took a deep breath. "Shondella . . ."

"Chill, I'm just messing with you. Fine. Apology accepted. Now, can I borrow five hundred dollars?"

Both Mama Tee and I cocked our heads at her.

She shrugged. "My car payment is due."

I shook my head, ignoring her request.

"You know Raedella don't have a job," Mama Tee snapped.

"I'm sure she has beaucoup savings," Shondella retorted as she plopped down on the sofa across from us.

"Yes, I do have some savings," I interjected, "but they're dwindling fast."

"I can get you on at Jr. Food Mart," Shondella said nonchalantly.

It took everything in my power not to burst out laughing. I knew I had hit rock bottom, but I didn't think I was under the ground, and that's where I'd be before I went to work at Jr. Food Mart. The old me probably would've let Shondella know that. But this was the new and improved me, or at least the I'm-trying-to-change me. After the incident with Felton, then the conflicting feelings with Rose, and the empowering message I had just heard, I determined that maybe forgiveness was the first step in getting over my pain.

"Thanks, Shondella. I'll keep that in mind," I said.

Both Mama Tee and Shondella looked at me like they couldn't believe what I'd just said.

We sat enjoying the silence for a few minutes. Then Shondella tossed a newspaper at me. "Hey, I forgot. I brought this for you."

"How'd you get a *Houston Chronicle* newspaper?" I asked as I caught the paper and snapped it open.

"One of my suppliers comes from Houston and I always tell him to bring me the newspapers."

"That's how she kept up with you all these years," Mama Tee said.

"Kept up with me? Why would you keep up with me?"

"Ummm, is that Mercedes calling? I think it is. I better go see what she want." Shondella raced out of the living room and out the back door.

"Why would she keep up with me?" I asked Mama Tee again.

"Because that's your sister, and despite what you may believe, she does love you." Mama Tee said it like it was the most obvious thing. She pulled herself up off the sofa. "You do need to think about what you gon' do with yourself now. My house got a ninety-day grace period."

"A grace period?"

"Yep. You have ninety days to stay here without working. After that, any able-bodied person in this house gets up and goes to work somewhere," Mama Tee said matter-of-factly. "So you think about that. I'm going to see Mrs. Miller up the road. She been under the weather lately. Be back after while."

Mama Tee's words weighed heavily on my mind after she left. I hadn't given much thought to what I was going to do with my future. I had no desire to return to Houston, and in fact, it no longer even felt like home.

I turned my attention to the television, where the six-o'clock news was just coming on. The red-headed anchor looked like she was about fifty years old. I remembered her from when I was growing up here. Linda Calvins was her name. I used to wonder why she never aspired to leave Sweet Poke, go to another market. She wasn't half-bad so I knew it wasn't because of her talent. I'd met her when I'd visited the station once with my high school class. When I'd asked her why she didn't leave Sweet Poke, she smiled and said, "Honey chile, Sweet Poke is home and there's no place like home." I remember looking at her like she was on crack or something. Who would've ever thought I would one day agree with her?

chapter 44

After the news went off, I glanced around. It was getting dark and the house was extremely quiet, which meant Shondella and her kids must have left. I stood up and the newspaper fell off my lap. I had gotten so caught up in my thoughts, I hadn't even read it.

I tucked the paper under my arm, then walked into the kitchen, where I made a cup of hot tea and a bologna sandwich. I grinned as I slapped mayonnaise on my wheat bread. I hadn't had a bologna sandwich in fifteen years. I eased down into the chair at the kitchen table and began slowly sipping my tea, nibbling on my sandwich and reading the paper.

I couldn't help but smile as I read the article at the top of the page. The headline was brazen: "Promising Politician Busted in Prostitution Sting." Myles did not look his usual dapper self in the photo. Maybe it was the handcuffs. Or maybe it was that he was being dragged out of a seedy motel by police officers. Either way, I thought it was poetic justice, especially when I scanned the article and realized Myles's career was probably over. Mama Tee always said that what goes around comes around, and it looked like Myles was about to get his.

I folded the paper just as Mama Tee walked back in.

"You reading about your ex, huh?" she said as she sat down across from me. "Told you that one was a snake."

I smiled. "Yeah, you did." I looked down at the paper. "You know, maybe Myles's arrest is payback for my baby. I know it probably sounds dumb, but he never wanted our baby. He never even asked me how I lost the baby." Myles had called a couple more times after his visit to Sweet Poke, but it was always to see if "you have come to your senses and are ready to come home," as he put it.

Mama Tee shrugged. "You never know. I always told you, ' "Vengeance is mine," said the Lord.' You don't have to worry 'bout nothin' 'cause the Lord will take care of it all."

I took in her wisdom. I was always amazed at her faith and vowed to work on mine. I still didn't understand why my baby didn't make it, but God knew what he was doing, I guess. Maybe He didn't want my child growing up with a selfish, amoral father like Myles. Or a messed-up-in-the-head mother like me.

"The Lord giveth and He taketh away," Mama Tee said, nodding. "Yes, He does."

"I just have to hope that one day He will see fit to allow me to redeem myself. I want a baby. I want to be a good mother. I want to prove that I can love someone unconditionally. And I want to do right what my mother did wrong. I don't know, call me crazy, but I think it's in me to be a good mother."

"I think you will make an excellent mother," Mama Tee said. "But you need to get a man first."

"Oh, no, a man is the least of my concerns. Maybe I need to work on me," I announced. "And once I work on me, I can have a baby without having a man. Yeah, a sperm donor or something. That way I'd get the kid without the drama." I smiled at Mama Tee. She was looking at me like I had lost my mind.

"What?" she finally said. "A what donor?"

"I would just go to a sperm bank and make a withdrawal."

Mama Tee fell back in her chair. "Lawd, have mercy. What is this world coming to? Raedella Dionne Rollins, if you so much as even think about having a baby like that, I'll never speak to you again. What would you tell that chile? 'Yo' daddy is donor number five'? Perish the thought."

I laughed at Mama Tee's reaction. At that moment I felt so happy. If Shereen could see me now, she'd think some alien had invaded my body. But I guess when you hit rock bottom, the only thing you see is up.

I thought about what was next for me. At this point, I had no idea what direction life would take me. Maybe I should try to get a job at Sweet Poke's lone television station. It was time for Linda to retire. I chuckled at the thought. I couldn't believe the mere thought of working there wasn't making my skin crawl. I think it was because I was more at peace now than I'd ever been in my life. There were no airs to put on, no high standards to maintain. I could just be me here in Sweet Poke. I had some serious thinking to do, but I knew I was going to do something.

Mama Tee had come out of her shock and was now watching me with a small smile on her face. "I'm glad you came home, baby girl."

"I'm glad you made me come home, Mama Tee." I sighed. "Originally, I felt like my life was over when I lost everything, but being back in Sweet Poke has reprioritized what's important. And being successful and rich just wasn't it."

"Umm-hmmm, I told you that. But you ain't never believed fat meat was greasy." Mama Tee took my hand. "Come on, let's go sit on the front porch. I want to sit in my new swing." I smiled as I got up and followed her outside. One of the few things I'd bought since I'd been back in Sweet Poke was a rocking-chair swing for Mama Tee. I had to fight her to let me throw out that old sofa and replace it with the swing, but she'd finally relented and I think she couldn't be happier. Now, if I could just get rid of the toilet.

We settled on the swing and gazed up at the clear, star-filled sky. Queen, Mama Tee's latest mutt, sat at her feet.

"I don't remember it being so peaceful here," I said.

"It's one of the things I love about Sweet Poke." Changing the subject, Mama Tee said, "You know, I talked with Mr. Williamson about you."

"Who is that?"

"His son runs the TV station here. Remember I used to clean his house when you were little?"

"Oh. What were you talking to him about?"

"You need a job, don't you?"

Funny that she would bring that up. "Actually, I was just thinking about giving them a call."

"Well, now you got a connection."

"But it'll be strange, a totally different environment. I've been to the big time."

"And in the end, it didn't mean diddly-squat."

I contemplated her words. "Yeah, but I don't know."

"You got any better ideas?"

"No, but—"

"Ain't no buts," she replied. "You need a job. You need to move on and get your own place. Now that your uncle Frank is gone, I needs my privacy. Deacon Baird gotta stuff a sock in my mouth when he come over—"

"Ewwwwwww!"

"Ewwwwwww what? You grown. I'm grown."

"Uh, Mama Tee, you're seventy-five."

"And?" She flashed a sly grin.

I couldn't believe we were having this conversation. "And Deacon Baird has got to be pushing eighty."

"He's eighty-one."

"That's disgusting."

"Actually, it's quite wonderful. That Viagra is a beautiful thing. But, back to what I was saying. You need to call Mr. Williamson's son. He's really looking forward to talking to you."

I was just about to protest again when I noticed Mama Tee break out in a big smile. I turned to see what she was looking at.

"Evening, Deacon Baird."

"Evening, ladies." He tipped his hat. "I was just in the area and thought I'd stop by and see if . . . if, umm, you had any . . . any wood you needed chopping, Ms. Rollins."

"I sure do," Mama Tee responded. My brow furrowed. It was well after dark. And if I didn't know better, I'd swear that was a seductive look in Mama Tee's eyes. "Why don't you come around back so I can show you where it is? Raedella was just about to run to the store."

"No, I wasn't."

"Yes, you were. I need some Karo syrup for those pecan pies I'm making tomorrow." Mama Tee stood up. She motioned for Deacon Baird to follow her. "Oh, and, Raedella, make sure you take the long way home. We don't want to disturb the good deacon while he's chopping wood."

epilogue

"That's it for our news tonight. Thank you for being with us. From all of us here at KLMD, have a great night." I smiled genuinely at the camera as the director faded to black.

I got up from the set. "Good job tonight, Jack," I said. "You really handled that technical glitch well."

"That's because I'm working with such a pro," Jack, the technical director, said. "Have a good night."

I bid Jack and the rest of the studio crew good-night and walked over to where Shereen was sitting. Her mouth gaped open. "I think I'm in the twilight zone. I mean, I don't know what is more shocking, you working in this hick town or you being nice to people."

I laughed and motioned for her to follow me. "Girl, this is the new and improved Raedella Rollins."

"And what's up with this country-ass name?"

I shrugged. "That's my name."

Shereen shook her head in amazement. "This is unbelievable. What was wrong with just *Rae*?"

"*Rae* was created to get me out of here. I'm not running anymore so I can go back to the name I was born with." I grinned at her awe. "Come on, follow me over here to my desk."

"Desk? You don't have an office?"

"Please, this is market number 198. An office is a luxury we don't get around here."

I smiled as Shereen continued to walk beside me, shaking her head. I had persuaded her to come visit me in Sweet Poke. Tomorrow would mark one year back home for me, and from the looks of things, I won't be going anywhere anytime soon.

"What is with this new attitude?" Shereen asked.

"You know, Shereen, losing everything that mattered to me was the most humbling experience of my life, but one I guess was necessary to get my life back on track."

Shereen was still having a hard time taking everything in. "So, what do you do around here when you're not at work? I know you ain't dating nobody around here."

"Hardly. Mama Tee has been trying to get me to date, fixing me up with Deacon Baird's son, a minister. But he wasn't my type. Nice guy, just something about being a preacher's woman didn't set right with me." I sat down at my desk.

"Besides, I'm not ready to date. I'm busy getting myself together. I pray a lot. Go to church every Sunday."

Shereen started coughing like she was choking to death. "Very funny," I said. "Yes, I have a wonderful relationship with God." I ignored her stares. "I had to confront my demons so that I can heal. I feel like a totally new person. I guess in a way I am. I'm getting to know Raedella first. Plus, I've established a relationship with an eight-year-old from across the tracks. Her mother abandoned her, too, and I have sort of become a big sister to her."

I smiled as I thought of Daysia. She was a joy to be around. It was funny; Shondella actually put me in touch with her, saying something about us being kindred spirits.

"Speaking of sisters, how are things with yours?" Shereen said as she leaned back in amazement.

"Things are so-so with us. We have our days, but for the most part, we act like sisters should."

"What about your mom?"

"Rose? She's still trying. She says she will never give up. I told her to save her energy, but deep down, I am kind of moved by her relentless efforts. Who knows what will happen with that? I have to admit though, her spending time with Justin has boosted his spirits, and that is having a wonderful effect on his recovery."

"Tell me again why you're working here?" Shereen leaned onto my desk.

"Linda retired and it's a job. Gotta pay the bills."

"What, you gotta pay for chicken feed?"

"Don't hate. Appreciate."

Shereen threw up her arms. "I don't believe this. You're even saying those old country, sayings, too. Good grief, you know you've changed."

"Yep, I know I've been changed," I responded with a smile.

"Oh, Lord, don't tell me you gon' burst out in a Negro spiritual?"

I laughed. "No, it's just that I'm happy. For once in my life I'm truly happy with myself."

"I guess," Shereen said, shaking her head.

"Not I guess. I know."

"It's just . . . this place . . . it's so . . . it's so . . . country."

"I guess you can take the girl out of the country . . . but you can't take the country out of the girl." We both laughed at that. Because now, more than ever, I knew just how true that was.

Reading Group Guide for
I Know I've Been Changed

Description: In just seven years, Raedella Rollins has reinvented herself from a small-town girl into the star news anchor at a Houston television station. When she left behind her hometown of Sweet Poke, Arkansas, she also left behind her family and all their embarrassing foibles. In Houston, her new friends and colleagues know her as the girl who has it all: fame, fortune, and the man of her dreams. Then everything changes when Raedella's eccentric relatives show up in Houston, and her carefully constructed world starts to crumble. But when everyone deserts her, Raedella finally realizes that no matter how wacky or bizarre, she's only got one family, and family is the only thing that counts.

Questions for Discussion

1. Describe Raedella at the beginning of the novel. What kind of person is she? How sympathetic are you toward her in the first few chapters? Is she a likable character?

2. As Raedella waits to board the bus that will take her away from Sweet Poke, her ex-boyfriend Reno tells her, "Sweet Poke is where you belong . . . you can't run from it, it's in your blood." How does Raedella's past in Sweet Poke affect the life she leads as Rae Rollins, television star, in Houston?

3. Discuss Raedella's relationship with Myles. What is your first impression of Myles? Does this impression change as the story unfolds? What are the first indications that Myles may not be what he appears?

4. After learning from Mama Tee that Justin is back in the hospital, Raedella must quickly compose herself and go on the air. "If there was one thing I was good at, it was that—shaking everything off and putting on my TV face." Why is Raedella so successful as an anchor and talk show host? Discuss the relationship between image and reality in Raedella's life in Houston.

5. Though a relatively minor character, Raedella's friend Shereen plays a major role in the story. What impact does Shereen have on Raedella's transformation?

6. Discuss Raedella and Shondella's relationship. What are the origins of the conflict between them? In spite of the obvious differences, do you see any similarities between the two sisters?

7. "Don't get me wrong," Raedella explains in the prologue, "I haven't completely stopped believing in God—I just don't think he makes frequent stops in Sweet Poke. If he did, everyone there wouldn't lead such miserable lives."

How does Raedella's relationship to God change as the story progresses? Identify three turning points in her spiritual transformation.

8. Relationships between mothers and daughters play a central role in *I Know I've Been Changed*. Discuss the many different versions of the mother-daughter relationship portrayed in the book, and the impact of these relationships on the central characters.

9. At the end of the book, Raedella is living in Sweet Poke and working at the local television station. She is still single, and still working out her relationships with Rose and Shondella, and it is unclear what will come next for her. Why do you think the novel ends this way, rather than with a more conventional "happy ending"?

10. Why does ReShonda Tate Billingsley choose to wait until the last chapters of *I Know I've Been Changed* to reveal the details of Jasmine's death? Why do you think Raedella remains silent about it for so long?

Activities to Enhance Your Book Club

1. Invite each member of your group to share a memory or artifact from his or her hometown. Give members a few minutes each to talk about where they come from, and how it has impacted who they are today.

2. Hold your discussion on I Know I've Been Changed over a soul food dinner. For recipe ideas, go to http://www.soulfoodcookbook.com/ or check out Real Men Cook, published by Simon & Schuster/Fireside Books.

3. Celebrate the spirit of Raedella's acceptance of her difficult past by asking each member of the group to share a humorous but embarrassing detail from her past. Examples may include everything from photos from an awkward age to stories about relatives' embarrassing behavior.

Questions for the Author

1. How did the character of Raedella Rollins take shape in your imagination? Did you conceive of her all at once—her history, her emotional transformation, etc.—or did she develop as you were writing the book?

2. Writers sometimes talk about their characters taking on "a life of their own." Did Raedella ever do something that surprised you?

3. How do you balance your life as a reporter with your work as a writer of fiction? Are these entirely separate activities for you, or do they somehow interconnect?

4. Which aspects of your own experience did you draw on to write *I Know I've Been Changed*? How much do you identify or not identify with Raedella?

5. In some ways, *I Know I've Been Changed* reads like a fairy tale in reverse. Raedella's dream job, dream marriage, and dream life dissolve, leaving her to confront realities that she has long denied. Do you see your writing as a critique of "fairy tale endings," or of fantasy in general?

6. The Reverend Simon Jackson and his daughter, Rachel, characters from your previous book, *Let the Church Say*

Amen, make a brief appearance in *I Know I've Been Changed*. Do you see a connection between the two books?

7. In your vision of the book, what role does God play in Raedella's transformation?

8. At the beginning of the book, Raedella is not a particularly nice person, and yet we care what happens to her. How did you manage to create a deeply flawed character who we still feel is redeemable? How sympathetic were you toward Raedella at the beginning of the book?

Visit www.simonsays.com or the author's website for answers to these questions.

Look for ReShonda Tate Billingsley's
award-winning debut novel

My Brother's Keeper

Available now
from Pocket Books

Aja glanced at her watch. It was nearing eight o'clock. She was starving and as usual, Roxie was late.

"Excuse me." Aja flagged down her waiter. "I'm going to go ahead and order an appetizer."

The waiter dragged himself over to Aja's table. He acted irritated, like he was mad about having to be at work. "Yes, ma'am. What'll it be?"

"Just a cup of gumbo and a Swamp Thing, please."

"Anything else?"

Aja shook her head. "No thank you—that'll be it."

The waiter gave a look of relief, seeming to be thankful that he didn't have to write anything else down. "You still waiting on somebody?" He pointed toward the empty seat across from Aja.

"Yeah, I guess she's just running late."

The waiter threw an exasperated look. "I'll have your Swamp Thing right out." He picked her menu off the table, then turned and walked off.

Good, I definitely need that Swamp Thing. The icy drink mixture of margarita, hurricane, and tequila was just what Aja needed to calm her nerves after a crazy day at work. Before she could even get out of the bed, her pager had started going off. Aja knew she shouldn't give her pager number to her clients, but she wanted them to know they could call her any time—and they usually did.

This morning it had been Octavia, near tears because her boyfriend, Javier, had walked out on her and she was eight months pregnant. Aja had managed to calm Octavia down and convinced her that Javier would be back, since he'd come back the last twenty times he had walked out. Aja really wanted to tell the fifteen-year-old she'd be better off if he didn't come back. All he was good for was making babies.

Aja really enjoyed her job as assistant director of The Texas Youth Authority, but she had to admit that sometimes she got too wrapped up in it. The Youth Authority was a social service agency for at-risk teens. Aja was supposed to step back and let her staff deal with the actual clients while she handled the administrative end and made sure things ran smoothly. But she never had been able to step back since she had been promoted from counselor. She had a roster of clients that she dealt with on a regular basis and since the organization was so short-staffed, none of the other counselors seemed to mind.

Octavia, what will it take to get you to see Javier is no good for you? Aja lowered her head and rubbed her temples as she thought of Octavia sitting at home crying her eyes out while Javier ran the streets. Octavia was by herself; her mother had put her out when she'd turned up pregnant. So now the teen was living with a sister who could care less what she did and only let her come live with her because she was counting on the welfare check Octavia would be getting once the baby was born.

Then, on top of everything else, Eric and Elise hadn't made up and it had been a whole week. Aja had called Eric before she left the house today, and her brother had still been in a funk, which put Aja in a bad mood.

"Roxie, why can't you ever be on time?" Aja glanced at her watch again. She was starting to get irritated.

"Speak of the devil and she shall appear."

Aja looked up at Roxie, standing over her, a huge grin plastered across her face.

"Hey, girl. Hope you didn't order without me." Roxie pulled out a chair and plopped down across from Aja. She looked great in a fuchsia shirt that exposed her firm stomach and black boot-cut stretch pants that looked like they were especially carved for her size-six figure. Her sandy brown hair was swept up into a ponytail, and she wore a pair of sunglasses on top of her head. Her high arched eyebrows set off her slightly slanted eyes.

Roxie had been Aja's best friend since their days at Texas Southern University in Houston. They'd both dated members of the same fraternity. Roxie had dated a guy named Warren, **and** Aja had been head over heels for Darwin. When they found out Warren and Darwin were cheating on them, they cursed the guys out, then got together and had a pity party to bond. After that, they became best friends, pledging to the same sorority. Both of them tried out and were rejected from the cheerleading squad. They moved in together their junior year and had been in each other's lives ever since. Aja was the maid of honor in Roxie's wedding three years before to a wonderful man named Brian. And she was also the godmother to Roxie's son, Brendan.

"Just one time. Just one time will you get somewhere on time." Aja tapped her watch and rolled her eyes in frustration.

"So whatcha eating?" Roxie completely ignored the irritation in Aja's voice. Roxie was free spirited and didn't let much get to her.

"Gumbo."

"Ewww! Why'd you order that? You know this restaurant don't use no seasonings."

"I happen to like it like that, okay?" Aja snapped. "And why don't you use correct grammar?"

"Dang. Why you so nasty? I'm sorry I was late okay?" Roxie poked her bottom lip out in a pouty expression. "You forgive me?" Aja shot a disgusted look. The waiter brought her drink and bowl of gumbo and set them down in front of her.

"Are you ready to order?" the waiter asked Roxie. He still had an I-don't-want-to-be-here look. Of course Roxie didn't care. She scanned the menu, taking her time, despite the waiter's obvious huffing and sighing.

"Yeah, I'll take the same thing my mean-ass friend is having." Roxie pointed to Aja's drink. "And bring me a bowl of crawfish bisque. That's just for an appetizer. I'm hungry, so I'll be ordering something else in a minute. I just don't know what I want yet." The waiter nodded—more like grunted—and then took off.

Roxie scanned the menu a little longer, then closed it and set it down. She tore open a pack of crackers, dipped one in Aja's gumbo, and popped it in her mouth. She grimaced at the taste. "Yuck! This is horrible!"

"You don't have to like it. I do."

Roxie cocked her head to the side. "Maybe this was a bad idea. I don't know if you're on your period or just plain irritable. But I didn't come here for you to be constantly snapping at me."

Aja's expression softened. "Look, I'm sorry. I just had a bad day at work."

"Well, don't take it out on me. Nobody told you to take that depressing-ass job in the first place. Everyone has problems, lives constantly falling apart, and everyone is ten seconds from killing themselves or somebody else. As if you need that shit. To this day, I swear I can't understand why you turned down that marketing job with Coca-Cola. That's what your major was in school. Not to mention the fact that you would've made twice as much as what you're making now. But no, you turned it down to work with juvenile delinquents."

"Those kids need me." Aja hated defending her work. It was something she did with great pride. It didn't pay the best of money, but it was her way to help young people out, the way she couldn't help her own family. Everybody had told her how stupid she was to turn down that Coke job, but she knew that it would never have made her happy. What she was doing with those kids made her happy.

"Yeah, yeah, yeah. What about your needs? When's the last time you had your needs fulfilled?" Roxie raised her eyebrows, leaned forward, and lowered her voice. "Come to think of it, when's the last time you had you some?"

"Some what?"

"Don't play dumb with me. Some nooky, some dang-a-lang, some good loving?"

"You sure have a filthy mouth to be a fifth-grade teacher," Aja laughed.

"Hell, I learned half this stuff from them. Now answer the question."

Aja sipped her drink. *When was the last time I had sex? Six months ago? Nah, that was Marcus, he didn't count.* They'd just fooled around. She'd played sick after she'd gone to the bathroom and saw that herpes cream in his medicine cabinet. That was one time Roxie's advice to always check the medicine cabinet paid off. Before that it was Troy, and that was more than a year ago.

"That long, huh?" Roxie said when Aja didn't answer. "You can't even remember, it's been so long. You've probably converted back to a virgin."

"Shut up, Roxie. You have a husband and can have sex every night."

Roxie took Aja's drink from her and slurped it up through the straw. "Honey, the only thing I'm getting every night is Brendan's bottle."

Aja snatched her drink back. "Could you order your own stuff please?"

"I did. That slow-ass waiter is just taking his time getting it to me and I need a drink. Those damn kids got on my nerves today."

"You talk about me? I will never understand why you became a teacher. You act like you can't stand those kids."

Roxie leaned back and rolled her eyes. "I can't. Bad-ass, no-home-training little bastards. But it pays the bills and I like having my summers off. Now, back to what I was saying . . . we're talking about you. I'm married. I don't have to have sex but once a month. Now, that brings me to the point of this dinner. Have I got the perfect man for you." Roxie flashed a huge grin.

There she goes again, trying to fix me up with someone.

Roxie had made it her goal in life to find a man for Aja, even though Aja tried to convince her friend she wasn't interested in dating. It was a mission she had taken on since their college days.

"Ummm, if I recall, your track record isn't good when it comes to selecting men for me. Remember Stanley?" Aja said.

"Oh yeah, the Omega. He was too fine and I thought he would be good for you."

"He was good for me, and Leslie and Lisa and Carla and God only knows who else."

Roxie started laughing. "I remember how Leslie threatened to commit suicide when she saw you and Stanley leaving the movies. And then Lisa told you how she had some incurable sexually transmitted disease, but she loved Stanley so much it didn't matter. She was standing outside our window hollering for Stanley to come down. Telling him she could never have children because of him, but she still loved him."

"Then you poured a bucket of ice cold water out the window on her. Told her to take her infected ass home," Aja recalled.

Roxie held her stomach as she doubled over with laughter. "That was too funny and too pathetic." Roxie caught her breath. "But that Carla took the cake. You remember how we dressed in all black to catch her on her way back to her dorm so we could give her a beat down for spreading all those rumors about you?"

Aja laughed at the memory, too. Roxie always had her back. The minute she felt like anybody had wronged Aja, Roxie would shelve that prissy mentality and get ghetto. "Yeah, I only let you talk me into that madness because I didn't think we'd actually go through with it."

"Awww, naw. I was game, all the way."

"I know you were," Aja responded. "You remember jumping out the bushes and grabbing Carla by her ponytail, then throwing her up against that building? You told her if she ever uttered my name again, you'd cut her throat. She was terrified. I was too, because for a minute I thought you were really going to do it."

"I would have," Roxie said, matter-of-factly. "Everybody knew if they messed with you, they messed with me. Hell, I would've cut Stanley's ass for the dog way he treated you but I could never get his big ass alone long enough."

Aja smiled. "But, remember, you were the one who insisted he was the 'perfect man' for me."

"Okay, so sue me. I was wrong on that one. And maybe a couple, twenty others. But this one—I've got a good feeling about this one." Roxie nodded her head, a look of satisfaction across her face.

Aja sighed. "Roxie, if I told you once, I told you a thousand times, I don't want a man."

"Well, what do you want? A woman?" Roxie said with a sly grin.

"Don't be silly. I just have more pressing things to deal with."

"Like what? Saving the world? Newsflash! It can't be done. I know you feel this overwhelming need to look after your family and save every wayward juvenile delinquent this side of the Mississippi, but sometimes you've got to take a little time for yourself."

Aja started eating, hoping her lack of response

would change the subject. She looked up at Roxie, who was throwing her a you-know-I'm-right look.

"So, how's your mother doing?" Aja asked. She hoped to get Roxie to talk about something else, but she genuinely wanted to know. Roxie's mother had all but adopted Aja when they were in school. Roxie came from a huge family—six brothers and three sisters. Her family had become Aja's family over the last few years. Aja made a mental note to call Roxie's mother when she got home.

"She's fine. Wondering when you're getting married. Now quit trying to change the subject. As I was saying . . . Look at you. You don't even fix yourself up anymore. You look like crap. No makeup—when's the last time you had a perm? And then you're wearing that Jennifer Beals *Flashdance* outfit. The only thing you're missing are the leg warmers."

Aja knew Roxie was right. She had smooth butterscotch-colored skin and defined features that were enhanced by makeup, yet she seldom bothered to put any on. Her curly brown shoulder-length hair was stuffed beneath an Old Navy baseball cap. She had on a pair of black leggings and an oversize gray sweatshirt, which hung off her shoulder, revealing the strap from her sports bra. Aja had been so concerned with everyone else that she had let herself go. She'd even put on a few pounds, which she was surprised Roxie didn't mention.

"I hope you didn't go to work like that," Roxie said as she surveyed Aja's outfit.

"Of course I didn't. I worked out after I got off, then I went home and changed. I just threw something on."

Roxie narrowed her eyes and turned up her lips in disgust. "You need to throw that mess away. Don't wear that again, please."

"Could you get off of me, please, and tell me why you wanted to meet me in the first place? It's the middle of the week. We never meet for dinner during the week. And you said it was important. I hope it's not about this so-called perfect man."

"Do you watch Channel 13?" Roxie asked out of the blue.

"What does that have to do with anything?"

"If you do, your date next Saturday won't be a blind one, at least for you."

"Date? What date?"

Roxie just smiled mischievously.

"Roxanne Bingham-Daniels, I told you about trying to fix me up. I don't do blind dates."

"Hey, like I said, if you watch 13, it won't be blind."

"And just why is that?"

"Because, drumroll please . . ." Roxie began banging on the table. People were beginning to stare, but Roxie couldn't have cared less. "Your escort for next Saturday evening shall be none other than Channel 13 Eyewitness News sports anchor Charles Clayton. Yes, behind door number one is a luscious, deep chocolate colored, sexy, *working* man, who wants to take you out."

Aja stared in disbelief. "You've got to be kidding me."

"Oh my, are we interested? Could it be?" Roxie chuckled. She leaned back with a look of satisfaction.

"Roxie, don't play, okay? First of all, Charles Clayton is all that, or at least probably thinks he is. Second of all, what part of 'I don't need a date' are you not understanding?"

"First of all," Roxie stressed, leaning forward and turning serious. "I'm not understanding this celibacy vow of yours. You're twenty-eight with no prospects. I know you want to have a husband and kids and all that. So you need to get started, before your eggs dry up." Roxie leaned back and smiled like she was an expert on the subject.

"You are so nasty," Aja laughed.

"Whatever. Listen, I didn't know this or I would've fixed you up a long time ago, but Charles and Brian went to school together. Brian swears he told me that, but my husband is always claiming he's told me stuff I don't remember."

"You don't," Aja interjected. "You have selective retention."

Roxie rolled her eyes. "Would you shut up and let me finish? Anyway, Charles came by the house this past weekend after playing golf with Brian. I overheard Charles mention to Brian that he had broken up with his girlfriend five months ago and is through mourning and ready to get on with his life."

"And you thought I'd be the perfect one to help him do that?"

"Girl, you know me so well. Hey, where's the waiter? I'm ready to order." Roxie looked around for the waiter, summoned him over, then ordered the fried alligator. After the waiter left, she turned back to Aja. "Anyway, I mentioned you to Charles and showed him your picture. You know, the one of us in Vegas last year? He thought you were cute and asked me more about you."

"And what did you tell him?" Surprisingly, Aja was on the edge of her seat. She was having a hard time believing Roxie, but she was excited nonetheless.

"That you were desperate, hadn't been screwed in a long time, and would probably give it up on the first date," Roxie joked.

Aja glared at her friend.

Roxie laughed. "What do you think I told him? You are every man's dream and if he is looking for a good woman, you were it. So are you interested?"

"Roxie, I just don't . . ."

"Good," Roxie cut her off. "He's going to pick you up at six-thirty Saturday night. Here's his number in case you want to talk to him before then." Roxie slid Charles's business card toward Aja with his home number written in the corner. "He's taking you to see that play, *Mama, the Rent Is Due and They Fixin' to Turn Off the Lights.*"

Aja took the card and laughed. "It's *Mama, I'm Sorry.*"

"Whatever, they're all the same. A bunch of folks overexaggerating and cracking on each other."

"Then why is it you don't miss one?"

"Cuz, they're still funny as hell. Anyway, don't give me any flack." Roxie turned serious. "Do this one for me, okay? If you don't like him, I'll leave it alone."

"What? Can I get that in writing? If this doesn't work, you won't pressure me about dating again?"

"Girl Scouts' honor." Roxie held up two fingers.

"You were never a Girl Scout and that is not the Girl Scouts' sign," Aja said.

"Whatever. You have my word. I won't pressure you about dating, at least dating Charles." Roxie grinned.

"But it'll work, girlfriend, I just know it will. As long as you do something with your hair and don't wear that getup." Roxie pointed to Aja's clothes, then nervously looked around. "I'm embarrassed to be seen with you my damn self," she kidded.

Aja playfully threw her napkin across the table. "You are such a butthole."

"Asshole, Aja, asshole. Nobody says butthole. I've got my work cut out with you. Don't be going and saying no corny stuff like butthole around Charles. He'll think you're a nerd."

"Okay, I'll make sure he knows I'm cool," Aja laughed. As usual, Roxie had made her feel better.